Praise for Emily March

"Feel-good fiction at its finest."

—Susan Wiggs, *New York Times* bestselling author

"A brilliant writer you'll love."

—Susan Mallery, *New York Times* bestselling author

"Emily March's stories are heart-wrenching and soul-satisfying."

—Lisa Kleypas, *New York Times* bestselling author

BALANCING ACT

"Gentle, wholesome, and satisfying, with pops of the unexpected, this tenderhearted tale with a touching, uplifting storyline will please March's fans and anyone looking for a captivating escape."

—*Library Journal*

THE GETAWAY

"Readers looking for feel-good fiction about a big, loving family will enjoy this.... March creates believable characters, and the Prentice family is an easy one to spend time with."

—*Booklist*

"An intellectually engaging and psychologically probing novel about a family returning from a dark place to a better one."

—*New York Journal of Books*

"The power of love and family shine through this heartwarming and relatable story of old wounds and new beginnings."

—Debbie Mason, *USA Today* bestselling author

"Heartfelt and satisfying."

—Annie Rains, *USA Today* bestselling author

Second Chance Season

Also by Emily March

The Getaway

Balancing Act

Second Chance Season

A Lake in the Clouds Novel

EMILY MARCH

FOREVER
New York Boston

Cover art by Debra Lill
Cover design by Daniela Medina
Cover images © Shutterstock

Forever
Hachette Book Group
1290 Avenue of the Americas, New York, NY 10104
read-forever.com
@readforeverpub

First edition: November 2024

Forever is an imprint of Grand Central Publishing. The Forever name and logo are registered trademarks of Hachette Book Group, Inc.

Library of Congress Cataloging-in-Publication Data

Names: March, Emily, author.
Title: Second chance season / Emily March.
Description: First edition. | New York : Forever, 2024. | Series: A Lake in the Clouds novel ; book 3
Identifiers: LCCN 2024023817 | ISBN 9781538707432 (trade paperback) | ISBN 9781538707456 (ebook)
Subjects: LCGFT: Novels.
Classification: LCC PS3604.A9787 S43 2024 | DDC 813/.6—dc23/eng/20240524
LC record available at https://lccn.loc.gov/2024023817

ISBNs: 9781538707432 (trade paperback), 9781538707456 (ebook)

Printed in the United States of America

LSC-C

Printing 1, 2024

To Helen.
Wait. I mean,
To Mary Lou.
Thank you. I love you. You're the best sister ever.

Part One

Chapter One

January

A SCATTERING OF SNOWFLAKES fell outside Raindrop Lodge and Cabins Resort in Lake in the Clouds, Colorado. Helen McDaniel turned away from the window, slung a tote bag over her shoulder, and exited the business office with a spring in her step. Life was good.

She and her sister, Genevieve Prentice, had just concluded their monthly update meeting with their innkeeper, Kelly Green. For more than an hour, they'd examined the books, studied occupancy and reservation data, and discussed personnel issues and any other problems that had popped up since their last meeting. Thankfully, Kelly's problem column was short. She excelled in her job. A little more than two years since Helen and Genevieve had taken on the task of renovating the dilapidated vacation property beside Mirror Lake, the business was thriving.

That fact hadn't gone unnoticed. Now Helen and Genevieve had a big decision to make regarding their inn.

Helen went to the lobby, where she planned to rendezvous with Genevieve, who had stepped outside to retrieve a file from her car following their meeting. Helen placed an order at the bar for their traditional, post-monthly-meeting Bloody Marys and then headed for the sisters' favorite chairs.

The deep-cushioned swivel rockers sat facing the large picture windows and the majestic vista beyond, yet near enough to the fire blazing in the large stone fireplace to allow those seated to feel the warmth. Helen snuggled in to wait and watched through the glass where the spruce and pine forest hugged the bank of a frozen Mirror Lake. Sunshine attempted to break through the clouds. The music piped in through speakers hidden high on the walls shifted to Fred Astaire singing about being in heaven.

"Appropriate," Helen murmured, humming along to the song.

She heard the sound of the front door opening and turned to see her sister hurry into the room, her cheeks red from the cold.

"Brrr…it is freezing out there," Genevieve said as she paused to grab two lap blankets from a big straw basket beside the fireplace. "I don't know if my Texas girl bones will ever get accustomed to the Colorado winters. I think we're done with the snow for now, however. The sun is coming out."

"Good. I'm ready for some sunshine," Helen replied, then thanked her sister as Genevieve passed her a soft, colorful throw. They settled into their seats, making small talk until the bartender arrived with their drinks.

"Thanks, Mike." Helen smiled and stirred the celery stick in her Bloody Mary.

"Let me know if you need anything else," the bartender replied, handing Genevieve her drink.

"Will do. Thanks." Genevieve took a sip and gave an appreciative hum. When Mike returned to the bar, leaving them in relative privacy, she stretched out her legs, crossed them at the ankles, and sighed. "Okay, I'm happy. This is my favorite spot in the lodge in winter."

Helen swiveled her chair to take in the vista of a snow-covered Granite Mountain rising above the frozen surface of Mirror Lake. "I know. It's a better view than what I have from my condo. Plus, we have our own personal bartender here."

Genevieve lifted her glass in a silent toast. "Are we lucky or what?"

"We are lucky," Helen agreed as the clack of billiard balls sounded from the game room on the far side of the inn's lobby. One guest groaned, and another chortled and chided about the unfortunate fall of an eight ball into a side pocket. "Although I'll be honest, I'm anxious to see what that Pennsylvania groundhog says next week. I'm ready for spring. The cold temperatures have bothered me worse this winter than usual."

Genevieve glanced at Helen, her eyebrows arched. "Did I just hear you admit to a sign of aging?"

"Of course not!" Helen schooled her expression to innocence and said, "It's those twelve pounds I lost last year. Remember that weight-loss bet you and I had? The wager that I won?"

"As if you'll ever let me forget it," Genevieve grumbled.

Helen fought a grin as she pursed her lips around her straw to take a sip of her drink. She had won the bet, but it wasn't a fair contest. She'd had a good twenty pounds she needed to lose.

Genevieve had lost six, all her extra weight—the witch. Genevieve looked ten years younger than her sixty years, slim and petite. She kept her hair the same golden blonde she'd been born with and wore it styled shoulder-length in feathered layers. Her gemstone green eyes had come from their father and had always been one of her best features. Genevieve was still a beautiful woman, inside and out.

She was Helen's only living sibling, her best friend, and her closest confidant. She was her most dearly loved Sister—with a capital *S*. Helen gave thanks in her prayers each day that

Genevieve's midlife crisis had given her a reason to make a new life and join Helen in Lake in the Clouds.

Helen pulled herself away from the brink of becoming maudlin by tugging her thoughts back to the weight-loss wager. She reached over, patted Genevieve's knee, and rolled out one of their mother's frequent sayings. "You'll do better next time."

Genevieve gave her sister the evil side-eye, then replied with another maxim: "This too shall pass."

"Don't borrow trouble."

"We'll cross that bridge when we come to it."

"Don't take any wooden nickels."

The sisters clinked their glasses in a silent toast to their mother, then settled back to watch as the sun finally broke through the clouds outside.

They'd had three new inches of snow overnight, but today's forecast called for clearing skies and sunshine by noon. Helen was glad about it. She hadn't been lying about the cold bothering her this year. Of course, it was no wonder, since she'd spent two weeks in Iceland in December chasing the Northern Lights. Probably all she needed was a long weekend somewhere warm.

She'd check her schedule and see how soon she could steal a few days away. Maybe Genevieve would fancy a quick trip to Florida or South Padre Island.

Before they planned another trip, however, they needed to deal with business, so following a few minutes of comfortable silence, Helen broached the proverbial elephant in the room. "So, what are we going to do about this offer?"

Genevieve released a heavy sigh. "I almost wish I hadn't answered the phone when our banker called last night. Making a decision this big is stressful."

The night before, a local real estate agent had called with an out-of-the-blue purchase offer for Raindrop Lodge and Cabins Resort. Her buyer wanted a closing date of March 1, though if they agreed to the sale, they'd delay closing until after Genevieve's daughter Willow's March 9 wedding to Noah Tannehill.

"I tossed and turned half the night thinking about it," Helen said. "Flipping this place has been on the table since the beginning. This particular offer aside, if we're going to sell, now is probably the time. Everything is in great shape."

"True," Genevieve agreed. "The renovation is complete. The books look great. It's an excellent offer, and I suspect it could be improved. You're an excellent negotiator, Helen."

Genevieve removed her celery stick from her drink and nibbled the end. "There's really no reason to keep the lodge. We're both busy with other things now, and since the prospective buyers have pledged to keep all our employees, we need not worry about Kelly and Mike and our other people losing their jobs."

"True." Helen readjusted her lap blanket so that it covered her feet. "I have my hands full these days being mayor. Your schedule is packed with play days with your grandchildren and overseeing our film festivals at the theater. Not to mention dating Mr. Hot-on-Horseback."

Helen referred to Gage Throckmorton, owner of the Triple T Ranch and Lake in the Clouds' most eligible widower.

Genevieve smiled smugly. She and Gage had publicly declared themselves officially a couple right after her birthday in November. "There is that."

"Speaking of the theater, what's next at the Emily?"

"Our Bogie and Bacall Festival starts on Valentine's Day and runs for two weeks."

"Ooh. I'll have to put that on my calendar," Helen said. "What are you showing?"

"*Key Largo* starts the festival. We end with *To Have and Have*

Not. We're still working on the rest of the schedule but intend to have a different film each night."

"Excellent." Helen licked at the salt on the rim of her glass. "You will show *Casablanca*, won't you?"

"Of course. I know it's your favorite."

"A tragic love story." Her heart gave a little twist because the phrase always gave her a fleeting memory of her first, her greatest, love. "That's my thing."

Genevieve's following words tugged her away from past sorrows. "We also have a week of classic cartoon matinees scheduled for spring break."

"I am down for that, too. Saturday morning cartoons were the best. I loved me some Yogi Bear and Road Runner. And, Bugs Bunny. He was my favorite character. Any chance you'll be showing Bugs Bunny?"

Genevieve gave her a side look and a grin. "Oh, *Looney Tunes* for sure."

"Good. That's so appropriate for us." As Helen stirred her drink with the celery stick, ice cubes clattered in her glass. "So, we're avoiding the subject at hand. Back to Raindrop Lodge."

Genevieve swallowed a long sip of her drink, then said, "We'd probably be foolish to turn this offer down. We'd make a significant profit."

"True," Helen agreed. "We never intended to be involved for over a year or two. Our plan from the beginning was to refurbish the inn, bring it up to operational speed, and flip it."

"I know." Genevieve's mouth twisted ruefully. "It's just that we've put so much time and effort into the place. We've made some lovely memories here. I don't know if I'm ready to walk away from the Raindrop entirely." She looked at her sister and asked, "Are you?"

Satisfaction washed through Helen. "No, I don't believe I am."

"So, we're going to turn down this offer?" Genevieve asked.

"That's my vote."

"Excellent." Genevieve beamed a smile Helen's way. "That was easier than I thought it might be."

They returned their attention to the outdoors, where sunshine had turned the snowy expanse an almost blinding white. Helen thought about the folders tucked into her tote bag. With the potential sale question behind them, it might be a good idea to give her sister a heads-up about the meeting Genevieve's daughter Willow had requested for later today.

But as Helen reached into her tote, Genevieve said, "Since that question is settled, I'd like to run an idea by you. I came up with it amidst all the tossing and turning last night."

"Let's hear it," Helen said.

"If we're committed to keeping the business, why not go all in? Think big. I believe we could really grow the business if we focused on making Raindrop Lodge a destination wedding venue."

Helen eyed her sister for a long moment. "You thought of this last night?"

"Yes."

"Did you call Willow and discuss the idea with her?"

Willow was a professional event planner. She'd moved to Colorado with her two young children at this time last year, and since then, she'd coordinated four weddings here at the lodge.

"No." Genevieve shook her head. "I wouldn't do that without talking to you first. Raindrop has been a partnership between the two of us from the beginning. I respect that. Any decisions to be made, we make together. I also thought we should deal with the immediate flip-it-or-keep-it decision independently of this idea."

"Would you have mentioned it if I said I wanted to sell?"

Genevieve shrugged. "I don't know. I might have changed my mind if you'd felt strongly about selling. Look, this is simply an idea I'd like you to think about. We're in no rush. It's not like Willow's plate isn't full as it is, what with her wedding on the horizon and trying to get the new house finished and furnished so they can move in when they return from their honeymoon."

Helen clicked her tongue, then lifted her drink in a silent toast. "All I can say is, like mother, like daughter."

When Genevieve gave her sister a curious look, Helen explained. "Willow came to me yesterday with a business proposal."

Genevieve sat up straight. "What kind of proposal? And why did she bring it to you and not me?"

"Don't get your knickers in a twist. She knew we had a three o'clock meeting here with the accountant yesterday. She came at three-thirty, hoping to catch us both. She didn't know that you would ditch me to go horseback riding with Gage."

"I didn't ditch you," Genevieve protested, her tone defensive. "I got my dates mixed up."

"Nevertheless, there's no reason for you to feel slighted. Willow left a folder for each of us to study. She has an appointment with a potential client here this morning. She wants to discuss her proposals afterward."

"Where's the file? What's in it?"

Helen removed one of Willow's folders from her tote. She handed it to her sister, saying, "The bottom line is this. You and your daughter have been thinking along the same wavelength. Willow is presenting us with two different business plans. One has her buying into the property as a partner. The second retains the current ownership status quo but puts Willow officially in charge of special events. Either way, she wants to focus on the destination wedding business."

"A partnership?" Genevieve's eyes went wide with surprise. "So, what did you tell her?"

"*Nada.* I wore my poker face. Didn't say yea or nay. Like you said a few moments ago, you and I are partners. We make decisions about the Raindrop together. I was getting ready to call you to discuss it when you phoned me with news about the offer. I didn't want to complicate that decision with the possibilities of this one. Not from the beginning, anyway."

"Smart," Genevieve agreed with a nod. "I'm glad we decided not to sell independently of family concerns. It's better to keep family and business separate as much as possible."

"Difficult to do in a family business," Helen replied, her tone dry.

"But better for relationships when we pull it off." Genevieve flipped open the folder and scanned the first page. "So, what do you think of her idea?"

"I like it."

"The destination wedding part or the partnership part?"

"I like both. What about you?"

Genevieve's green eyes brightened with pleasure. "I love the thought of bringing her in as a partner. If she expands the business, she should have a piece of it."

"I agree." Helen folded her arms and nodded with satisfaction.

Lifting her gaze from Willow's proposal, Genevieve said, "This is exciting. I've grown to love this inn. Sometimes I'll make an impromptu visit to the Raindrop to sit in the lobby and visit with our guests. People can be so interesting. And the weddings make me happy—especially since Willow is there to deal with all the problems that erupt—large or small. So, how should we handle this?"

Helen sipped her drink, savoring the spicy tomato flavor as she considered the question. "I didn't do more than glance at her paperwork, but knowing Willow, she's presenting us with well-considered proposals. I suggest we let her make her presentation, tell her we want her as a partner, and then let our respective attorneys hammer out the details."

"That sounds like an excellent plan." Genevieve flipped to the second page of Willow's proposal. "She wants to change the name. Reflections Inn at Mirror Lake. I like it."

"I do, too," Helen agreed. "So, do you have time to meet with her this morning? Or do you have a lunch date with the hunky rancher?"

"I'm free." The smile on Genevieve's lips faltered just a bit as she added, "We're going to dinner tonight."

"Oh yeah?" Helen waggled her brows. "Having a sleepover afterward?"

"No!" Genevieve snapped. Then, in a more tempered voice, she added, "I'm not sleeping with Gage."

Helen drew back. "Something going on there that you haven't told me about, sister?"

Genevieve shrugged. "Not really. We only recently agreed that we are officially dating. And we're doing it the old-fashioned way."

"Old-fashioned," Helen repeated with a snicker. "What does that even mean? Does he take you parking somewhere on his ranch, and you steam up the windows? I imagine it's not easy to crawl over the backseat at this age. Your knees!"

Genevieve chastised her with a look. "Very funny."

"Be fair. I remember when you were dating David. It didn't take him long to get into your—"

"Stop. Gage isn't David, and I'm certainly not the same woman I was in the 1980s."

"What does age have to do with anything? There are lots

of positives to having sex at our age. No worry about getting pregnant is a good one."

"Enough." Genevieve scowled at her teasing sister. "I'm not discussing this with you, Helen."

"Spoilsport. I'm not asking for details. Well, actually, I'd love details so that I can live vicariously through you. I'm alone, and Gage Throckmorton is such a hunk."

"Oh, for heaven's sake. The only reason you're alone is because you want to be alone. All you need do is snap your fingers, and every unattached man in your retirement community will come knocking at your door. Probably some of the married ones, too."

Helen waved the comment away. "As if I'd want anything to do with those old men. Have you heard about the STD rates at that retirement city in Florida? Shocking, I'm telling you! No, I'm good with a fantasy man at this point in my life. And let's face it. Gage is—"

"When is Willow due to arrive?" Genevieve interrupted, pointedly changing the subject.

Helen gave in, glancing toward the cuckoo clock mounted on the wall beside the lodge's front doors. "Any minute. She said she's meeting potential clients at ten thirty. I don't know any more details."

"Oh, I know about these clients." Genevieve tucked her daughter's business plan back into the folder's pocket. "Maybe that's why weddings were on my mind at three o'clock this morning. We have a new referral from Celeste. A couple is looking for a wedding venue, and Angel's Rest is already booked for their date."

Their friend, Celeste Blessing, owned and operated Angel's Rest Healing Center and Spa in Eternity Springs, another small mountain town about an hour's drive from Lake in the Clouds.

An experienced innkeeper, Celeste had been Helen and Genevieve's mentor, guiding them through the process of becoming successful innkeepers as the sisters took on the project of making Raindrop Lodge shine again.

Helen nodded with satisfaction. "Perfect. We can visit with Willow after she's finished with the lovebirds and then have lunch." Rattling the ice in her nearly empty glass, she added, "Shall we have a second one to celebrate?"

"You're talking my language, sister," Genevieve said. She signaled to the bartender. Moments later, he delivered another round of Bloody Marys.

Genevieve held up her glass. To the tune of The Dixie Cups' "Chapel of Love," Genevieve sang her own lyrics. "Gonna build a business, and we're gonna get 'em ma-a-ar-ried."

Delighted, Helen clinked glasses with her sister and joined in, singing, "Gee, I really love this and can't wait to get 'em ma-a-ar-ried. Goin' to build a business of love."

The sisters shared a snicker at their silliness, then returned their attention to the view beyond the windows. Genevieve mused, "Do you know what the lunch special is today?"

"I don't, but I can check. I need to powder my nose, anyway." Helen set her glass on the side table and rose from her chair. "I'll be right back. Do you want some munchies now? Crackers and cheese, maybe?"

"Sounds perfect. Thanks."

After a visit to the ladies' room off the lobby, Helen made her way through the café and into the kitchen, where a mouthwatering aroma greeted her.

"Something smells delicious," she said to the cook, whom they had stolen from a local diner last year. "Is that the lunch special stewing on the stove?"

"It is," the cook replied. "Beef stew. The soup of the day is tortilla. And our sandwich special is a Reuben."

"I may have to have a little of everything. In the meantime, Genevieve and I would like some cheese and crackers to hold us over. Mind if I help myself?"

"Be my guest." The cook made a welcoming gesture and added with a teasing tone, "After all, it's your lodge."

"But it's your kitchen," Helen replied as she opened the refrigerator. "I know my place."

A few minutes later, Helen whistled the Dixie Cups tune as she departed the kitchen carrying a small charcuterie board she'd put together. Softly, she sang the legit version of "Chapel of Love," and she'd just glanced at the cuckoo clock near the registration desk to check the time when the front doors opened, and her niece stepped inside.

Helen beamed a bright smile at Willow Eldridge, soon-to-be Willow Tannehill. "Hey, sunshine. Perfect timing. Your mom and I are ready to discuss your ideas about the Raindrop as soon as you're free."

"Excuse me?" Willow said in a voice that wasn't Willow's. "Are you speaking to me?"

In that instant, Helen noticed three things. First, Willow's hair had grown four inches since Helen last had seen her. That was yesterday. Second, her coat sported a Houston Astros logo, and Willow was a Colorado Rockies fan. She wouldn't be caught dead wearing Astros gear.

The third and final sign that Helen had misunderstood the situation was that a man had followed Willow inside, and the masculine hand now taking hold of Willow's didn't belong to Noah Tannehill.

Helen bobbled her charcuterie. This wasn't Willow.

Chapter Two

ZOEY HILLCREST WATCHED SHOCK enter the mature woman's mossy green eyes. The cheese board she held teetered, and Zoey lurched forward to intercept it. Ever quick on his feet, Cooper beat her to it, rescuing the charcuterie before it hit the floor. That he lost only two small squares of cheese and a trio of grapes in the process demonstrated his dexterity.

The woman was stylishly dressed in a thigh-length, geometric-patterned sweater in shades of green over slim jeans and knee-high leather boots. She shoved her fingers through her short, auburn hair and dropped her gaze. She shook her head, which sent her large gold hoop earrings swaying, then gave Zoey a second look. "You're not Willow."

"No, I'm Zoey." She guessed this woman to be in her mid-sixties, and the confusion in her expression brought dementia to mind. Gentle compassion washed through Zoey as she asked, "What's your name?"

"Helen." She raised her hand to cover her mouth and murmured, "I can't believe it."

Helen's bewilderment tempted Zoey to reach out and hug her. She was a hugger by nature, which often came in handy for her professionally, but she'd learned to read the room. A hug wasn't the appropriate response here today. Instead, she made her tone friendly, saying, "We have an appointment with someone named Willow. I love your earrings, by the way. I'd wear big hoops every day if I could, but I work with children, and the little ones like grabbing my earrings."

Helen's hand shifted from her mouth to her earring, but her gaze didn't move from Zoey. Cooper interrupted the odd moment by returning the charcuterie board to Helen.

While Helen thanked Cooper, Zoey took that opportunity to glance around the room. A wide-eyed teenager stood behind a registration desk, gawking at them. She smiled at the young man, stepped toward him, and said, "Good morning. We have an appointment with your event planner. Where can we find Willow Eldridge?"

"Uh...," responded the teenager. "I don't know. I haven't seen her today. Wow."

That wasn't very helpful. Zoey hoped this trip hadn't been a waste of time. She'd loved the look of Raindrop Lodge when they drove up, but she didn't want to trust the biggest day of her life to a business with poorly trained front-facing employees.

"We are a little early," Cooper pointed out.

"True." Neither Zoey nor Cooper could stand being late, so they invariably arrived early. It was one of the many ways they were compatible. Addressing the teenager, she said, "Where should we wait for—"

Before she finished her sentence, she heard the lodge's front door open. Cooper glanced over his shoulder and murmured, "Whoa."

"Hello," came a feminine voice from behind her. "I'll bet you are Zoey and Cooper. I'm Willow Eldridge. Welcome to Raindrop Lodge."

Zoey turned around.

Willow's welcoming smile froze. So did Zoey's.

Whoa is right. Zoey's gaze swept Willow Eldridge from head to foot, then back up again. The woman could be her sister. Maybe even her twin.

For a long moment, the two women stared at each other. Same green eyes. Same high, prominent cheekbones. Similar tall, lithe builds. Same blond hair color, though Zoey wore hers in a longer style. She thought Willow might be a few years older than she.

Deep inside herself, where childhood dreams never wholly died, a spark of hope flared to life. Zoey was an only child. What if...?

Then the woman named Helen broke the spell by laughing. "Lord love a duck," she said. "I've always heard that everybody has a doppelgänger. It looks like the two of you found yours." She stepped forward, delight replacing the confusion on her face and making her look younger. She extended her hand toward Zoey. "I'm Helen McDaniel, one of the owners of this resort. I apologize for my brain freeze. I honestly thought you were Willow when you walked in."

As Zoey shook Helen's hand, the younger woman said, "I thought you were Willow, too. Only, *I'm* Willow." She extended her hand to Cooper. "Willow Eldridge."

"Cooper MacKenzie," he replied, shaking Helen's hand first, then Willow's. "This is my fiancée, Zoey Hillcrest."

"It's very nice to meet you both," Willow said. "It's always nice to get a referral from Celeste Blessing." To Helen, she added, "They'd hoped to have their wedding at Angel's Rest, but their date isn't available."

"Ah, yes. My sister told me Celeste was sending someone our way. When are you getting married?"

"August seventeenth is our preferred date," Cooper replied, his brown eyes warm and friendly.

"Of next year?"

"No, this year," Zoey clarified, sharing a rueful smile with her fiancé. "We didn't know we were hunting a unicorn when we looked for an available venue in Eternity Springs."

"We have an open date on their weekend," Willow informed Helen.

"That's good." Helen glanced over her shoulder and called out, "Genevieve, come meet our visitors." To Zoey and Cooper, she explained. "Genevieve is my sister and Willow's mother. As you probably surmised, Raindrop Lodge and Cabins Resort is a family business."

Zoey watched as a woman seated near the fireplace looked up from reading a stack of papers. She rose from her chair and started across the lobby. She was an attractive woman—blond, slim, and petite—and Zoey guessed Genevieve was the younger of the two sisters.

Zoey recognized the moment when Genevieve got a good look at her. The polite smile on her face melted like ice cream in the hot summer sunshine. She spoke in a shocked tone of voice. "Oh my."

Helen piped up. "If Zoey weren't so obviously younger than Willow, I'd ask if you and David accidentally left a twin behind at the hospital when Willow was born."

"Well, thank you very much, Auntie," Willow said, folding her arms.

Helen shrugged and winked at Zoey when Genevieve added, "Yes, Helen. Thank you very much."

Zoey shrugged. "If I'm younger than you are, Willow, it's not by much."

"That's it." Willow clapped her hands. "You're my new best friend. Zoey, Cooper, allow me to introduce my mother, Genevieve Prentice."

Genevieve shook their hands, saying, "Welcome to Lake in the Clouds. I agree that the resemblance between you and my daughter is striking. Perhaps our family trees connect somewhere in the past. We moved here from Texas. Any Texas roots in your family?"

"Not that I know of." But, then again, Zoey didn't know what connections might be found in a family tree, did she? "We live there now, but I grew up in Florida. My dad moved to Houston for work when I went off to college."

"Lots of people are moving to the Lone Star State these days," Willow observed.

"Lots of Texans moving to Colorado," Helen pointed out. "Or at least keeping a second home here to escape the summer heat."

Cooper grimaced. "I grew up in Michigan. My first summer in Houston almost killed me. It's why I lobbied for a mountain location for our summer wedding."

"Speaking of your wedding," Willow said with a smile, "perhaps we should get started on our meeting. If you would join me in my office, I'd like to hear your thoughts. I'll show you around the property once I understand your needs."

After taking their leave of the two sisters, Zoey and Cooper followed the wedding planner down a short hallway and into an office that offered a breathtaking view of the lake and mountains beyond. When Zoey could drag her gaze away from the wall of windows, she noticed four framed photographs decorating the room's other three walls. They depicted scenes from different weddings.

Zoey stepped closer to study the photos. "What a gorgeous setting."

"That photo on the right is the first wedding we hosted here at Raindrop Lodge," Willow shared. "It was my older brother's wedding to the most wonderful woman—the most patient woman—in the world. She needs that patience to put up with my know-it-all bro."

"So says the little sister," Cooper wryly observed.

"You betcha." Willow's grin was wide and winsome. She reached into her desk, withdrew a pair of spiral-bound books, and handed one to Zoey and Cooper. "This is our idea book. You'll find more photos here."

Willow opened a notebook and picked up a pen. "Now, we confirmed that August seventeenth is your big day?"

"Yes." Zoey shared a smile with Cooper, then added, "We could move it back a week if necessary, but you said you are open on that date?"

"We are. So, let's add the rest of the basics. Estimated size of your guest list and wedding party?"

They discussed their wants and desires for the next twenty minutes or so. Cooper's interest in wedding-related details didn't surprise Zoey. He was a detailed kind of guy—precise, organized, and decisive. He was a problem solver and a decision-maker. And smart as a whip, of course. The man didn't lack confidence. All were qualities that made him such an excellent orthopedic surgeon.

Cooper claimed that Zoey was the better diagnostician, and she wouldn't argue the fact. Medicine was a blend of art and science, after all. In addition to information gleaned from a physical exam and testing, Zoey relied on intuition, empathy, creative reasoning, and subjective judgment to identify her patients' ills. A good percentage of her patients couldn't tell Zoey what hurt. Such was the life of a pediatric emergency physician.

Thinking about work threatened to dim her shine, so Zoey focused on the wedding planner.

Willow Eldridge shut the notebook where she'd recorded Zoey and Cooper's answers to her questions. "I think we've covered everything I need to know now. Ordinarily, I'd give you a tour of the facilities at this point. Are you okay with that? It's cold outside and—" She glanced through her office window. "Oh, good, the snow has stopped. The complete tour will take us about half an hour, though I can do the highlights in fifteen minutes."

"I don't mind the cold," Zoey said. "And Cooper loves it."

"May I offer you hats and gloves?"

"We have some in our pockets," Cooper explained.

They all rose, donned their outdoor gear, and exited the office. Willow led the visitors down a long hallway toward a door that opened onto the lodge's large lake-facing covered patio. Halfway there, Cooper leaned close to Zoey and murmured, "She even walks like you."

Zoey replied with an elbow to his ribs. "Stop watching other women's butts, Dr. Mac."

"It was an innocent observation," he defended, a teasing twinkle in his brown eyes as he added, "I am blind to any female derrière but yours."

Zoey snickered and gave an exaggerated roll of her eyes. "In that case, one must be thankful that you're an orthopedist rather than a gastroenterologist."

He slipped his arm through hers. "Seriously, though, even Willow's gait is similar to yours. It's eerie."

Zoey focused on Willow and tried to see what her fiancé saw. Since how a person walked fell under Cooper's area of expertise, Zoey couldn't fault him for noticing.

The wedding planner pushed open the door, and Zoey quit

thinking about walks as bitterly cold air swooshed inside to greet them. Zoey shivered in response to the chill and the excitement building inside her. Despite having an understanding that they would marry after Zoey completed her medical education in June, they hadn't been officially engaged until Cooper had asked her to marry him on Christmas Eve. Since then, she'd been working killer hours at the hospital. She hadn't had much time to think about the wedding before boarding the plane for Colorado yesterday.

Now, Zoey's imagination fired as they stepped onto the deck and took in the vista before them.

The overcast sky was clearing off, revealing patches of brilliant blue sky above the ice-white surface of Mirror Lake. "It's beautiful here," Cooper observed.

"Wait until you see it in summer when the lake isn't frozen." Willow pointed toward the horizon. "Granite Mountain, there in the center, and the two peaks surrounding it maintain a snowcap year-round. In the summer, you'll often get enough wispy clouds around the peaks to have an explosion of color at sunset. In August, you'll have swaths of wildflowers on the mountain. Seeing it all reflected on the lake surface steals your breath."

Cooper took hold of Zoey's hand. "I'll bet it does."

"I can picture it," Zoey said. "I love flowers. If I hadn't gone into medicine, I might have worked as a florist. I worked in a flower shop as a teenager, and I loved it. I want to have lots of flowers at our wedding."

"We can certainly do that." Willow's tone grew matter-of-fact. "You indicated you prefer an evening wedding. Sunset on August seventeenth is at eight-oh-one p.m. If we plan to start your ceremony ten minutes earlier, you'll be saying your vows at the pinnacle of the show. However, that makes for a late start.

You could begin earlier and plan for your first dance at sunset. It's a trade-off. It's something you'll need to discuss."

"You looked up the sunset?" Zoey asked. "You're very thorough."

"Details are my job," Willow said with a smile. "I can't guarantee sunshine and a spectacular sunset on your wedding day. That is God's doing. But I feel confident enough about the weather to promise Mirror Lake won't be frozen in August. If that has occurred in the past, it has not happened in recorded history. And mid-July to mid-August is the sunniest part of our year."

The sound of a barking dog attracted Zoey's attention. Out on the snow-covered ground sloping toward the frozen-over lake, a young boy dressed in a navy-blue ski jacket, red hat, and yellow gloves threw a stick for a medium-sized dog with a golden coat. The sight made her smile.

As much as Zoey appreciated the magnificence of a colorful sunset, she found the sight of a healthy child doing healthy childhood things more beautiful. She didn't get enough of that in her everyday life.

"This way," Willow said, leading them toward a set of wooden stairs at the center of the deck. She greeted a couple seated in oversized log rocking chairs near a pyramid-shaped patio heater and asked if they were enjoying their visit to Raindrop Lodge.

She's confident, Zoey thought. Such a question could invite complaints, so she must not be worried that her guests' responses might reflect poorly upon the lodge.

The woman in the rocker nodded enthusiastically. "We're having a fantastic time," she said, her voice heavy with the sound of the Carolinas. "Everyone is so nice and welcoming. The food is excellent, too. This hot chocolate is some of the best I've ever had."

"The complimentary cookies they serve in the middle of the afternoon aren't half-bad, either," her male companion added. "Do you know what kind they're making today?"

"I do," Willow nodded. "It's Saturday. Saturday is Snickerdoodle Day."

"Chocolate chip is my favorite, but Snickerdoodles work." The man saluted with his steaming mug of hot chocolate.

They moved toward the center of the patio, where a broad set of stairs led down to the ground that sloped gently to the lakeshore. Willow turned toward Cooper and Zoey, wearing a satisfied smile. "Just for the record, those weren't ringers but real guests with real opinions." After waiting for a beat, she added, "Though I think I'll suggest our baker whip up a batch of chocolate chip cookies to serve along with Snickerdoodles this afternoon. We aim to please here at Raindrop Lodge and—"

A chirp sounded from Cooper's pocket, a ringtone he and Zoey both recognized. Their gazes met briefly. She nodded as Cooper stepped away, saying, "Excuse me."

Zoey gave Willow an apologetic smile. "Cooper is an orthopedist, and that's his answering service calling. He may be just a minute, or this may take a while."

"A doctor?" Willow opened her notebook and made a note. "I missed that detail. I usually ask the career question early in our initial discussion. I skipped it completely. Can you give me his contact information?"

Zoey rattled off the name and address of his group practice, office number, and personal cell phone. Willow noted everything, then asked, "And yours?"

Zoey gave Willow the name of the hospital where she worked, along with its main number and address. "That information is good until the first of July. I complete my fellowship in June, and I'm not sure where I'll be working after that."

Admiration glowed in the wedding planner's eyes as she said, "So instead of Mister and Missus, you'll be Doctor and Doctor. That's awesome."

"It's been a long journey. Cooper and I met in California while we were doing our medical residencies. When I moved to Houston for my fellowship, he still had a year to go in his program. So, we did the long-distance thing for a year. He joined an orthopedic practice in Houston two years ago."

"Do you plan to stay in Houston?"

"For now, yes. My dad is there. I think Cooper would like to return to a cooler climate at some point. He grew up in Michigan and likes the snow. I'm still deciding where I want to work and when I want to start. We're planning a nice, long honeymoon. A month."

"That sounds divine. Where are you going on your honeymoon?"

"The South Pacific."

"Ooh, I'm jealous. My aunt Helen traveled there not too long ago. You should talk to her if you have any questions."

"I'll tell Cooper. The honeymoon is his responsibility. We both work crazy hours, but he has a little more time than I do. This long weekend we've stolen for wedding planning is the last we will have until I finish my program."

At that point, Cooper caught their attention with a wave. He muted his phone and called out. "This is going to take some time. Why don't you two go on and finish the tour? Zoey can fill me in later."

"Okay," Zoey replied. As Cooper retreated indoors, she nodded toward Willow. "Lead the way."

"Okay, then." Willow turned to face the lake. "Before we move on, I want you to picture standing in this spot in August.

The snow is gone, the grass is green, and the lake is a brilliant sapphire blue."

"Like in the photographs on your wall and your website."

"Exactly. However, you need to know that the photographs don't show the improvements we have scheduled for completion before your wedding day. In a straight line centered from this staircase, fifteen feet from the water, we are building a pergola, which we'll use as a wedding arch. We'll be able to leave it bare or cover it in the flowers of your choice."

"Oh, I love that." Zoey clasped her hands. She was so excited! "I am all about flowers."

"The pergola is a nice addition, I think. If a bride wants a grand entrance and isn't afraid of stairs, we can begin the bridal march here. Otherwise, you can choose wherever you wish to begin. There's a stone path you can't see beneath the snow, and we'll place an aisle runner atop it—or not—depending on preference. The lodge has a ground-level side door that offers egress, and we'll place potted plants to shield our bride's arrival until she takes her place at the end of the aisle. The space is infinitely customizable, and if you have a vision, we're happy to work with you to bring it to life."

"A rose-covered wedding arch is right up my alley," Zoey said, excitement humming in her veins. "That's going to be gorgeous."

Willow's voice held a note of wistfulness as she said, "I think so, too. It's almost enough to make me want to delay my own wedding until summertime. I'm getting married in March."

"I noticed your engagement ring. It's beautiful."

"Thank you. It's my fiancé's grandmother's ring. I didn't know I would love a sapphire engagement ring until he gave me this one, but I adore it."

"Just like Princess Di's."

Willow laughed. "Not quite on the same scale, but I wouldn't trade it for anything."

Zoey understood. She felt the same way about her own engagement ring. Although Cooper had never admitted to it, she believed that he'd waited so long to propose to her because he'd wanted to save up to buy her the perfect ring. He'd come from humble beginnings, and despite all the scholarships he'd earned, the astronomical cost of medical school meant he'd finished his education owing significant debt. A proud man who was careful with his money, Cooper had offered her a ring he'd owned free and clear when he went down on one knee. She subconsciously fingered the square-cut diamond and asked the wedding planner, "Are you getting married here at the lodge?"

"Our reception will be here. The ceremony itself will be at the church we attend in town. We're staying closer to home and spending a week in Sedona for our honeymoon. I have two young children, and I'm not ready to travel overseas without them."

"That's understandable," Zoey said. "Are they staying with your mother while you're gone?"

"Yes. She was willing to watch them for longer than a week, but my fiancé nixed that idea. He said he'd miss them too much if we went away for longer."

"That's sweet."

"Noah is going to be a great dad. My kids love him." Willow recognized the unspoken question in Zoey's eyes and explained. "Their father died in a car accident a few years ago."

"That must have been very hard."

"It was. But life is good now. Second chances are a blessing."

"That's true." Zoey saw it every day in the emergency room. So often, her job was to give her patients the opportunity for a second chance. When she was successful, life was good. All too often, though, all she had to offer was heartbreak.

It wore on a woman more than she had anticipated.

Zoey shook off the melancholy that the thought provoked as she followed Willow to a four-person utility vehicle parked beneath the patio deck. "If not for the new snow, I'd suggest we walk, but we had three inches overnight."

While driving down to the ceremony site, Zoey's excitement rekindled as they discussed what Raindrop Lodge offered as a wedding venue. They reviewed seating options, lighting choices, and musicians on the lodge's recommended vendor list. They considered the catering menu and the cakes. Willow then showed Zoey the area they used for receptions, including where tables would be set for dinner and the spot currently hidden beneath the snow where the dance floor lay.

At that point, Willow said, "Now, I'd like to show you another spot. Should we buzz back and pick up Cooper?"

Zoey checked her phone. "No. He'd text if he were free."

"All right, then. Into the woods we go." Willow whipped the vehicle around and headed away from the lake toward the lodge. Zoey noticed that a man, a young girl, and two more dogs had joined the boy and dog she'd watched earlier playing fetch. The boy continued to throw a stick, but the little girl tossed a bright yellow tennis ball. The man carried three pairs of ice skates.

As the UTV passed closer to them, the trio waved. The little girl called, "Hey, Mom! Guess what? Anna has learned how to fetch!"

Willow returned the wave and called, "Hurray!"

"Your daughter?"

"Emma. And my son, Drew; my fiancé, Noah; and our three dogs. The puppies have been to obedience school this morning just down the road from here. The dogs are doing great.

Learning a lot. It's really too bad that the instructor doesn't work with little boys in addition to canines. I'd enroll Drew in her classes. Is it too much to ask that a nine-year-old boy picks up his underwear from the bathroom floor after he showers? I don't seem to be having much luck with that particular lesson lately."

Zoey grinned as Willow added, "Noah is teaching them to ice skate."

"They make ice skates for puppies?" Zoey teased.

Willow snorted. "Probably. I haven't looked, but people tend to treat their pets like humans these days. Allow me to clarify. The kids and Noah are going skating. I imagine the dogs will go sliding because it's still early days in obedience school, and leaving them behind is almost impossible."

Watching the children, Zoey knew a twinge of envy. She and Cooper hoped to have children in the next few years.

The two women fell silent as the vehicle entered the woods. The distance wasn't far, but it was as if they'd crossed the threshold of a new world. Willow pulled the UTV to a stop and switched off the engine. "Looks like the trees intercepted most of the snow. Are you okay with a short walk? A bit of it uphill? Nothing too strenuous, I promise."

"I'm up for that."

They exited their ride, and Willow gestured for Zoey to follow her. Soon, the evergreen firs and pines gave way to a stand of aspen. Ahead, Zoey spied a high-backed wooden glider beneath a canopy of winter-barren branches. Willow gestured toward it and said, "I spent so much time here this past fall that Noah built this and put it here for me. Our home is not far away as the crow flies. It's a nice hike when everything's not frozen."

They took their seats. Willow gave the glider a gentle push and didn't seem in any hurry to continue her sales pitch. Zoey didn't have many moments of inactivity in her life these days, so she decided to take advantage of this one. She relaxed into the glider, closed her eyes, and breathed a glorious but chilly breath of fresh air.

The peace from the forest washed over her. Into her. She tilted her head back and stared upward. Straight white tree trunks rose high into a bright blue sky. "It's like a cathedral."

"You see that, too!" Willow turned a delighted smile her way. "This is my favorite spot on the whole property. It's not in-your-face majestic like the lake surrounded by snowy peaks, but it's equally magnificent to me. The creek runs just to the north of here. When it's not deep winter, the sound of white water rushes and rumbles through the woods like music. Like a hymn. Being here makes my heart sing."

"I can see why."

They sat silently for a few minutes before Willow sighed deeply and said, "I have plans for this place. I don't know if I'll be able to pull them off, and I won't use them as part of my pitch to you because it would take a miracle for us to get it ready before your wedding. However, I wanted to share this spot with you so you know we have this hidden gem. We can do a private pre-wedding picnic in the woods for you and Cooper or have a special event for your wedding party. We're only limited by our imaginations." After a moment's pause, she added, "Well, that and your budget, of course. And the cell service. Phones can't pick up a signal here."

Zoey grinned. She liked Willow Eldridge. She loved Raindrop Lodge. She and Cooper needed to talk it over first, but she would love to say her wedding vows beneath a flower-covered pergola beside Mirror Lake. "So, tell me about your plans for this space."

Willow glanced at Zoey and cautioned, "As I said, it's all

dreams right now, and dreams take time to build. Even if everything goes smoothly, it won't be ready in August."

"I hear you."

"Okay, then." Willow straightened. A dreamy smile played on her lips as she gazed around the forest.

"I want to build a chapel out of stone, wood, and glass in these woods. I want it to be called the Glass Chapel, so our architect must give us lots and lots of glass. And we need some windows to open so we can hear the creek bubbling and the leaves quaking. I want it to be part of nature but something more. Something inspirational."

"Oh, Willow. You paint a lovely picture."

"Thank you, although I don't feel like my description does justice to the vision I have in my head. Celeste Blessing recommended an architect she assures will bring my idea to life. I just have to land my pitch to my mother and aunt."

"Well, you've convinced me. I know nothing about owning and operating a mountain lodge or an event-planning business, but I have good instincts about people. I suspect you are very good at your job. If you think a glass chapel is—"

A faint voice floated through the trees. "Willow? Willow!"

"Mom?" Alarm flashed across Willow's face, and she met Zoey's gaze. "Something's wrong."

Chapter Three

WHEN GENEVIEVE PRENTICE'S HUSBAND left her widowed at the age of thirty-eight with four children to raise, she'd learned to persevere. In the twenty-two years since that horrible day, she'd weathered her fair share of frights, emergencies, terrors, and crises concerning her loved ones. She'd even starred in a couple of those situations herself.

But nothing—*nothing*—tore her up like hearing a grandchild's cry of pain.

Her baby's baby, who needed her mother.

Genevieve had followed the utility vehicle's tracks until she found it parked at the entrance to the woods. She knew Willow had a place out this way that she loved to visit—a spot where her phone didn't get a signal—but Genevieve didn't know exactly where it was.

She'd followed the tire tracks until she spied the utility vehicle parked in the woods. After that, she climbed from her own UTV and trailed the pair of footsteps deeper into the woods until the scarcity of snow on the ground made the two women's tracks more difficult to determine.

Genevieve wasn't a hunter, but she was a mama bear of a nana. She studied the forest floor carefully and managed to follow the trail. She hoped.

She called her daughter's name every few steps, then stopped and listened. Nothing.

"I swear, I'm getting everyone whistles for Valentine's Day," she muttered. Maybe she'd also look into what could be done to get a cell tower built in this direction. Her sister was mayor. Couldn't Helen do something about cell towers? "Willow! Where are you?"

Sound floated toward her. "Mom?"

Not too far away. *Thank God.* Genevieve shouted. "Willow, come to me! We need you."

Genevieve stopped moving and waited for her daughter to find her. Shortly, she heard the crunch of twigs and leaves beneath footsteps. "Mom? Sound out!"

"Here!" Genevieve said even as she spied figures moving toward her. When they were close enough that she could see the panic on her daughter's face, Genevieve led with the vital information. "It's not too serious. Emma got tangled up with one of the pups on the ice and fell. She hurt her ankle."

"Oh, Emma," Willow cried. "My poor baby."

"It's our good luck that an orthopedic surgeon was on hand," Genevieve continued. "He said to tell you he suspects it to be a simple fracture, and he's gone to the hospital with Noah and Emma."

"A fracture? She broke her ankle?"

"Cooper is an excellent doctor," Zoey assured Willow. "Your daughter is in good hands."

"He certainly relieved my mind." Genevieve sent a grateful smile Zoey's way.

Willow closed her eyes and massaged her temples. "Was it

Thor? I'll bet it was Thor. That dog is such a troublemaker. And Cooper went along to the hospital? That's so kind of him."

"He's a great guy," Zoey said. "And seriously, he's a wonderful doctor. Great with kids. Sports injuries are his jam."

Genevieve hugged her daughter and then handed her a set of keys. "I'm parked right behind you. Give me your keys, then take my buggy and go, Willow. Head straight to the parking lot. Helen is watching and waiting with your bag and car keys."

"Drew?"

"We've got him. Don't worry about anything here. And drive carefully! Only one family member is allowed in the hospital at a time. Family rule."

"Yes, ma'am. Thanks, Mom. Zoey, I'm sorry—"

"Not necessary. Go see to your child."

Genevieve added, "I'll finish the tour, honey. Go give Emma a kiss from Nana."

Willow took off in the direction of the UTVs. Genevieve watched her go, then exhaled a sigh. "Well, this has been an exhausting half an hour. Do you mind if I take a few minutes and catch my breath before we start back to the buggy?"

"Take all the time you need. Do you want to sit down? The glider isn't far."

"My daughter has a glider tucked away out here? I knew she had a spot but didn't know it included furniture. I'd love to sit a bit. Please, lead on."

The hike to the bench wasn't far at all. Genevieve wasn't physically tired so much as she was mentally whipped. She hadn't slept well the night before, struggling with the decision to sell the inn, so she hadn't been in top form when she first heard Emma's scream of pain. The last half hour or so had sapped her energy. And if she were honest, the day drinking hadn't helped.

Genevieve sank onto the glider. "Goodness. I'm afraid we are not showing you our best side in our effort to earn your business, Zoey."

"Not at all. The Raindrop would be a fabulous place to get married. You can't ask for a prettier setting. Honestly, it's more scenic than Angel's Rest."

"Better than Angel's Rest? Be still my heart. Oh, I do like you." Genevieve patted Zoey's knee. "I really want to be Celeste Blessing when I grow up."

"I don't blame you. She's great. Willow has been great, too. I'm the last person to criticize a mother rushing off to care for her injured child."

Genevieve leaned her head back and closed her eyes. "Thank you. That's sweet of you to say. Cooper mentioned you are a physician, too?"

"I am. My specialty is pediatric emergency medicine."

"What could I do to convince you and Cooper to move to Lake in the Clouds? We need a new generation of talented doctors in town. Willow told me not long ago that her pediatrician plans to retire this fall." Giving Zoey the side-eye, she added, "I can get you a great discount on the wedding."

Zoey had never considered practicing medicine in a small town. Sitting here in these woods, she had to wonder why. "The weather would appeal to Cooper, that's for sure. I'm afraid our leaving Houston wouldn't make my dad happy. The hospitals we work in are only minutes apart."

"Your father is a doctor, too?"

"Yes, but he's not budging from Houston. He's a cancer researcher at MD Anderson."

"A noble occupation."

"He's really good at it. Gifted. Unfortunately, he works all the time. I wouldn't see him nearly so often if I didn't work so close by. When I was in med school in California, visits were rare. I missed him."

It didn't escape Genevieve's notice that Zoey failed to mention her mother, but she felt she'd pried enough. Right at this particular moment, anyway.

She could always put Helen on the job.

Genevieve couldn't help but be a little curious about Zoey Hillcrest. Her resemblance to Willow was uncanny. However, right at this moment, she was more interested in her education than her pedigree. "It's been a while since I've dealt with a broken bone. How long will our Emma be out of commission?"

"It depends on the severity of the break, of course, but you can figure on six to twelve weeks."

"That poor baby. She'll still be dealing with it at her mother's wedding. Poor me, too, since I'm keeping the kids while Willow and Noah honeymoon. Emma's brother has a history of injuries, but this is Emma's first serious incident. She'll be traumatized."

"She's how old?"

"Five."

A frown creased Zoey's brow. "And Willow's getting married when in March?"

"March ninth," Genevieve said.

"Emma is likely to be out of a cast by then. She'll be accustomed to it even if she's still in one."

"That's good to know. And speaking of weddings, let's get back to yours. I've lazed around long enough." Rising, Genevieve invited Zoey to join her with a wave. "Let's continue with our tour, shall we? What questions do you have about Raindrop Lodge or our special event capabilities? I'll do my best to answer them. Has Willow taken you by the cabins yet?"

"We haven't gotten to that part of the tour."

"I'm happy to show them to you. Or would you prefer to

return to the lodge, have something warm to drink in front of the fire, and wait so Cooper can join us?"

"I'd love to see the cabins. No telling how long Cooper will be."

Genevieve pursed her lips. "We have completely thrown you off your schedule, I'm sure. Do you have other appointments today?"

"Actually, we don't. We thought we'd spend the rest of the day sightseeing between here and Durango. We have a flight home from there tomorrow afternoon."

"In that case, the Raindrop would love to offer you a complimentary room and dinner tonight, along with tickets to a showing of *It Happened One Night* with Clark Gable and Claudette Colbert at Lake in the Clouds' historic theater, the Emily." Noting Zoey's spark of interest, Genevieve added, "It's our special Thank You, Doctors MacKenzie and Hillcrest package."

Zoey laughed. "While I can't decide about our wedding venue without speaking to Cooper first, I can make the executive decision to accept your kind offer. I don't think I've ever seen a Clark Gable movie."

Genevieve halted abruptly and clapped her hand against her chest. "Seriously?"

"No," Zoey said with a laugh.

"Oh, sweetheart. He was my first movie star crush. You'll love the movie tonight." They arrived at the utility vehicle, and Genevieve climbed behind the wheel while Zoey took the passenger seat. Genevieve asked her guest, "So, who was your first movie star crush?"

"Legolas in *Lord of the Rings.* Orlando Bloom. My dad got me the DVDs for my birthday when I was ten, and I spent my whole summer in Middle-earth."

As Genevieve started the motor and put the UTV into gear, she noted that, once again, Zoey Hillcrest didn't refer to her mother. Genevieve found that she was curious about the young woman's family. A natural reaction, she figured, considering how closely Zoey resembled Willow.

Genevieve exited the woods and headed cross-country toward the section of the property where the stand-alone cabins were located. She and Helen had renovated the original buildings and added four more after purchasing the resort. A quick check of the dash revealed that Willow had indeed left her ring of master keys.

"Isn't this cute?" Zoey said when Genevieve pulled up to Cabin Number 6.

"Six is a one bedroom, one bath. We have eighteen cabins—ten one-bedrooms, seven twos, and one three-bedroom. It's Number 17 and our only cabin to have two baths. It's rented this weekend, but our website has photos of its interior."

"Yes, I've seen them," Zoey said. "It looks so cozy."

"My sister and I had fun decorating," Genevieve said as she unlocked the door. "Each cabin is a little different, but they all have a fireplace, kitchenette, and rockers on the back porch."

Zoey's enthusiastic reaction to Cabin 7 and the two-bedroom Genevieve showed next had her preening. After viewing the adjacent playground area and the tennis and pickleball courts, they returned to the lodge, where Helen awaited them. She'd kindly had a small square table moved from the dining area closer to the fireplace. The heat from the roaring fire felt heavenly to Genevieve. She glanced around for her grandson. "Where's Drew?"

"He's downstairs in the game room," Helen replied. "I gave him a bag of quarters for the pinball machine. He's happy as a clam."

"Good. I'm going to run down and check on him. I'll be right back. Any word from Willow or Noah?"

Helen shook her head. "Not yet."

Genevieve hurried downstairs and soon discovered that the boy was indeed happily occupied. She challenged him to a game of pinball and won. Putting off his request for a rematch, she returned to the lodge's main floor. She found Helen and Zoey standing before the fireplace, their hands outstretched toward the warmth. Zoey glanced over her shoulder. "I've had a text from Cooper. Willow arrived safely, and she was with her daughter and Noah. Cooper said to tell you that Emma is doing well. He is going to head this way soon."

"Do we need to pick him up?" Genevieve asked.

"No. He'll bring Willow's car back."

"Good." Genevieve sank into a club chair with a heavy sigh. "Well, Zoey, I don't know what to say besides thank you. Believe me when I tell you this is not how we ordinarily run our sales presentations."

"Honestly, I've liked it." Zoey tucked a long blond curl behind her ear. "Not that Emma got hurt, of course, but you've treated me like family."

"Hard not to when you appear to be Willow's long-lost sister," Helen observed. She gave Genevieve a considering glance, opened her mouth to speak, then apparently reconsidered and abruptly shut it. She took a seat on the small sofa perpendicular to Genevieve's chair.

Genevieve knew her sister and could predict what Helen wanted to say. She'd probably been thinking back to events more than thirty years past and running numbers. Genevieve did not doubt that Helen would get her answers before Zoey Hillcrest rode off into the sunset—most likely never to be seen again because seriously, after today's circus, who would trust the Raindrop with their wedding?

And speaking of that...if they decided to make the wedding business a focus, they should seriously consider going forward with rebranding like Willow suggested. Raindrops and wedding days weren't a popular combination. "Zoey, we're thinking about changing the name of our resort. Would you prefer to be married at Raindrop Lodge or Reflections Inn at Mirror Lake?"

"Oh, that's pretty," the young woman said. "I'd vote for the new name."

Helen shot Genevieve a look of frustration, which told Genevieve that her sister wasn't ready to let her doppelgänger questions go. Genevieve understood. She was curious, too, although Helen was probably chewing on some suspicions that David had cheated on Genevieve and had a love child. Genevieve didn't believe that one little bit.

However, she and Helen did have three brothers, all now deceased. People always said that Willow had a lot of Bennett in her. Since Zoey had accepted Genevieve's lodging offer, Helen would have her chance to pry. *Good.* Her sister was better at it than she was.

Genevieve didn't for a moment think she'd heard the last of Helen's inquiry into the status of hers and Gage's sex life. In fairness to Helen, Genevieve had previously discussed such matters with her. Pre-David and post-. But this time with Gage was different.

She was different.

She wasn't sure what she wanted or needed at this point in her life.

Genevieve loved spending time with Gage. She had feelings

for him, and those feelings were growing, but she was perfectly happy taking it at a tortoise pace. She'd been single a long time. She'd made one great big fat change in her life recently when she sold her home and most of her belongings and moved to Colorado. She didn't need to rush into another one.

Besides, Gage had his own issues. He was now on better terms with his children than when Genevieve first met him. But his daughter didn't like the fact that her father was dating, now two and a half years since losing his wife to cancer.

Why am I worrying about this now?

Dismissing the disturbing thoughts, Genevieve rose and picked up the lunch menu on the small square dining table nearby. "Well, I don't know about y'all, but I can use something to eat."

She gave the menu a quick scan. "Looks like tomato soup is our soup of the day. I will have a bowl of that and a grilled cheese sandwich. Zoey, could we order something for you?"

"No, thank you. I'll wait and have lunch with Cooper. I will check out the menu, though."

Genevieve handed her the paper. "How about something warm to drink? Coffee? Tea? Hot chocolate?"

"I'd love coffee. Black, please."

Genevieve glanced toward her sister. "Helen?"

"Hot chocolate."

"Got it. I'll be right back." Genevieve crossed through the lobby to the cafe where she placed the order. A new server had come on shift since Emma's accident, so Genevieve spent a few moments answering her questions about the events. When she returned to the fireplace seating area, she found her sister and Zoey in the midst of a conversation.

"...father was a small-town lawyer, but his brother was a general practitioner in another even smaller town in Texas not far from the Dallas/Fort Worth metroplex," Helen said. "In those days, you had to go to the city to see a specialist, so Uncle Ray did a little bit of everything—minor surgery, setting broken bones."

Genevieve set her tray down on the square table nearby. She offered her sister the mug of hot chocolate as she said, "Uncle Ray delivered a lot of babies, too. He loved delivering babies."

Helen frowned down into her drink as Zoey accepted her coffee from Genevieve. "I sometimes regret not choosing obstetrics as a specialty," Zoey said. "When it came time to make a choice, I was in love with the adrenaline rush of emergency medicine. But I always gravitated toward children, so I added the pediatric subspecialty. Sometimes, I wish I'd chosen pediatrics from the beginning. It would be nice to watch the littles I treat in the ER grow up."

"Is it too late to change?" Helen asked.

Zoey shrugged. "I've invested a lot in this specialty. It would be a waste to abandon it before I even get started."

"What's wasteful is spending your life doing something you don't enjoy," Genevieve observed.

"It's not that I don't enjoy the work," Zoey defended. "I'm just... well... tired. I need to get to the end of June, when I complete the fellowship. Then I'll have a nice long break when all I'll need to worry about is enjoying our wedding and honeymoon."

Having served her sister and guest, Genevieve sat at their table and spread her napkin across her lap. "That sounds like an excellent plan."

Helen, bless her heart, then asked the question Genevieve was curious about the most. "Will your mother be helping with your wedding planning?"

"No. Honestly, I'm not certain we'll invite her to the wedding."

Genevieve and Helen shared a quick look that silently

conveyed shock, curiosity, and the nudge to find out more. Genevieve said, "That's . . . um . . ."

"Harsh, I know." Zoey sipped her coffee, then explained, "She left us when I was young, and she's been an inconsistent part of my life since. If I send her an invitation, I'm inviting drama."

Genevieve clicked her tongue. "That's a shame."

Zoey gave a fatalistic shrug as Helen inquired, "No stepmother to fill that role?"

"No. Dad never remarried. Cooper's mom is nice. She'll be a great mother-in-law, but we don't have that type of mother-daughter relationship where we would expect her to be involved in wedding arrangements."

"Well, as long as you have an excellent wedding planner, you won't need much help," Genevieve pointed out. "With Willow overseeing the event, a bride can do as much or as little as she wishes—if we haven't scared you away from the Raindrop, or rather, Reflections Inn at Mirror Lake, that is."

Zoey grinned. "I'm not scared. I just need to talk everything over with Cooper."

Genevieve swallowed a bite of the sandwich and then informed her sister. "I've offered Zoey and Cooper complimentary accommodations for tonight. Dinner and tickets to the Emily, too."

"Wonderful." Helen folded her hands and beamed at Zoey. "You'll love the Emily. I think our suite here in the lodge is open for tonight. Would you prefer that or one of our cabins?"

"The lodge, I think."

"Excellent choice. And dinner reservations? We have a local steak and seafood restaurant that's highly rated. How does that sound?"

"Perfect."

After that, the talk turned to other activities the couple

might enjoy on a chilly afternoon in Lake in the Clouds. Genevieve finished her lunch, and when Helen offered to show Zoey the Mirror Lake Suite, Genevieve went downstairs for the pinball contest. Drew eventually won in a three-out-of-five match. Genevieve had just returned to the main floor when the front door opened, and Cooper MacKenzie stepped inside. Zoey and Helen were nowhere in sight.

"How's everyone doing?" Genevieve asked Cooper.

"Emma's doing great. Your orthopedist knows his stuff."

"We're lucky to have Dr. Knowles in town. He's semiretired and only works during ski season. Once spring thaw happens, he hangs out his gone-fishing sign. What can you tell me about Emma's injury?"

"Very little," he said with a sympathetic smile. "I'm not her doctor, so what I can share is limited. That said, I did get a quick look at the X-ray before I stepped back from professional mode when Dr. Knowles made it in, and I'll tell you not to worry."

"Okay. Wonderful. I'm so relieved."

"Good." He glanced around the lobby. "Now, I'm back to being a groom, and I am hunting for my bride. She texted me she's in the Mirror Lake Suite?"

"Up the stairs and to the left. It's the last room at the end of the hall."

"Great."

Cooper started to turn toward the stairs, but Genevieve stopped him with a touch on his arm. "Dr. MacKenzie," she said, using his title to emphasize her point, "thank you so much."

"Hey, Noah had everything under control, but I'm glad I was able to be of assistance. According to my text messages, it netted me some perks. I understand I get a gander at Claudette Colbert's gams tonight. Lucky me."

"She did have some pretty glamorous gams," Genevieve

replied, smiling. "Be sure to let us know if we can do anything to make your stay more comfortable."

After Cooper disappeared upstairs, Genevieve visited for a moment with a foursome from Iowa playing eight ball in the billiards room before going in search of her sister. Peeking into the innkeeper's office, she asked Kelly if she'd seen Helen. Moments later, at Kelly's direction, she joined Helen in the lodge's conference room, where she quickly ascertained that her sister was on a phone call with her assistant in the Lake in the Clouds' mayor's office.

Genevieve sat across the desk from Helen and waited for her to finish the call. She eavesdropped as Helen agreed to meet with the local tourism board and scheduled a lunch with a city councilman the following week.

When Helen set down her phone, she met Genevieve's gaze and said, "What a day."

"It's definitely been eventful."

"Any more news about Emma?" After Genevieve summarized her conversation with Cooper, Helen nodded. "Good. I like that young man. I hope they decide to get married here. How bad do you think we screwed that up?"

"Hard to tell. I think Zoey likes us, but who knows?"

Helen reached for the handbag she'd left on a credenza and removed a small notebook, which she handed to her sister. "I had a few minutes, so I consulted with Mr. Google. Don't judge me. I was curious. Read the last page."

Genevieve turned to the indicated notation and read a date. "And this is . . . ?"

"Zoey Hillcrest's birthdate."

"Okay. And I should care why?"

"She's more than a year younger than Brooke."

Brooke was Genevieve's youngest child. "Okay," Genevieve repeated. "And I should care about that why?"

"Because David got his vasectomy when Brooke was a month old!"

"Helen!" Genevieve tossed the notebook onto the conference table. "Seriously? You seriously thought Zoey Hillcrest might be my husband's love child?"

"No, not seriously," her sister said in a defensive tone. "But in the words of Ronald Reagan, trust, but verify."

"Oh, for heaven's sake. We're not talking nuclear weapons."

"No, but it would darn sure be a nuclear bomb in your family if it happened to be true. Personally, I don't want to negotiate another one of those, Genevieve. We're still dealing with the fallout from the last one."

"You're ridiculous."

"No, I'm not. Zoey Hillcrest could be Willow's twin!"

"No, she's Willow's doppelgänger. It's a thing."

Helen shrugged. "Well, now we know for certain, and you can forget about that nagging little worry."

"I didn't have a nagging worry."

"If that's true, it's only because you haven't had a moment to brood about it yet."

Genevieve rolled her eyes. "Whatever. Look, I made reservations for them at Vista Ridge, took care of the check, and arranged to have tickets at the Emily box office in their name. Can you think of anything I've overlooked?"

"I think that's the perfect amount. Anything more might look like a business bribe rather than a personal thank-you."

"Good point. Well, I promised Drew another game downstairs, but before I join the pinball wizard, I wanted to confirm you're planning to be at book club at my house on Tuesday?"

"I'll be there with bells on," Helen replied.

"What are you bringing for snacking?"

"A veggie plate with a Greek yogurt dip."

Genevieve gaped at her sister as her stomach sank. "Seriously?"

"Oh, for heaven's sake, Genevieve. I'm planning to bring Mom's sheet cake as usual."

Relieved, Genevieve wiped her brow dramatically. Mom's sheet cake was the sinfully delicious chocolate concoction their mother used to make. The recipe called for two unusual ingredients that made the cake uniquely delicious. The Lake in the Clouds crowd loved it when the cake appeared on the dessert table.

The Bennett sisters did not share the recipe, keeping the special ingredients secret even from Genevieve's children. Family tradition dictated that the recipe be passed down in one's will, and Genevieve and Helen had sworn to honor the custom.

But there would be hell to pay at the book club if neither brought the chocolate cake.

"Okay, I'm going to—" A knock on the threshold interrupted her. She glanced over her shoulder to see Zoey Hillcrest standing in the doorway. The young woman sparkled, and Genevieve couldn't help but smile at her.

"I'm sorry to interrupt," Zoey said. "Cooper and I headed off to explore Lake in the Clouds. I wanted to let y'all know that we have discussed it, and we would like to get married here at the resort."

"That's wonderful," Helen said.

"Fabulous," Genevieve added. "Willow will be thrilled."

Zoey beamed at them. "I'm really excited. I know Willow has her hands full at the moment, and I don't want to call and interrupt her, but I'm hoping we could squeeze in a short meeting tomorrow before Cooper and I leave for the airport at ten. Around nine, perhaps? I figure you'll speak with her at some point this afternoon. Would you ask her?"

"Absolutely. I'm sure nine o'clock will be fine with her. Why don't you plan on it, and if she can't make it work for some reason, I'll have her call you."

"Good deal. I am so happy we found the Raindrop or, should I say, Reflections Inn at Mirror Lake?"

The Bennett sisters shared a glance, and then Genevieve said, "Reflections Inn at Mirror Lake it is."

Helen rose, moved around her desk, and hugged Zoey. The move surprised Genevieve. As a rule, Helen wasn't a hugger. Not with guests, anyway. Genevieve *was* a hugger, though, so she naturally followed her sister's lead. Once the group embraces ended and Zoey stepped away, Genevieve was surprised to see tears in her eyes.

"It's going to be a beautiful wedding, Zoey," Genevieve assured her. "You are going to be a beautiful bride."

"Thank you. I hope so."

"I know so," Helen insisted. "Because, Dr. Zoey Hillcrest, you are one of our brides. Welcome to the family."

Part Two

Chapter Four

April

ZOEY'S HEART POUNDED AS she strode away from the emergency room, the grieving mother's sobs still ringing in her ears. She was angry. Furious. She was so effing tired of stupid, careless people making stupid, careless decisions that cost the youngest and most vulnerable their lives.

"What made me think I wanted to do this stupid job anyway?" she muttered. Stupid. Stupid. Stupid.

Her shift had ended an hour ago, so she hurried to the locker room and retrieved her purse, slamming the door with a metallic bang. Eight minutes later, she screeched her tires as she punched the gas, accelerated onto the freeway, and headed home.

She was taking the long route to the townhouse she'd shared with Cooper for the past two years. Well, a year and three-quarters. He'd be home already. It was Thursday, an office-hour day for him. He'd be rested and relaxed and ready to interact when she arrived home. Invariably, his office days were good days.

Some days, that totally ticked her off.

Zoey should have gone into orthopedics or, better yet, plastic surgery. Then she could spend her days doing boob jobs and nose jobs and plumping lips instead of dealing with dead toddlers.

"Cabinet latches," she muttered. "What's so hard about putting latches on cabinets where you store your drain cleaner?"

Maybe she should ditch medicine altogether and find a flower shop to run.

She rolled down the window and let the air blow through the car, the sound system belting classic rock. She continued three exits past the one leading home and only exited the highway and turned toward home when she judged her blood pressure had lowered back to a normal level.

She hit the garage door opener, and the door slowly lifted. Zoey was surprised to discover that Cooper's car was gone. Inside, she found a note on the mudroom door.

> *Your dinner is in the oven. On a dessert run. Will be right back.*
>
> *~C~*

"Yum," Zoey murmured. She followed the tempting aroma of balsamic chicken toward the kitchen, where she kicked off her shoes, poured a glass of red wine, and removed a plate from the warming oven. Fresh broccoli and a side of pasta. The man had been busy.

She was halfway through her meal when she heard him enter the townhouse. Zoey expected him to be carrying a quart of ice cream from the creamery just outside the neighborhood. Peach ice cream was her fiancé's favorite food group. Instead, the bag he carried sported a grocery store's logo. She smiled up at him. "The chicken is delish. Thank you."

Cooper studied her closely. "You're welcome. You doing all right?"

She knew right then that he'd called the hospital. He probably spoke to the ER nurses' station, and someone told him about the toddler. "I'm okay. What's in the bag?"

"Italian cream cake."

Yes, he'd definitely called the hospital. Italian cream cake was Cooper's way of taking care of her. Not a bad way at all. "You're spoiling me. Better stop it, or I won't be able to fit into my wedding dress."

"Yeah, not hardly. I'll bet you've lost ten pounds since Christmas."

Though he said "Christmas," they both knew he meant since their return from Colorado on their wedding venue trip. That first week back, she'd lost seven patients in the ER. Seven! From car wrecks, an accidental shooting, a backyard pool incident, and a bicycle wreck. It had been a perfectly horrible week. Then, a respiratory virus turned into pneumonia and knocked her on her butt. She'd missed three weeks at the hospital. Since then, she'd all but lived at work as she played catch-up on her training, which left her exhausted and pining for more time with Cooper. Seemed like they hardly saw each other anymore.

Zoey took a sip of her wine and then shrugged. "Every bride wants to lose weight before her big day."

Cooper chose to change the subject after that, and he shared news about a mutual friend from their days as resident physicians as they dug into the cake. She was loading dishes into the dishwasher when the doorbell sounded. Glancing at Cooper, she asked, "Are we expecting someone?"

"Not me. Keep eating. I'll see who it is." He strode toward the front of the house.

A moment later, Zoey heard the low murmur of masculine

voices. It was too soft for her to identify the visitor. She wiped her mouth with her napkin, her gaze on the doorway. Spying the new arrival, her face lit up. Tall and fit, he had sandy blond hair with a touch of gray at the temples and laugh lines at the edges of his blue eyes. "Dad!"

"Hi, sunshine," Adam Hillcrest said, his smile easy and warm.

Zoey slid off her chair and all but ran toward her father. His strong arms enveloped her in a comforting hug, and a measure of the tension within her flowed away. Her dad loved her unconditionally. He'd been the one person she could count on her entire life.

"This is a nice surprise."

"Actually, it's not."

Zoey pulled away from the hug and stared up at him. Her father looked at Cooper. "You have any whiskey?"

"Sure." Cooper turned to get it while Zoey asked, "Daddy, what's wrong? Are you sick?"

"No, I'm fine. Nothing is wrong with me." He sighed, then said, "This is about your mother."

Zoey took a deliberate step backward. Now she understood why he'd asked for the drink. A discussion about Jennifer Hillcrest was invariably helped by booze. Zoey resumed her seat at the bar.

She hadn't heard a word from her mother in probably three years. That had been a phone call to tell Zoey that Jennifer was getting married again. "What has she done this time? Another breakup? Another bankruptcy? Another arrest?"

"No, honey. This time, I'm afraid it's different. Zoey, your mother has cancer."

Zoey went still.

Her father continued. "She contacted me about six weeks ago and told me she'd been diagnosed with stage four lung cancer.

She was being treated at her home in Florida, but her doctors were not hopeful. I arranged for her to be evaluated at the hospital, and she's been accepted for a clinical trial. She begins treatment tomorrow."

The hospital he referred to was the one where he worked as a researcher, MD Anderson Cancer Center. Adam continued. "She asked that I wait until now to share the news with you."

While Adam went into detail about Jennifer Hillcrest's condition and the treatment plan, Cooper sat beside Zoey and took her hand. Adam answered the medical questions Zoey and Cooper posed, then, following a brief moment of silence, Zoey summarized. "So, she's terminal."

"I'm not prepared to make that pronouncement. We're making advances every day, and I've seen this team perform miracles in the past."

And this, Zoey thought, was the difference between an emergency room physician and a medical researcher.

"But it is serious," Adam continued. "Otherwise, I wouldn't have thrown this into your lap. I know the timing could be better."

"There's the understatement of the night," Cooper muttered. He gave Zoey's shoulder a gentle squeeze, signaling his support.

The final months of a fellowship were beyond busy and filled with stress. On top of the make-up hours at the hospital from her illness in addition to the regular full work schedule, Zoey had end-of-program exams on her horizon.

Adam's rueful grimace acknowledged the point Cooper had made while Zoey's thoughts shifted from the medical to the personal. "What about Gary? Is he with her?"

Adam took a sip of his drink. "Well, apparently, her husband passed away a couple of years ago. She's been living in Florida."

Really? The last Zoey had heard, Jennifer had been living in

North Carolina. Zoey filled her cheeks with air, then blew out in a rush.

Adam shot his daughter an apologetic look and then put the cherry on top of the reason for his visit. "Honey, your mother asked me to ask you to visit her."

"I see." Zoey sat back in her chair, her thoughts spinning. "I see" was a silly thing to say. She didn't see anything. That's the way it had always been with everything where her mother was concerned.

Zoey had been six years old when Jennifer Hillcrest left her husband and daughter for the first time. She'd stayed gone three months before showing up again without notice or really any repentance that Zoey had noticed. Five months later, Zoey woke up one morning to find her gone again.

Adam allowed his wife to return to live with them one more time when Zoey was nine. When she left again less than a month later, Zoey's dad told her mom never to come back. Their divorce had been finalized the day before Zoey's tenth birthday.

"I don't know how to explain your mother to you," her father told Zoey when he shared the news. "I know she loves you, but I think she has her hands full trying to care for herself."

"Do you still love her?" Zoey asked.

He let the question dangle unanswered for a long time. Finally, he said, "No, sweetheart, I don't. But listen to me. What's between your mother and me is separate from your mother and you. My feelings have nothing to do with your feelings for your mother or hers for you. She's no longer my wife, but she will always be your mother."

"So, it's okay for me to love her still?"

"Of course, baby. I won't ever try to interfere with that."

Zoey had nodded. She'd believed her dad. Back then, she'd believed in her mother, too.

She'd believed her mother would one day love her enough to speak the truth. Twenty years later, she was still waiting.

Her mother was a mystery. She'd told both Adam and Zoey tales about her past over the years. Little of what she'd said had turned out to be true.

Jennifer had claimed to be an orphan when she'd met Adam, the young, nerdily handsome, smart-as-a-whip college student who bought doughnuts at the shop where she waitressed. Theirs had been a whirlwind romance, she'd told her daughter. They'd been two young people drawn together by his daily sugar craving and her attraction to a brilliant mind.

Turned out that Jennifer was one area in his life where Adam wasn't so brilliant. Though neither of her parents ever admitted as much to Zoey, she could do the math, and their marriage had been the result of an accidental pregnancy. Zoey had often wondered if Jennifer had seen Adam as a meal ticket and gotten pregnant on purpose.

She did believe that, for a while, her mother had tried to make the marriage work. Zoey had memories of love and laughter in their home. She knew her father had suffered when Jennifer went away.

Only when Adam eventually decided to divorce her did he discover through the legal process that Jennifer Beaudine Hillcrest didn't actually exist. She admitted to being a runaway who'd assumed a false identity and used a fake ID when she'd married Adam. She'd refused to reveal to either her husband or her daughter the truth about who she was or where she came from. While she married twice more after Adam—that Zoey knew about, anyway—she'd kept the Hillcrest surname.

And now, Jennifer Hillcrest was dying and finally—finally—wanted to see her daughter. Zoey had given up asking for visits a decade ago. "Has she given up, then? Does she want to say good-bye?"

Adam shook his head. "No, not at all. She's ready to fight, which is one of the reasons I recommended her for this trial. We know how stubborn she is."

Zoey studied her father. How did Adam feel about Jennifer's return to their lives under these circumstances? Facing this prognosis? She honestly couldn't tell.

"Look, sweetheart, I'm not about to tell you what to do. If you choose not to see her, you won't hear one word about it from me. I believe you had a right to know this information, but Zoey, you don't owe her anything."

Well, except for my life.

Cooper draped his arm around Zoey's shoulder in silent comfort and support. She drew in a deep breath, then released it slowly with a sigh. "I'll go see her. I'd regret it if I didn't. Who knows, maybe she'll finally come clean about her family background."

Maybe Zoey would finally discover why her mother left her, why she'd never loved Zoey enough to stay. Why Zoey had never been good enough.

"If you want answers from her, I'd recommend you go tomorrow," Adam suggested. "This treatment will hit her pretty hard. She won't be in the mood for a heart-to-heart once she's into treatment." He paused a moment, then added, "That's assuming she'd ever be in the mood for a heart-to-heart."

Zoey considered the next day's schedule and inwardly sighed. "I'll go during lunch tomorrow. Will I see you there?"

Adam shook his head. "No. I'm leaving tomorrow for the conference in Brussels, remember?"

Zoey snapped her fingers. "Your big presentation. I can't

believe I forgot about that." Her father was going to be gone for a month.

"She didn't forget," Cooper said, rising and crossing the room, headed for their bedroom. Over his shoulder, he said, "She bought you a gift. I was going to drop it by your place on my way to the gym in the morning."

Delight filled Adam's face. "You bought me a present?"

"*We* did." Zoey gazed at Cooper with loving gratitude as he returned carrying a gift-wrapped package. *He'd even wrapped it, too. Oh, Cooper. You are the most thoughtful man.* "It's for the plane trip."

Adam unwrapped an advance reading copy of his favorite thriller writer's upcoming novel. His chin dropped. "Whoa. How did you get your hands on this?"

Delighted with his reaction, Zoey beamed as Cooper explained. "The daughter of one of my partners is roommates with the author's daughter. Zoey got the idea to ask for an autographed book. This is what he sent."

"It's signed to you, Dad," she pointed out.

"Well, I'll be damned. Thank you, sweetheart." Adam shook Cooper's hand and clapped him on the shoulder. Then he gave Zoey a big hug, whispering in her ear, "I'm sorry, baby. Remember, though, she is not your responsibility. She gave up that right years ago."

"I know. It's okay. I'll be fine. I hope you have a great trip, Dad. Break a leg at your presentation and enjoy your well-deserved vacation." It was the first extended vacation he'd planned to take in years.

"Thanks. I'll be back in six weeks. I'll keep in touch by phone and e-mail. I'll check with the hospital about Jennifer, and I'll keep you informed so you don't need to concern yourself. You take care of your business at the hospital and get ready for that big party we're having in August."

Her father left Zoey and Cooper's place a short time later. Exhaustion hit Zoey when the door closed behind Adam, and she murmured, "I'm toast."

"I can imagine." Cooper slipped his arms around her and pulled her close. "Want me to go with you tomorrow?"

Zoey let herself relax into him and considered the question. More than anything, she'd like answers from her mother. "Thank you, but I don't think so. This might be my one chance to find out about her family."

Cooper pressed a kiss against her temple. "I know that's important to you."

Zoey had tried to explain to him in the past about the hole in her soul caused by not knowing anything about her family history. Her dad came to live with her grandparents through a closed adoption. Her mother had been a nameless runaway who had lied about everything important. All of her life, Zoey had yearned for roots.

Cooper was a good man who loved her, but she didn't expect him to truly understand this part of her. He knew his bloodlines. He had parents and grandparents who'd shared with him a family history going back generations.

Zoey sighed and said, "Yes, it is."

The following day in the first hour on the job, Zoey dealt with a severe burn case, an accidental choking, and a poisoning before leaving the ER to deal with administrative issues for a couple of hours. She next stole forty minutes to study for her exam. Throughout the morning, her tension grew. By the time she climbed into her car for the short drive to MD Anderson, her nerves were strung tight as a guitar string.

Fifteen minutes later, standing in the hospital room doorway,

Zoey studied the woman lying in a bed. Jennifer Hillcrest had aged since she'd last popped into Zoey's life some three to four years before. She was thin, her once-dark hair now peppered with gray. Her head turned. Their eyes met.

A lifetime's worth of yearning swept over Zoey.

"Well, look at you," Jennifer said. "Aren't you a pretty thing? I'd forgotten that you have your grandmother's eyes."

My grandmother's eyes. It was the first such remark Zoey had ever heard. "Hello, Jennifer."

She didn't call her "Mom" or "Mother." Jennifer had forbidden that early on. She'd claimed to have been too young to be a mother. *"We'll be friends, you and I, Zoey. That's what we'll be."*

Such a liar she'd been. Zoey needed to remember that today.

She walked into the room, a strange combination of a little girl out of her element and an experienced physician well accustomed to hospital rooms. Uncertain of what to say or how to begin, she retreated into safe Dr. Hillcrest territory. She checked the readings on the machines monitoring Jennifer's condition.

"So, am I alive?" Jennifer asked after a moment.

"Looks that way to me."

"Your father tells me you are a doctor, too."

"I am. I'm a pediatric emergency physician."

Jennifer closed her eyes and rested her head back against her pillow, a faint smile on her face. "In that case, you should be my doctor. Even after all these years, I'm still a child."

Well. What was Zoey supposed to say to that? She shoved her hands into her jacket pockets and said, "Dad told me you wanted to see me."

"Yes. He warned me that you might not be keen about the idea, so I'm a little surprised to see you here."

"Honestly, that makes both of us."

"Sit down, Zoey. I do have a few things I'd like to say to you. Dying gives a girl perspective." She watched her daughter closely for a reaction, but Zoey had been a physician long enough by now to keep emotion from showing on her face.

Jennifer continued. "Knowing I'm about to meet my maker makes me think I should try to right some wrongs in my past."

A conversation can't wipe out a lifetime of neglect, Jennifer. Nevertheless, Zoey was interested to hear what her mother had to say. To a point. She took a seat beside the bed. "I'm on my lunch break. I can only stay about fifteen minutes."

"So, you want me to hit the high points?"

"That would be good."

Jennifer studied Zoey for a long minute before she began. "More than anything, I wish I could have made a life with you and your father. I tried to make it happen. I truly did. But the die was cast long before I met Adam, I'm afraid."

Zoey shifted in her chair. Did she believe anything her mother said?

"For a little while, I harbored some hope. I thought perhaps that things could change. That you and your father could save me." She closed her eyes and said, "It wasn't meant to be. It was better for you and your father that I left. For that, I want to tell you that I'm sorry. I don't believe I've ever said it before."

No, she hadn't. A flood of emotion washed through Zoey. She was nine years old again, and her mother was packing her bag. Zoey hadn't understood it then. She didn't understand it now. "Why? You said you want to right some wrongs. Tell me why you left, Jennifer."

Her mother's mouth shut. Her lips flattened in a grim line. She shook her head, refusing to answer the question, and shifted her gaze to stare out the window.

So much for making amends.

The exchange set the tone for Zoey's visits from that day forward. Nevertheless, she returned to the hospital daily, always hoping for answers to her lifelong questions.

"You have your grandmother's eyes," Jennifer had said. Who was this grandmother? Who were your people? *Do I have family anywhere?*

May

Helen braked her car to a stop in front of the newest and most isolated cabin on the Reflections Inn at Mirror Lake property—their luxurious honeymoon cottage. Or, at least, it would be luxurious once they added the final touches. The structure itself had been completed. What was left for her and her partners to complete was the fun stuff.

Some of which she had loaded into the back of the SUV.

As she switched off the engine, Helen's phone chimed with a text. Genevieve was running late, and Helen should expect her in twenty minutes. Helen replied with a thumbs-up emoji. A second text from her sister announced BIG NEWS INCOMING. Helen tucked her phone into her jeans pocket and murmured, "That's interesting."

She unloaded the first of four large tubs she had stored in the back of her SUV and carried it into the cottage. Just as she set the box on the sofa that had been delivered the previous day, her phone rang. The ringtone identified the caller to be Nicole Vandersall.

Nicole was Lake in the Clouds' assistant city manager and Helen's right-hand woman. The former librarian and mother of two had moved to Lake in the Clouds following a divorce to be closer to her widowed mother, a neighbor of Helen's in the Mountain Vista Retirement Community condos. Helen had been impressed by Nicole's organizational skills, the kindness she showed her ailing mother, and how she handled her teenage daughters. Shortly after winning the mayor's race last August, Helen had convinced the city council to hire Nicole to serve as Lake in the Clouds' city manager. Hiring Nicole had proved to be one of the best decisions the city had made in decades.

Nicole learned fast, and she'd been a great help to Lake in the Clouds' mayor pro tempore, Celeste Blessing, while Helen had been away last December. In April, when the Bennett sisters had popped over to visit Paris for a week, Nicole stepped up and performed the mayor's duties seamlessly. If Helen were being brutally honest, Nicole made a much better mayor than she.

She set the phone on the coffee table and connected the call, putting it on speaker. "Hello, Nicole."

"I'm sorry to bother you, Helen, but we have another wildlife problem on Main Street."

Helen closed her eyes and sighed. "Bears again?"

"Cougars."

"What?" Helen's eyes flew open as she straightened in alarm. "We've never—"

"The two-legged kind."

"Oh."

Nicole elaborated. "A group of six women is in town for the Rodgers and Hammerstein Film Festival at the Emily. They're staying out at Reflections."

Well, damn. Helen slumped down onto the sofa.

Nicole continued. "I am told that Gage was having pizza with his sons and daughter at the bowling alley. Our tourists appear to have begun their three-martini lunch well before noon. They started harassing the Throckmorton family."

"What sort of harassment?"

"Flirtation on steroids."

"Oh dear. Was Scamp there? Gage's young grandson?"

"No," Nicole replied. "All involved were adults, thank goodness, because three of the cats sprang. They swooped in, sat on the guys' laps, and attempted to steal kisses."

"Oh, for crying out loud."

"The men managed to extricate themselves, but in the melee, Gage's daughter threw an elbow that caught a tourist's nose. Blood gushed, and the visiting team went wild."

Helen scowled and asked, "What is wrong with people?"

"I blame social media. Anyway, they've been detained on a drunk and disorderly charge. The plan is to keep the . . . I hesitate to call them ladies . . . in jail long enough to sober up. The Throckmortons aren't pressing charges, although Lindsay wasn't happy because her shirt got ruined, and Gage apparently was hot under the collar about having his family lunch interrupted."

"I imagine he was. I don't think he often gets together with all three of his kids. These chicks are lucky he's not demanding they be charged with sexual assault."

"True, that," Nicole agreed. "Well, with any luck, this incident is over, but I thought I should give you a heads-up because you're the mayor, and they're staying at Reflections. I asked Chief Roberts to let you know once they're sprung from lockup."

"Thanks, Nicole. I appreciate it." Helen dropped her head back and stared up at the ceiling. "Is there anything else I need to know about before the council meeting tonight?"

The two women briefly discussed a couple of city business issues before ending the call. As Helen returned her phone to her pocket, a chuckle escaped her. She'd have to tease Zach about this the next time she saw him.

Zach Throckmorton was the eldest of Gage's three adult children and the owner of the company that had transformed the Bennett sisters' investment property from a tired and outdated tourist camp to a working-toward-five-star resort.

Helen headed back outside to retrieve another box when she spied her sister approaching in her crossover SUV, which was also loaded with storage tubs. Genevieve pulled up behind Helen's vehicle. The moment she switched off the motor, Helen asked, "So, let me guess. Your big news involves your boyfriend and cougars."

"What?" A wrinkle of confusion creased Genevieve's brow.

"You haven't talked to Gage?" Helen lifted a tub from her SUV.

"No, but I am headed out to the ranch after I leave here. We're going horseback riding up to some scenic viewpoint he wants to show me. You said 'cougars'? Was someone hurt?"

"No. Everyone is fine." As she relayed the story about the out-of-control tourists, Helen eyed her sister more closely, noting the way she glowed. Surreptitiously, Helen checked her sister's left ring finger. Still empty. So, Gage hadn't popped the question. Helen expected a marriage proposal would come sometime this year, although Genevieve didn't appear to be expecting one imminently. Helen believed her sister would have mentioned the possibility if she thought one was on the near horizon.

Genevieve continued, "He's having lunch with his children."

"I know." Perhaps the purpose of his family lunch had been to inform the Throckmorton progeny of Gage's intention to propose prior to the fact. If that was the case, Genevieve was obviously oblivious. So, why the glow? "What's your big news?"

Genevieve's shine went incandescent, and her emerald eyes sparkled. "Willow is pregnant."

The news was an unanticipated arrow to Helen's heart. She bobbled the tub in her arms as a wave of pain seasoned with jealousy radiated through her.

The emotion shamed Helen. As always, she powered through it. She pasted a smile upon her face and tried—seriously tried—to make it genuine. "Congratulations, Nana. That was fast."

"Happened on their honeymoon."

Helen did a few quick calculations as she carried the storage container toward the cabin's front door. Her niece had married in early March. "She's due in December? How is she feeling? Do they know yet if it's a boy or a girl?"

"She says she's feeling great. No morning sickness and that early pregnancy fatigue is easing. I think it's too soon to know the gender. Nevertheless, she told me they've decided to wait until the baby is born to find out." Genevieve grabbed her own tub and followed Helen into the Honeymoon Cottage.

"They're waiting?" Helen set the tub down with the ones she'd brought inside earlier. "That's unusual in this day and age."

Genevieve set her burden next to Helen's tubs in the kitchenette. "Willow and Noah think waiting is a better option for Drew and Emma. One of them is going to be disappointed, and they won't be as focused on whether they have a brother or a sister when there's an actual baby to play with."

"Well, I'm thrilled for them and for you, too. That'll be three new babies in three months, with Jake and Tess's twins due in October. Speaking of your eldest and his wife, how is Tess feeling?"

"She's doing better. She says she's only throwing up once a day instead of three times."

"That poor girl."

"She's been pretty miserable. But I keep telling her it's all worth it in the end. She'll get two precious bundles." Genevieve waited for a beat and added, "I won't mention what a pain in the butt adult children often are."

"I thought you were getting along well with your offspring right now," Helen said, arching a questioning brow.

"I'm thinking about Gage. His up-and-down relationship with Lindsay is in the valley again. That's the reason behind today's pizza summit at the bowling alley." Genevieve's expression turned rueful as she added, "He was hoping to improve the situation before they all head off to Alaska on their family vacation."

"Well, who knows? Maybe the cougar brawl will unite father and daughter and facilitate healing."

"Maybe." Genevieve gave her sister a doubtful look.

Helen doubted it, too. She also had her suspicions about why Gage's daughter had a bee in her bonnet these days. Genevieve might be blind to the rancher's deepening feelings, but Helen could spot the development from a mile away.

And Gage's daughter didn't like her widowed father having a new woman in his life.

Genevieve wasn't blind to that. The twenty-something-year-old woman had made her feelings clear last year when her father praised Genevieve during the opening gala for the Emily. While she might not have a personal beef with Genevieve, Lindsay Throckmorton Higgins clearly thought it was too soon for Gage to move on with his life where romance was concerned.

Eyeing her sister, Helen considered keeping the gossip she'd picked up yesterday at the nail salon to herself. But, no, Genevieve shouldn't be caught off guard. "I heard a rumor that she's moving back to town."

Genevieve's head snapped around. "Who?"

"Gage's daughter."

"What?" Genevieve's eyes went round and a little buggy. "Lindsay and Frank are moving to Lake in the Clouds?"

"Sometime this summer, so tweeted a little birdie in my ear."

That tidbit obviously sent Genevieve's mind to spinning. "Is Frank joining a bank here? Are they going to live at the ranch?"

"I don't know."

"Who's the birdie? Is this for real?"

Helen explained about being drawn into a conversation with the sister of the wife of Gage's ranch manager while seated next to the woman in pedicure chairs at the nail salon. The woman proved to be a rabid gossip.

Genevieve tried to act as if the news hadn't disturbed her, but Helen wasn't fooled. Genevieve would have to figure out what she wanted from Gage Throckmorton, and she would need to do it quickly.

While her sister was busy figuring out her wishes, dreams, and desires, Helen needed to go to work on her own. Somehow, some way, she needed to come to terms with these old emotions that all these new babies were stirring up inside her.

Well, first things first. She and Genevieve had a honeymoon cottage to decorate.

While her sister went outside to get the last tub from her SUV, Helen rolled her shoulders, stretching her taut muscles, and did some forward thinking. When Genevieve returned with the bucket, she said, "So, we have a number of Christmas-season weddings booked. And at Thanksgiving, too, I believe. Willow will need maternity leave. We'll have to put our contingency plan into action."

"I know." Genevieve carried a tub labeled "Bedding" into the bedroom and set it on the king-sized bed. "It's good that we prepared for this possibility when we decided to expand the wedding business. Willow said she'd start interviewing for an assistant coordinator next week."

"Thank goodness," Helen said, relieved. "Kelly said that

Willow has needed help for weeks now. Once we put the architectural drawings of the Glass Chapel onto the Reflections Inn website, wedding inquiries exploded."

"It's going to be such a beautiful building," Genevieve said as she removed the lid from her tub. She hummed with pleasure when she spied the duvet cover lying on the top of a pile of bedding. "And this place is going to be perfect."

"Dare I say we've improved on the Honeymoon Cottage at Angel's Rest?"

"Only because we totally ripped off Celeste's ideas. Our baseline was near perfection. You ready to get decorating?"

"Let's do it," Helen said as she released the lid on a tub containing bath towels.

They spent the next hour dressing the cottage. They'd chosen a soft, romantic color palette of sage, bronze, and copper tones. They hung curtains on the windows and pictures on the walls. They placed dishes and glassware into cabinets and stocked the pantry with paper goods and picnic supplies. Once the bed was made, towels stacked, and the rugs spread upon the floor, they finished with the little touches that added romance to comfort—scented candles, branded soaps, bubble bath, and lotions made specifically for them by Heavenscents out of Eternity Springs.

Once done and with empty crates returned to their vehicles, they stood side by side in the middle of the main room and surveyed their handiwork. "It's perfect," Genevieve said with a sigh. "Don't you think it's perfect?"

"Yes, I do. However, I expect we will have a few adjustments to make after Willow and Noah's quality-control visit this weekend."

Helen smirked. "Aren't we lucky to have our own pair of newlyweds in-house to ensure we got it right?"

Genevieve took another long look around, then spoke confidently. "Oh, we got it right. So, what's next on the list?"

"Well, I'm headed back into town. A box of merch for our Christmas market booth arrived just as I left this morning. I'm anxious to inspect the contents."

Genevieve's eyes lit. "Oh yeah? What merch? From what vendor?"

"The glass tree ornaments. It's our special order from Whimsies."

Genevieve clapped her hands in delight. "Ooh. I want to come and have a look."

"Don't you have a horseback riding date?"

"Yes, I do." Genevieve's lips twitched with mirth. "I'm dying to hear his version of the cougar attack."

"And you get to share Willow's big news."

"True. Although, I admit I'm a little hesitant to do so. He's already jealous that we're having twins in October. The man wants more grandchildren." She paused a moment and considered. "You know, I wonder if that's why Lindsay and her husband are moving to Lake in the Clouds? Maybe they're ready to have a baby and want to be around family."

Babies, babies, babies. Helen stifled a sigh. She might as well get prepared. With three new grandchildren on the way, infants would be top-of-mind for Genevieve for the next year or so. "Well, I'll put the tree ornaments in our storage unit after I inspect them, so come by whenever you'd like. You have a key."

"I'll do that."

The sisters shut and locked the cottage door, hugged good-bye, and went their separate ways. At the intersection of the highway and the entrance to the resort, on a whim, Helen turned away from town and toward the scenic alpine loop. Twenty minutes later, she pulled off at an overlook high above

Lake in the Clouds, exited her vehicle, and took a seat on a wooden bench. She fixed her gaze on the valley below, but she didn't really see the town. Nor was she more than minimally aware of the moisture that swam in her eyes and eventually overflowed.

She loved her little sister. Truly, she did. She loved Genevieve with her whole heart. The woman was her confidant. Her traveling buddy. Her best friend. Almost every time, Genevieve had been there for Helen when Helen needed her. Through the divorces—all three of them. Through the miscarriages—four of those. She'd been there when Helen had her professional triumphs, too. Making partner, the mentoring award. Her race for mayor. Genevieve was—like their father used to say—good people.

And today, Helen was pea-green jealous of her.

Genevieve had babies—four of them. She had grandbabies, two with three more on the way. She'd had one successful marriage to a handsome man to whom she'd been the sun and the stars, and now another fabulous man had gone head over heels for her and soon would pop the question. *Just see if he doesn't.*

And Helen, all she had was memories. Once upon a times. And what-ifs.

What if.

Those had to be two of the saddest words in the English language.

Summer of 1973

"What if you don't tell your parents?" Billy Poteet whispered in Helen's ear.

She playfully shoved him away. "They'd find out anyway. You know they would. Someone would tell them, and then I'd be grounded for life."

"But it would be worth it, don't you think?" He winked at her and slid his hands around her waist. "Imagine it. Fireworks booming against a starlit sky, the reflection of colors on the surface of the lake. You. Me. A blanket." He pulled her close, bent his head, and covered her mouth with his.

Helen wrapped her arms around his neck and gave herself up to the pleasure of his kiss. They stood shielded from view of the swimmers at the neighborhood pool by a hedge of junipers. His tongue slipped past her lips, probing and exploring, stoking the fire inside her until she melted against him with a moan.

Helen was in love.

Billy Poteet was a man, a high school graduate as of three days ago. Too old for barely-fifteen-year-old Helen, her father had decreed after she'd introduced him to Billy on Christmas Eve. Edward Bennett had forbidden her to date the senior basketball player who bore a striking resemblance to Hollywood heartthrob Robert Redford. Of course, that had only made the relationship more exciting, and Helen had been a rule-breaker from the beginning.

The shrill trill of a whistle interrupted the spell. The head lifeguard at the end of the hedge called, "Hey, you two. The runts in the kiddie pool can see you, and the mamas have complained. Break it up!"

Startled, Helen pulled her mouth away from Billy's. She could feel the warmth of a blush sting her cheeks. Billy only laughed and stole another quick kiss. Then with his summer blue eyes glinting down at her, he flashed a boyish grin. "Guess I'd better go cool off."

He ducked around the end of the hedge and ran toward the

swimming pool, letting out a yell as he leaped into the air and cannonballed into the water.

It was the first day of a truly glorious summer.

Since her father's Christmastime edict, she and Billy had been careful to keep their relationship quiet. Their efforts had been complicated by the fact that her brother Paul was a classmate of Billy's. He was an overprotective older brother, which meant they'd spent the entire spring semester sneaking around.

Luckily, Paul had joined their older brother John in Austin this summer as they both were taking summer classes at the University of Texas. Helen's job babysitting her younger sister and brother gave her a first taste of real freedom. Her sibs wanted to spend every day at the pool, and the lifeguards did the babysitting.

Nine-year-old Genevieve was clueless about her sister's romance, as was six-year-old Mark. They ran in packs with classmates at the pool, paying Helen little attention. It was a perfect situation.

Billy and Helen took full advantage of it. He was even able to talk her into the Fourth of July rendezvous at the lake. She'd secured an invitation to spend the weekend at a friend's lake house. He and two of his buddies rented a houseboat for the weekend.

They'd watched fireworks together and later, created some of their own. It was Helen's first time, and Billy had made it perfect for her.

She floated through the summer in the throes of first love, and determinedly refused to think about what would happen in the fall. Because Billy wasn't simply going off to college like her brother. Billy was joining the Marines. He was scheduled to leave on September twenty-fourth.

The magical summer officially ended when the mid-August start of school meant the idyllic days at the swimming pool came to a close. Helen greeted the beginning of her sophomore year in high school with a growing sense of distress. She'd never felt so alone as when she walked through the hallways at her school, knowing Billy wouldn't be meeting her at her locker between classes or sitting with her at lunch. If she felt this lonely while he was still in town, how would she manage once he left for basic training?

When they met in the parking lot at the football stadium before the game on the second Friday of September, he presented her with the traditional ribboned mum that girls wore to school on football game days. Ordinarily, florists delivered the mums on Thursdays. Billy had to deliver his in person so that her parents wouldn't see it. Helen opened the mum box and burst into tears.

"Oh, baby, what's the matter?" he asked, pulling her into his arms. "Did I not get a big enough flower? Did you want more ribbons? More cowbells?"

"I don't want you to leave!" she wailed. "Why did you have to go and join the Marines? Why couldn't you have stayed here and gone to college at Midwestern? What if you go off and forget about me?"

"Oh, baby. I'm not going to forget about you. I love you! I'm doing this for you...for us. The Marine Corps is going to give me all sorts of opportunities."

"Yes," she snapped. "Like dying in Vietnam!"

"Now, Helen. I won't be sent to 'Nam. The war is over. The Paris Peace Accords were signed in January. They're bringing troops home, not sending new ones over there. I told you that my recruiting officer told me that when I'm finished with all my training, I'm just as likely to be stationed Stateside as anywhere else."

"Is that the truth?"

Billy shrugged. "It'll be okay, I promise. I'll come home on every leave, and I'll write you and call you."

"Oh, that'll be just great," she declared. "I can see my dad handing the phone over to me when a Marine calls."

"We'll find a way. Haven't we managed since Christmas?"

"Yes, but—"

"No buts. It's all good, sunshine. I'll miss you like hell, but I promise these next three years will fly by. Before we know it, you'll be graduating. And then, we can get married."

"Married." It was the first time he'd mentioned marriage.

Helen lifted her head from his shoulder and gazed up at him with hopeful wonder in her eyes. "Married?"

"Yeah." His expression turned fierce. "You don't think I'm gonna let some other guy make time with you, do you? Look, I know you are smart as a whip and will want to go to college. We will make that work, too. I want a future with you, Helen. I want to be your future."

My future. Our future. Married. "I love you, Billy."

"I love you so damned much, Helen. Promise me you're not gonna forget me after I leave."

"Forget you!"

"Yeah. Maybe take up with the captain of the football team."

Helen tenderly cupped Billy's cheek. "Jeff Jarrett? What would I want with that loser?"

Grinning, he turned his head and pressed a kiss to her palm. Helen swallowed hard and swore, "I promise I won't forget you, Billy Poteet. You're my hero. I will love you forever."

He closed his eyes. "Now that's what I wanted—no, I needed—to hear."

Helen could see the truth of the statement gleaming in his eyes. A whirlwind of emotions blew through her. Fear, hope, yearning, and regret—more feelings than she could put a name to. Yet, strongest of all, most consuming of all, was love.

She needed to show him. Now. Helen rose up on her tiptoes and pressed a quick kiss against his lips. "You know, Billy, it's a beautiful night. What if we skipped going into the game?"

A million years later, seated alone on a bench above Lake in the Clouds, Colorado, thrice-married and thrice-divorced... childless...oh, dear Lord...childless, Helen Bennett McDaniel grieved for the only man she had ever truly loved with her whole heart. She grieved for her hero, her hopes, and her dreams.

Helen grieved for the family she and her Billy had lost.

Chapter Five

Houston

ZOEY WAS BURNING HER candle at both ends—and in the middle, too. She spent, on average, twenty hours every day in one hospital or another, and she did most of her sleeping in the chair beside Jennifer's bed. In the past seven weeks, something inside her had changed. She'd grown to hate being in hospitals. She didn't like the work anymore. She didn't like the people with whom she worked.

She didn't like herself.

She hadn't been treating Cooper very nicely. She was freezing him out and pushing him away. She wouldn't talk to him. She wouldn't let him offer comfort. She wouldn't even eat the food he went out of his way to make for her. Cooper didn't deserve that. He was worried about her.

For the first time in her life, she'd flunked an exam. For the first time in her professional career, she'd lost her temper with colleagues during a particularly needlessly tragic case. On top of all that, she was avoiding her dad. Adam didn't deserve that, either. He'd gone above and beyond the call since he arrived home from his conference a week ago, taking shifts at Jennifer's bedside when Zoey had to be at the hospital, and she knew he'd rather be just about anywhere else. Zoey thought her mother was managing to break her father's heart all over again. That's what she was doing to Zoey.

Same song, second verse. Twenty-second verse. Too many verses to count!

Zoey didn't know how to fix things. She didn't know how to fix herself.

She told herself things would get better soon. She'd be done with the fellowship in just over a month. By then, based on her mother's doctor's best guess, Zoey's vigil beside Jennifer's bed would be behind her.

Jennifer had been unable to tolerate the experimental treatment. Her condition had deteriorated quickly, and she'd been moved to hospice care the week before. Nevertheless, she continued to cling to life. Jennifer Hillcrest was running away from death as hard as she'd run away from everything else in her life.

And Zoey still didn't know why the running began. She still didn't have the answers she wanted more desperately with every passing day. Oh, she'd discovered a few bits and pieces while sitting beside Jennifer's bed daily, but nothing concrete. As Jennifer's time ran out, so did Zoey's. It was making Zoey miserable. It was making her angry. Cooper was about to blow a gasket, too.

Last night, with her mother mostly insensate due to the pain meds she was on, Zoey had finally cut her visit short and come home to catch a few hours of sleep. She'd slept fitfully, tossing and turning the entire time. Twenty minutes ago, Cooper had rolled from the bed with a curse and headed for the shower.

Now, she sat with her legs crossed on the right side of the king-sized bed they shared. The low-pitched hum of an air conditioner died as the unit cycled off, and a heavy silence descended on the room. An emotion that was as hot and heavy as the air on this muggy morning in June rolled through her.

She suddenly felt naked in Cooper's Michigan Wolverines T-shirt as her fiancé emerged from the bathroom wearing a towel around his waist. Zoey tugged the smoke-colored sheet up over her lap. Judging by the set of his jaw, a confrontation was coming.

She didn't blame him. How could she expect him to understand when she didn't understand herself?

Having donned a pair of running shorts, Cooper turned toward her, obviously braced for battle. He set his hands on his hips. "Did you really go off on Martin Green yesterday?"

Zoey stiffened in shock. "How did you find out? Do you have spies in the ER?"

"He's a doctor in my practice who was there to see a patient. He is my friend. He knows that you are my fiancée, so he called to warn me. He said scuttlebutt around the ER is that you are one more eruption away from flaming out of the program with less than a month to go. Is that true?"

Sullenly, she folded her arms. "He shouldn't have called you. That's totally unprofessional."

"Well, there seems to be a lot of that going around your hospital," he snapped back before closing his eyes and taking a deep breath. He walked over to his nightstand and pulled a slip of paper from beneath his phone. He handed the paper to Zoey.

She read a name and an address. "What's this?"

"She's a therapist. She has an opening this afternoon at four o'clock if you will concede to take it."

A therapist. Her stomach rolled. "I'm scheduled to work this afternoon."

"Dr. Lawrence is available to cover for you."

The sick feeling in her stomach transformed into anger. Zoey threw back the covers, climbed out of bed, and glared at Cooper. "You've got a lot of nerve, Dr. MacKenzie. I haven't asked for your input. It's not your place to interfere in my professional life or pick out my effing shrink!"

Frustration flared in his brown eyes. "Maybe it's not, but somebody needs to do it because you're not taking care of business yourself. I love you, Zoey, and you're scaring me. You need sleep. You need help. Let me help you."

The fight went out of Zoey as quickly as it had come. "I just need to get through these next few weeks."

"If you don't kill yourself first. You're not a hospice nurse, Zoey."

"She's my mother, Cooper."

A hint of temper joined his frustration. "Is she? Is she really? It seems to me that the aloe vera plant you keep on the windowsill fills that role as well as the woman you're vigiling yourself to death for."

"I don't think 'vigiling' is a word. And you don't understand."

"No, I don't." He dragged his fingers through his hair. "You won't tell me. You won't talk to me."

Zoey opened her mouth, then shut it without speaking. She didn't know what to say to him. She had no explanation for her actions. She knew she was blowing up her career and maybe her relationship, too, but she couldn't seem to help it. Wasn't certain she even cared. "My mother is dying, Cooper. She's dying, and she has no one else to care for her."

He went down on his knees in front of her and took hold of her hands. "Honey, she does. She has hospice professionals. Your father sits with her. I've offered a dozen times to sit with her in your place."

"But she has no one who loves her."

"And whose fault is that?"

Zoey closed her eyes. He was right. Jennifer Hillcrest had created her solitary existence through her own actions. Or, more concisely, her lack of actions.

Cooper said, "Sweetheart, I know this isn't about me. Nevertheless, it's tearing me up to watch what she's doing to you. You've told me what it was like. She's never been there for you. Never once. Not when you had an emergency appendectomy. Not when you graduated from high school. Not when you earned your white coat. She's never been there when it matters, and it hurt you! You can't let her take this from you, too."

"That's why I have to be there now."

"That makes no sense. You're ready to throw everything away because of her."

"I'm not throwing anything away," she protested, even as her stomach made a sick roll.

"Aren't you? You're a ticking bomb. If you can't talk to me or to your dad, then talk to a professional before it's too late. Otherwise, I'm afraid another visiting physician will ask you another stupid question, and you'll explode again. They'll boot you from your fellowship a month short of graduation."

"Fine. If that happens, it won't be the end of the world. So, I won't be an ER pediatrician. I'll still be a doctor." If that's even what she still wanted.

He released an exasperated sigh, dropped her hands, and stood. Staring down at her, he snapped, "And you'll be making half of what you could be making for the rest of your career."

Feeling defensive, she lifted her chin. "It's not all about the money, Cooper."

He opened his mouth, then shut it. His lips stretched into a grim line.

"What?" she challenged.

"Not all of us are lucky enough to have family who can pay for our education. Having medical school debt on top of college debt is a heavy burden."

"Not all of us are lucky enough to have a two-parent family who was there for us," she fired back. "You don't understand what it's like, Cooper. Your folks might not have had much money, but they were there for you. Your mother was there for you."

"Yes, she was. Yours wasn't. I get that. But I don't understand why you feel like you have to be here for her now under the circumstances you are facing. She doesn't need a pediatrician. She needs palliative care, which professionals are providing."

"*I* need her. *I* need this time with her. It's my last chance to find out who I am!"

"You know who you are! You are Doctor Zoey Hillcrest, a strong, tenacious, brilliant, beautiful woman. You're the woman I love."

"That's not enough."

He jerked back as if she'd hit him. After a moment's pause, he said, "Well. Okay, then."

A wave of despair rolled over Zoey. "I'm sorry. I didn't mean that the way it sounded. Try to understand, Cooper. I need your support. I need to understand why I wasn't enough for her. Why she couldn't love me. I need her to tell me that."

"Oh, baby. You are breaking my heart. She hasn't told you those things in the past. What makes you think she'll tell you now? What are you going to do if she doesn't?"

"I'll deal with it."

"Will you? I hope so, but right now, I'm less than confident. That's why I want you to take an hour and talk to a therapist. You need help, Zoey. I've tried to help, but this is beyond me."

He folded his arms and stared at her without speaking for a

long moment. Zoey's heart began to pound. Quietly, he asked, "Will you please take the therapy appointment? Do this much, if not for yourself, then for me?"

She didn't have it in her to delve into the riotous emotions boiling inside her. It wasn't just her mother dying or the answers to questions she might or might not get. It was more. It was her misery at work. It was the fear that had been eating at her for months, fear she recognized existed, but didn't understand. "Not today. I can't today."

Cooper's expression went grim. "If not today, then when?"

"When it's over."

"When what is over?" he asked, a note of bitterness in his tone. "Us?"

Maybe. She didn't know. She didn't know anything about anything right now. She sucked in a quick breath. Her voice trembling, Zoey asked, "Cooper, please, I need your support."

Sadness and another emotion Zoey did not want to name dimmed the light in his eyes. He nodded once and grabbed his sneakers off the floor. "Okay, then. I'll be here."

To pick up the pieces. Though he didn't say it aloud, she heard the message loud and clear.

Cooper turned away from her, dressed quickly in hospital scrubs and his sneakers, then headed for the door. "Call me if you need me."

The flatness in his voice conveyed that he didn't expect to receive a call from her.

"Have a good day, Cooper," Zoey called after him. His response was a wave. Moments later, she heard the front door open and then close firmly.

She managed to hold her tears until she took her own shower, at which point the sobs erupted. She slid down the tile wall and sat on the floor, her arms wrapped around her legs, her face buried against her knees as the hot water pounded her. Zoey didn't cry often, but when she did, it was ugly. She sobbed until the hot water ran cold, grieving for her mother, herself, and the relationship she'd always desired but never had. Crying over the cracks in her relationship with Cooper these last months had created.

Finally chilled to the bone, her tears exhausted, she exited the shower to the ringing of her phone. It was the hospice facility.

Her mother was awake, aware, and asking to see her.

Twenty minutes later, Zoey entered her mother's room. A nurse was seated beside the bed, filing her mother's nails with an emery board. She gave Zoey a sympathetic smile. "Hi, Dr. Hillcrest. She asked for pain meds shortly after I called you. So..."

The nurse shrugged, and Zoey nodded that she understood. The "aware" part of the phone call might no longer be in evidence. "I'll take over for you, Liz."

The nurse rose and handed Zoey the file. "I hope you have a nice visit."

Zoey took a seat and picked up her mother's hand. She was shaping the nail on her ring finger when Jennifer's eyes flickered open. Her eyes shifted and focused on Zoey. "You came."

"I did. How are you feeling?"

Her tone was thready and fragile as she replied, "Drugs in the eighties were more fun. I'm thirsty."

"Well, we can fix that." Zoey lifted the covered tumbler from the nightstand and guided the straw to her mother's lips. Jennifer sucked weakly and then grimaced. "Hot."

"I'll add some ice."

The ice bucket was empty, so Zoey carried it down the hall to the machine in order to fill it. Returning to her mother's room, she removed the lid from the tumbler, added ice, and then filled it with bottled water. When she looked up from her task, she found her mother watching her. Jennifer said, "You're not like me."

Zoey didn't know how to respond to that.

"More like Becca than me. That's good."

Zoey felt her heartbeat speed up. "Becca?"

"My sister. She was smart, too. Like you. Like Adam. You're mostly Adam." She closed her eyes and added, "I'm glad."

Her mother had a sister named Becca. Zoey licked her dry lips. "Was Becca older or younger than you?"

"Younger."

That's something. Casually, Zoey asked, "What was her last name?"

One corner of Jennifer's mouth lifted in a crooked smile. "Good try, smartypants."

Zoey wanted to fling her mother's hand away and throw the nail file across the room. She quashed the childish reaction and gently went to work on shaping her mom's little fingernail.

Keeping her voice calm, she asked, "Why did you ask to see me this morning?"

"Because I trust you to tell me the truth."

Wish I could say the same.

"How much longer do I have?"

Zoey had thought she'd cried out her daily ration of tears already. Apparently not, because her eyes suddenly stung. "I honestly don't know."

"You've looked at my chart."

"It's not my specialty," Zoey said, shaking her head. "I'm not qualified to say."

"Guess."

"Okay, but a guess is all it is. Maybe a couple of weeks."

Jennifer turned her head away and looked out the window.

Following a moment of silence, she nodded. "More than I expected, to be honest. I think maybe it's a generous guess. Thanks for being here for me, Zoey. It's more than I deserve."

"Will you please tell me who you are?"

Jennifer glanced back at Zoey, met and held her gaze. "No."

Then she closed her eyes.

Zoey rose and stood beside the bed, fighting back tears. She was so pissed and so sad and so exhausted and so…so…she didn't know what she was feeling. Maybe Cooper's shrink could tell her.

Maybe she should go talk to the woman after all.

Zoey remembered the name, so she googled the number and placed the call. The afternoon appointment had been filled, but the doctor was willing to meet with Zoey that evening. Zoey agreed to the time, disconnected the call, then dialed the hospital. Following a somewhat uncomfortable conversation with her boss, she agreed to work the overnight shift. Afterward, she wanted to crawl under a bed and hide.

Instead, she stepped into the hall and called Cooper. He didn't answer, of course. He was in surgery this morning. Zoey waited to be connected to his voice mail.

"Hi. It's me. I wanted to let you know that I have an appointment with Dr. Rios late this afternoon. I'm going to have to work the overnight shift, so I won't be home tonight. I guess I'll see you sometime tomorrow." After a moment's hesitation, she added, "I love you. Bye."

Zoey then returned to her mother's bedside. Jennifer lay still and quiet. Zoey took the opportunity to pull out her laptop and review for her upcoming exam. She was knee-deep in administrative policy and procedure rules when Jennifer's eyes opened once again. This time, though, the lucidity was missing.

When her mother began murmuring, Zoey made out only

nonsensical words. Nevertheless, as she'd been doing since her vigil began, Zoey pulled up the recording app on her phone and set it on the bedside table. Then she opened a file on her computer that she'd titled "Mom" and began to list each legible word her mother spoke.

Gibberish, she thought glumly, until she heard "Becca" and then a new name—"Harry."

"Harry?" Zoey murmured. She made the note and underlined it twice. Rising from her seat, she moved closer and concentrated, but her mother had, for the most part, fallen silent. So hard was she listening that when she heard the light rap on the door and then its opening, she didn't glance away from her mother.

A deep, raspy voice asked, "Zoey?"

Cooper? Here? This time of day? Startled, she jerked up and twisted around. He stood just inside the room and looked haunted. Everything inside her went cold. "What's wrong? Who's hurt?"

"Nobody's hurt."

"Then why are you here instead of in surgery?"

His gaze shifted past her to the bed. "I'd like to speak with you for a few moments the next time she's sleeping peacefully."

Zoey glanced at her mother. "She seems to be settling. Let's give her another few minutes."

"Okay. There's no one in the conference room. I'll get some coffee and wait for you there. Would you like a cup?"

"Sure."

Less than five minutes later, Zoey decided her mother was soundly sleeping. It took another couple of minutes for her to work up the courage to join Cooper. She wasn't sure she wanted to know whatever had put that haggard expression on her fiancé's face.

Maybe she had crossed a line with him this morning. Maybe he'd decided to break up with her after all.

Well, fine. If he can't understand my situation, then good riddance.

Really, maybe this was all for the better. They hadn't exactly had the best of relationships over the past few months, had they? If she were being perfectly honest, things between them hadn't been easy since she got sick in February. She'd blamed it on stress, but maybe what really had happened here was that it highlighted weaknesses in the relationship.

They'd have to call off the wedding. Oh, joy. At least the invitations hadn't gone out, though they had sent Save the Date cards with information about the location in February, right before she got sick.

Despite her bravado, Zoey's stomach was churning as she leaned over, kissed her mother's forehead, and exited the room, turning toward the conference room down the hall. Outside that door, she paused and drew in a deep breath. She could do this. She told parents their children had passed. Nothing could be harder than that.

She hated doing it, too.

She'd thought that those children whose lives she saved would offset those that she lost. It *should* work that way. She did save lives in the ER. Why didn't she find that rewarding?

Why was she thinking about work now when her fiancé was about to dump her?

Maybe she should call off the wedding first. Get out in front of it. Be the dumper rather than the dumpee.

You've got this, Zoey. You are Jennifer's daughter. Becca's niece.

Whoever the hell they are.

You're a mental case. That's what you are. Cooper is right. You should be in a psychiatrist's office right this very second.

And he shouldn't be dumping her now while her mother was dying during the last few weeks of Zoey's fellowship.

Zoey stepped into the conference room, braced for battle but trying to hide it. Cooper stood at the coffee machine, filling a paper cup. A second cup already sat on the conference table. Zoey's gaze fastened on it. Calmly, she asked, "Is that for me?"

"Yes."

She didn't need any more acid in her stomach, but holding the cup gave her something to do. He took a seat across the table from her and set his cup in front of him. Neither of them sampled their drinks.

Zoey decided to wait for him to speak first. Instead, he picked up from the floor a white paper shopping bag with handles that she had not previously noticed. He set the bag on the table and shoved it toward her. "What's this?"

Not a calling-off-our-engagement gift, surely.

Cooper nodded toward the bag. "I made some calls and tracked these down. I think this would help you a lot."

Zoey couldn't read the expression in his eyes as she reached into the bag. She pulled out a box. A single-party DNA test. Her brows arched, and her gaze briefly flew toward a stoic Cooper before returning to the bag to retrieve another one of the boxes. Another test kit. Five more boxes, including different tests and different manufacturers of the identical test. He'd covered every available base.

He was suggesting she put her DNA into the wild and see what turned up.

Zoey recoiled from the idea. It was something she'd considered and rejected in the past. "This is a Pandora's box."

"It could be. But you need answers, Zoey. I see that now. You told me that previously, your father gave you his blessing to do this, so maybe now is the time."

What Cooper said was true. Adam Hillcrest had no pressing desire to learn his former wife's true identity. That ship had sailed years ago. However, he didn't oppose Zoey's going down that road if that's what she wanted to do.

"I can't take my mother's DNA. It's probably illegal. It's definitely an invasion of privacy."

"What's she gonna do? Sue you? Look, she owes you answers. If you want them, I think you should take advantage of the tools that science has provided."

"I can't do it, Cooper. It would make me feel scummy."

"Okay," he said with a shrug. "Then you test *your* DNA. See if you find out anything that way."

Zoey thought about her mother's ramblings. She thought about her computer file with the notes she'd made. "I've never thought it was a good idea to put private information out there in the ether. You don't like the idea, as I recall. We've talked about it in the past."

"True. But if this is the only way for you to get the answers you need, maybe it's worth the risk." As Zoey picked up one of the boxes and began reading the back, he added, "Look, Zoey, it's become obvious to me that you need the answers. However, I'm not trying to pressure you. I simply wanted to make it easier for you. This is totally your decision."

"Thank you. This means a lot to me, Cooper." Acting on instinct, she reached across the table and squeezed his hand. "Did you get my voice mail?"

"I did. I'm glad you're going to talk to Dr. Rios. I hope it helps." Rising, he said, "I've got to get back to work. I hope you have an easy shift tonight. I'll see you in the morning at home."

He left without giving her a good-bye kiss, which was unusual. Zoey let out a slow breath. Okay. Well. At least the wedding was still on.

For now, anyway. He might not have come here today to break up with her, but things were obviously not right between them. Had their relationship been healthy, the thought of breaking up wouldn't have popped into her brain so easily. But it wasn't healthy. It might not be on hospice, but it was definitely in intensive care. Except, she hadn't been giving it care, had she? *What kind of doctor are you? A lousy one. That's kind of the point, isn't it?*

Sadness, shame, and regret washed through her, and she closed her eyes against a flood of tears. If she started crying now, she wouldn't stop.

When Zoey returned to her mother's room a few moments later with a heavy heart and the sack full of DNA kits in tow, Jennifer was stirring again. Zoey grabbed her notebook and sat with her mother until long after she'd quieted. When Zoey finally left the hospice facility and headed for the hospital, she wasn't looking forward to the shift. She had, however, made one momentous decision.

She dropped a pair of envelopes containing DNA samples into the mailbox on the corner.

Jennifer Hillcrest passed away three days later while Zoey worked her shift at the hospital. She left a handwritten will leaving all her worldly goods to her only relative, her daughter, Zoey.

Chapter Six

June

GENEVIEVE GAZED DOWN AT the scissors in her hand, and a memory flashed into her mind. She'd been four years old—maybe five—when she'd sneaked the scissors from the kitchen junk drawer, crawled beneath the table, and cut her own hair. Her mother had shrieked with horror when she spied the results. Genevieve had earned her first spanking for that one because the scissors were a big no-no. That had been in the 1960s, back when parents still spanked their children.

A rueful smile touched her lips. That had actually been her one and only spanking. She'd been a good little girl, the polar opposite of her big sister.

Helen had been a wild child in her teens. While their parents managed to keep their sons in line, their rebellious elder daughter seemed to befuddle them. Helen had been grounded a lot. She missed her curfew regularly. Genevieve remembered the fights they'd had around the Bennett house—especially between her sister and her dad. Finally, someone—the school counselor, maybe—suggested a "cooling-off period," and Helen went to live with Uncle Ben and Aunt Grace in a small town west of Fort

Worth for a semester. That seemed to suit everyone—except Genevieve. Mom and Dad had quit their constant fighting, and Helen had really liked her new school. She'd liked it so much that she'd lived with their aunt and uncle until she finished high school. She'd never really moved back home.

Genevieve had missed her sister, but honestly, the six-year age difference between them at that stage of life had been huge. She'd liked having a bedroom to herself more than she'd liked Helen to be around. It had been a good move for Helen. She'd buckled down as a student and ended up an extremely successful attorney.

It had been when Helen was in law school and Genevieve in high school that the two sisters had grown close. Genevieve gave Helen full credit for that. She'd made a real effort to become Genevieve's friend, confidant, and advisor during her high school years. Genevieve was grateful to this day that she'd had the counsel of her big sister during those challenging times.

"Hey! Earth to Genevieve," Helen called from the doorway, snapping Genevieve from her reverie. "You gonna stand there all day? Folks are getting restless."

"Sorry. I'm coming." Genevieve shut the desk drawer and exited the office of her latest passion, the Lake in the Clouds Community Museum. Moments later, she ducked under the red ribbon stretched across the front door and joined her sister on the front steps where a crowd of fifteen to twenty people gathered to watch their mayor officially open the small town's newest historical attraction.

Genevieve handed the scissors to Helen. "I can't believe I left the monster-sized scissors I purchased for today at home. I'm so disappointed."

"Don't fret. As long as these aren't as dull as the black-handled pair in Mom's junk drawer when we were growing up, they'll do the job. We can use the big scissors when you open your next project."

"I don't have a next project."

"Pshaw," Helen replied, giving her eyes a roll. "Haven't I seen home-decorating magazines all around your house? Isn't your television tuned to HGTV exclusively these days?"

Genevieve shrugged. "Gage wants to make some changes at the ranch. He's asked me to help him when he gets home from his fishing trip with his sons."

"When are they due back?"

"Next week, I believe. Their plans were flexible based on how good the fishing proved."

A man in the crowd called out, "Would you girls quit your lallygagging? Let's get this show on the road."

Helen turned an exaggerated glare on the speaker. "Hold your water, George. This museum is worth the wait."

"Yes, George," called a woman whom Genevieve believed was a member of Helen's bowling league. "It's not even ten yet. The ribbon cutting is scheduled for ten o'clock, and if the mayor starts her speech before the church bells ring, we won't be able to hear her."

On cue, the bells from the Methodist church across the street began to peal. When the sound died, Helen moved forward to the edge of the front steps and addressed the crowd of friends, neighbors, constituents, and a sprinkling of family.

"Happy Founders Day, Lake in the Clouds!" she said. "The revitalization of our downtown district is exciting to watch, and I am proud to be part of it. That said, it would be wrong of me to take credit for either the idea or the execution of the creation of this Community Museum. It's been the dynamic duo's project from the get-go. You all know who I'm talking about—my sister, Genevieve Prentice, and your assistant city manager, Nicole Vandersall. Genevieve brought the idea and the research to our city council, and then Nicole accepted the project manager's hat. They've spent the past three months working tirelessly in order to meet an ambitious grand opening deadline of our annual Founders Day celebration."

The crowd applauded. Genevieve and Nicole waved their thanks. Helen held up the scissors saying, "All I did was sign the checks, so I think one of you two ladies should do the honors."

Genevieve gave Nicole a little push forward. "The scissors are yours." To the crowd, she added, "She did the lion's share of the work."

Helen nodded enthusiastically and added, "That's the way Nicole rolls."

A flush stained Nicole's cheeks as she accepted the scissors. "Oh, Helen. You are too sweet."

At that, Genevieve quipped, "Sweet as lemon juice."

Helen made a show of rolling her eyes at the old tease from her baby sister. "Don't you mean lemonade?"

"No, I don't think so."

The crowd chuckled, and when Nicole cut the red ribbon, added applause and a spattering of hurrahs. Then Helen linked arms with her sister and city manager, and together they stepped inside the museum lobby. They approached the ticket window, where they each bought a ticket for entrance into the exhibits. "No special treatment or perks for anyone," Helen declared when asked about the purchase. "In Lake in the Clouds, everyone gets equal treatment."

"Only since you won the mayoral election," Genevieve added.

The sisters exchanged self-satisfied smiles as one of Helen's neighbors at the retirement home piped up. "What? No senior discount?"

"Entrance is a whopping four dollars, Paul," Helen replied. "Don't be such a cheapskate."

Nicole piped up. "We do have Two-dollar Tuesdays, which will feature a new mini-exhibit every week. Also, the Taco Bus will be parked out front on Tuesdays. On good weather days, we'll set out some tables and chairs on the sidewalks."

"It'll be a little sidewalk café." Genevieve stood on the right of the exhibit entrance, and at Helen's direction, Nicole stood on the left. They personally welcomed each of the visitors and basked in the warm glow of congratulations for a job well done.

Helen made sure to direct as much praise as possible toward Nicole. Genevieve knew that her sister had plans for her protégée. Helen had no intention of running for reelection. She had accomplished the goals she'd set when she'd made her decision to run for mayor, and she was ready to move on. Nicole Vandersall needed to be the next mayor of Lake in the Clouds. Sooner rather than later.

Recently, Helen had confided to her sister that she'd put her legal training to good use by doing a deep dive into Lake in the Clouds' election policies and procedures. Once she'd passed the halfway point in her two-year term, Helen could resign and appoint Nicole to serve out her term as mayor until the next election. Doing so would set up the younger woman to win the next contest. Nicole worked well with the current city council and city manager, and Helen believed the team could be counted on to continue the improvements she'd put into place.

And Helen's work here will be done. What her sister would do with herself afterward, Genevieve hadn't a clue. Retirement was proving to be a problem for Helen.

Not that Genevieve knew what project she'd jump into next, either. Helping Gage redecorate his ranch house would be a favor, not a project. However, in the past year, she'd come to trust that she would find something to occupy her time and make her feel as though her life was of value.

After the last of the visitors entered the exhibit space, Helen slipped her arm through Genevieve's and said, "Show me your museum, little sister. I understand there's an entire section dedicated to the Throckmorton family and the Triple T Ranch?"

Genevieve nodded. "Yes. Gage groused for a week before the interview with Nicole to talk about the history of the Triple T. He told her he'd give her half an hour, and then he talked for over two."

"Well, the man has a lot of history of which to be proud," Helen said. "According to Nicole, he was too cute about how much museum space was to be dedicated to the ranch."

Genevieve nodded in agreement. "She wanted to use the entire second floor. He made it a condition of his donation—both the significant chunk of change and the artifacts—that his family heritage isn't displayed more prominently than others. He insisted that 'It's a *community* museum—focus on the community.'"

"That sounds like Gage."

Genevieve gave a satisfied smile as she explained, "Nicole managed to wrangle a little extra out of him. She's dedicated one room to special-themed exhibits that she's planning to update twice a month. Believe me, when she devotes an exhibit to family china, she'll include the Throckmorton treasures."

"Family china exhibit?" Helen made a *Home Alone*, two-handed face clap. "I never would have guessed that your museum would feature a family china exhibit."

"Ha. Ha." Genevieve's lips twitched as she added, "It's scheduled for September."

"I can't wait." Helen plucked an exhibit flyer from a display as they entered the first exhibit room.

Genevieve's concept for the Lake in the Clouds Community Museum was to tell a narrative of the history of the town through stories about the families who'd settled in the area and built Lake in the Clouds. Nicole had suggested that they organize the tale according to eras, beginning with the pioneers and town founders—the Throckmorton family among them—and ending with a section dedicated to newcomers. Each section had a kid's corner of interactive, thematic activities. In the last section, they intended to rotate families in and out based on local participation in order to keep the content fresh.

Genevieve believed they'd created a museum that encouraged one to dawdle and read and study. She was proud of it.

"Y'all have done a spectacular job," Helen said to Genevieve as they exited the Roaring Twenties through the World War II section and entered the postwar to Y2K portion of the exhibit.

"Thank you." Genevieve's gaze landed on the wedding portrait of a couple whom she recognized at once as retired sheriff Darrel Sears and his wife, June, who owned and operated the hair salon Genevieve frequented.

They were the cutest couple. Darrel stopped by the salon every day and brought his wife a single red rose. The romantic gesture made all the salon's patrons swoon. For her part, June had made it a practice to leave Darrel little love notes inside his personal items and/or spaces each day. Everyone said you could always tell when Darrel found his note because he got a little extra spring in his step.

Genevieve had known the pair had been high school sweethearts, but seeing the proof displayed here made her smile.

It also brought David to mind. Had David lived, would he still be bringing her roses? Pink roses, because one time she'd told him she loved pink the best, and he'd never bought her anything else. Every Valentine's Day, every birthday, every wedding anniversary, he brought her pink roses. Truth be told, she wouldn't have minded having yellow or red in the mix. She'd loved him dearly, but romance hadn't been his forte. If he'd lived, Genevieve believed they'd still be together and in love. He might be retired, and they might be living in a small town somewhere. However, she could not under any circumstances picture him gifting her with a flower each day.

Genevieve would have liked a little more romance in her marriage, but in David's defense, she hadn't made him aware of that fact. She'd wanted him to know, to want to make such gestures on his own. To know her well enough that he'd make them without her having to ask. Having to ask took the shine off the rose, so to speak.

She gave a little self-deprecating laugh. Why had her mind wandered off in this direction this morning anyway? She didn't have romance on her mind as a rule.

Because you're missing Gage. He's been away for over three weeks, and you miss him.

It was true. The man didn't send her a rose every day, but he'd sent her half a dozen postcards from Alaska. She watched her mailbox like a hawk every day.

Genevieve sensed Helen's presence behind her. Without taking her gaze off the photograph of the Sears, Genevieve said, "I think that in your capacity as mayor, you should create an award for Lake in the Clouds' most romantic couple. Name it after Darrel and June Sears. Maybe it'll inspire people to add more romance into their lives."

Genevieve's heart gave a little lurch when a deep-timbred male voice softly asked, "Is that a hint, Genevieve?"

Helen watched Gage Throckmorton approach her sister with a smile on his handsome-though-weathered rancher's face. While she couldn't hear what he said to her, whatever it was caused Genevieve to whirl around and light up like the sun.

Genevieve said, "Gage! I didn't think you'd be back until next week. This is a lovely surprise."

"We got in late last night. I intended to be here for the ribbon cutting, but your son-in-law waylaid me this morning with a bunch of papers I needed to sign. Almost made me wish I hadn't hired Noah as my business manager." He took hold of her hands, leaned down, and kissed her briefly but publicly on the lips. "I missed you."

"I missed you, too." A rosy blush stained Genevieve's cheek as she darted a gaze toward her sister.

Helen held back a snort. Genevieve was still getting accustomed to PDAs from Gage. Her husband, David, had been a reserved man in public. In contrast, Gage was a toucher. If Helen hadn't sworn off being a buttinsky where Genevieve's relationship with the rancher was concerned, she'd warn Gage to dial it back a bit.

Genevieve might appear confident and at ease with Gage, but the more her feelings for him grew, the more skittish she became. Helen had seen how much her sister had missed Gage while he was away. The woman was falling. However, Helen also knew her sister. If Genevieve felt rushed in any way, she'd back off. Right now, based on her observations of the pair, Helen put the odds of the relationship succeeding long-term right at 50/50.

The rancher spotted Helen and gave her a nod. "Hello, Helen."

"Welcome home, Gage," she replied. "How was your trip?"

"Really nice. Alaska is beyond beautiful, and I had some quality male-bonding time with my boys and grandson."

"Did you catch a lot of fish?" Genevieve asked.

"We did. All but wore our fishing gear out. That's one reason we came home a day early. Also, I wanted to be here for Genevieve and today's grand opening."

Genevieve beamed. "Have you seen the Triple T Ranch section of the exhibit yet? It's wonderful."

"I breezed through it, but I didn't look at anything. I was searching for you. I'm anxious to check it out, though."

Genevieve glanced at her sister inquiringly. Helen said, "You go with him, Genevieve. I have a quick city council meeting scheduled before the parade, and I'm going to do some breezing through the rest of the exhibits myself."

"You sure?" Genevieve asked, a faint line creasing the space between her brows. "I don't want to ditch you."

Helen gave Genevieve's arm a reassuring pat. She recognized that as her sister's relationship with Gage developed, Genevieve took extra care to ensure that Helen didn't feel like the proverbial third wheel. "No ditching involved. You kids have fun. I'll see you tomorrow at the book club meeting."

Genevieve snapped her fingers. "I almost forgot about that. I still need to read the last two chapters of this month's book."

"Glad you mentioned that," Helen said. "I almost asked you what you thought about the surprise twist at the end."

"What surprise twist? I love surprise twists."

"Read the book and call me tomorrow if you want to chat before the actual chat." Helen smiled up at Gage and added, "I'm glad you are home. She missed you."

He smiled and tipped his imaginary hat, then they turned to retrace their steps while Helen moved forward toward the section of the exhibit focused on families who were part of Lake in the Clouds during the post-WWII years until the turn of the century. She smiled when she saw the console TV with a two-button remote control. When she was growing up, her best friend's family had something similar. One button shifted the channels forward in numerical order. The other shifted backward. Helen had been quite impressed.

She could almost hear her father's gruff response to her enthusiastic description of the device. *Sounds like something that'll find its way into the sofa cushions like lost change. Besides, why would anybody need a contraption to change the TV channel? That's what kids are for.*

The smile on Helen's lips lingered until she drifted on to a display that highlighted the Mayer family, and her gaze lit on a shadowbox containing a Purple Heart medal. Mounted next to it was a reproduction of the front page of the *Lake in the Clouds Gazette.* Its headline declared, "Local Serviceman Killed in Vietnam."

Reading it catapulted Helen into the past. She was suddenly fifteen again, buying a drink at the neighborhood convenience store. She'd just counted out the exact change and placed it on the counter next to her wild cherry Slurpee when her gaze strayed to the stack of newspapers on the counter.

She'd read the headline just above the fold. Her head had spun. Her knees had buckled. She'd fainted dead away.

When she came to a few moments later, the concerned store clerk had already called her house looking for help. Helen had fled the store, barely making it to the parking lot before she doubled over and vomited just as her father arrived to get her in his sedan.

Reliving the moment in Lake in the Clouds, Colorado, over half a century later, Helen's eyes filled with sudden tears. She turned around and headed for the exit, brushing past Genevieve and Gage without speaking.

On the sidewalk, one hand braced against a lamppost for support, Helen lifted her face toward the sunshine. Warmth kissed her cheeks and seeped into her cold bones as she fought back the tears. It took longer than a full minute to collect herself, but eventually, peace eased past the pain.

"Whoa," Helen said softly with a sigh. That had certainly been a blast from the past.

She drew in a deep breath, exhaled in a rush, and repeated the exercise twice more. She was feeling shaky. She'd taken no more than a dozen steps before the sound of a familiar voice stopped her.

"Auntie! Wait," Genevieve's daughter Willow called. "I saw you coming out of the museum. Are you okay? What's wrong?"

Helen halted and turned toward her niece while pasting on a smile. "Hello, sunshine," she said. "I'm fine. What are you up to?"

"You're not fine," Willow accused. "You're crying."

Helen swiped at the tears on her cheek. "Oh, don't pay me any mind. I just had a little moment. How are you feeling? Any morning sickness?"

"I'm fine," Willow snapped with more than a little exasperation in her tone. "Don't do that, Auntie. No deflecting. You never cry. Why now? What are you having a moment about? Talk to me."

Helen hesitated. Ordinarily, she'd talk to her sister, but Genevieve was occupied with her beau. She and Willow had always shared a special bond. Willow was the closest thing to a daughter Helen would ever have.

Tears stung Helen's eyes. *Oh, Billy. I would have loved to have had your little girl.*

She cleared her throat and slipped her arm through Willow's. "Are you up to taking a little walk with me, sunshine? I'd like to take a look at the parade entrants before the party starts. When you're mayor, you're too busy politicking to enjoy the show."

Willow gave her a searching look, then nodded. "I would love to walk with you."

The Lake in the Clouds Founders Day parade was scheduled to kick off at noon. At last count, four floats, one marching band, a handful of antique cars, and more than a dozen red, white, and blue bedecked golf carts and ATVs were registered to participate. They expected the largest crowd in history to watch the event. Helen couldn't have been more pleased.

The two women didn't speak as they walked down the street and past the courthouse at the center of town, headed toward the parade staging area, which was three blocks off the square. As they approached the first float—a display of American flags throughout history—Helen focused on the Old Glory flag and said, "A newspaper clipping in your mother's museum triggered an old memory this morning. I was reminded of my first love. My first heartbreak. Have I ever told you about my Billy?"

Willow gave her an intent look. "The college baseball player?"

Helen's smile went soft and wistful. "No. That was my first husband, Rex."

"Oh yeah. Fastball Rex." Willow's green eyes sparkled with interest. When they completed their walk around the flag float, she added, "I don't recall you ever talking about a high school boyfriend. I don't think Mom has ever mentioned a friend of yours named Billy."

Helen moved toward the second float lined up for the parade, the downtown merchants' float covered in bunting and balloons and a huge American eagle. "Genevieve was still a little girl when I dated him, and she only met him once." An old, never-forgotten anger rolled through Helen, and she inadvertently picked up her pace as a result. "Our parents didn't approve of him."

They viewed the veteran's float in record time. Willow obviously picked up on Helen's pain, and her tone was gentle as she asked, "What happened?"

Helen strolled on toward the third float, a project by the theater club at the high school, where riders would be dressed in Colonial America costumes. "Billy was whip-smart, near the top of his class. He'd been raised by his single mother, and tragically, she was killed in a car wreck during his senior year in high school. That happened not long before I met him."

"So, he had no parents? I cannot imagine how hard that must have been. After Dad died, losing Mom was always my greatest fear."

Helen gave Willow's arm a comforting pat. "I know. When I met him, Billy was a little lost. I think he needed me. We drifted together during the fall semester and had our first official date going to church together on Christmas Eve. That's when I introduced him to Mom and Dad. That's when your mother met him, too."

"Why didn't your folks approve of him?"

"They said it was because he was too old for me. He was a senior, and I was a freshman." Helen shook her head. "It was more than that, and I knew it. My father was a class-conscious snob. He was an Ivy League–educated attorney whose family had been early settlers in our hometown. Billy Poteet was a poor boy who grew up in a single-wide trailer parked on the wrong side of the tracks."

"So, they wouldn't let you date him?"

"It was expressly forbidden. I was threatened with all sorts of ugly consequences if I continued to see Billy."

Willow knew Helen. "So, of course, you didn't stop."

"I absolutely didn't stop. The whole forbidden fruit thing made sneaking around all the more exciting."

They moved on to the fourth and final float in the parade. The VFW float had been used recently during the town's Memorial Day parade. It showcased the Armed Forces flags and honored Lake in the Clouds' veterans. It had been such a hit that Helen had asked the VFW to join today's parade, too.

Helen understood they expected to have seven riders today, the eldest a wheelchair-bound Vietnam vet. Her gaze settled on the Marine Corps banner, and her heart gave a twist.

"My parents were wrong about him. Billy was a good guy. After his mother died, he could have stumbled, but he didn't. He was determined to make something of himself. He stayed in school and graduated. He was awarded a full-ride scholarship to study petroleum engineering at Texas A&M. He had a summer internship lined up at one of the oil and gas companies in town."

A car horn sounded, interrupting the tale. Helen and Willow both waved at the occupants of a convertible bedecked with the local high school colors. Helen observed, "Will Sumpter is a great school mascot. He loves wearing that bear costume."

"I heard that he wore it to the Sunshine Diner this morning," Willow said as they watched the convertible maneuver to take its place in the parade queue. "Gave some tourist kids a thrill."

Helen halted beside the VFW float and reached up to grab an American flag trimmed in gold fringe as her thoughts returned to the discussion at hand. "Billy was going to go far. I'm sure of it."

Willow gave Helen a sharp look at her use of the past tense verb. "Did your Billy have a problem in college?"

"I'm afraid he never got to go to college. The day he was scheduled to start at the oil and gas firm, he got a call telling him not to bother coming in. Not only was the job not happening, but neither was the scholarship."

"Why?" Willow demanded.

"B.S. reasons." Helen released the Stars and Stripes and moved on. Upon reaching a movable set of stairs that allowed access, she climbed up onto the float. She took a seat on a bench beside the Marine Corps scarlet standard. "I think Billy knew that someone behind the scenes was pulling strings, especially after he got a call from a Marine recruiter."

Willow watched her aunt closely as Helen traced the circumference of the blue globe near the center of the flag. "I was clueless. I was devastated. I had made my peace with his going three hundred miles away to college, but now he was headed to San Diego for basic training. After that, who knew where?"

Willow's brow furrowed, and Helen anticipated the question she expected her niece was about to ask. "Not Vietnam. Technically, the war was over. The Paris Peace Accords had been signed in January. The recruiter assured Billy he wouldn't be sent to Vietnam."

"Was he lying?" Willow asked.

Helen shrugged. "We'll never know. Billy was killed in a training accident in California in November."

"Oh no." Willow climbed up the stairs and moved to take a seat beside her aunt. She took hold of Helen's hand and gave it a comforting squeeze.

"I learned about his death from an article in the local newspaper. That's what set me off this morning. A Lake in the Clouds family lost a son in Vietnam, and the newspaper clipping about it is on display."

"Oh, Auntie." Willow rested her head on Helen's shoulder. "I can't imagine how horrible that must have been."

"I was inconsolable. To make matters worse, I learned that my father had pulled strings to get both the job offer rescinded and the scholarship revoked."

Now Willow sat up straight and pulled away, staring at her aunt in shock. "My grandfather did that to you? That's awful!"

"It was, wasn't it? One of my brothers had ratted us out to Dad, and he decided Billy needed to go far away. The joke ended up being on him, though, because Billy named me as his next of kin in his paperwork for the Marines, so Dad got to pay for Billy's funeral expenses."

"Oh, Auntie. I'm so sorry. That must have been so terrible for you."

Helen patted Willow's knee in a silent thank-you for the support. "I held a grudge against Dad for a very long time. Things were ugly around the house, so I eventually went to live with my aunt and uncle, and I never really went home again."

"I've never heard this story. Why is this the first time I've heard about your Billy?"

"I seldom talk about him. Even after all of these years, the wound is still raw." Helen's gaze shifted from the flags gracing the float to the flagpole rising above the courthouse, where the Stars and Stripes fluttered in the gentle breeze. "I don't know what would have happened to us had my father not interfered. We were young. Too young. Too inexperienced. Chances are we wouldn't have stayed together if he'd spent that summer working in the oil business and gone off to A&M in the fall. But I'll never know that. I've always wondered if Billy Poteet was the one. My forever guy. He's owned part of my heart my entire life. Through all of my relationships."

The moment was interrupted by the arrival of a van sporting the Mountain Vista Retirement Community logo. The door opened, and a grizzled elderly occupant wearing an Army beret called out. "You gonna ride with us today, Mayor Helen? Or are you up there dusting?"

"Not dusting. Squirreling away M&Ms for you to enjoy

during the ride." To make the statement true, Helen opened her handbag and removed a handful of M&M mini-packs, which she set at the base of the Army banner. Then Helen and Willow climbed down from the float and spent a few minutes exchanging small talk with the veterans who were preparing to take their places.

When they were away from the staging area, Helen reached out and gave Willow a quick, hard hug. "Thank you for listening, sunshine. I needed to talk about Billy and tell our story today. I'm so glad you were here."

"I'm glad I was able to help." Willow returned the hug, then clarified, "Mom knows this story, though, right?"

Helen hesitated. She'd opened up a can of worms today, hadn't she? It wouldn't be fair to ask Willow to keep this conversation to herself, but Genevieve wouldn't be pleased when she heard about it. "Like I said, your mother was still a little girl when all this went down, and our family never spoke about it afterward. I probably would have confided in her once she was older, but then our father died. She idolized him. I didn't see the sense in spoiling that. And honestly, I did my best to put it all behind me. I'm good at compartmentalizing. I locked my memories of Billy away, and I seldom let them out."

"You should tell her, Aunt Helen."

Helen sighed heavily. "I know. I will."

But she'd do it in her own sweet time.

Chapter Seven

July

ZOEY STOOD WITH HER arms folded as she stared out of the townhome's living room window where Houston's humid summer heat radiated off the driveway. Behind her, Cooper paced the room. They'd been at this for almost half an hour.

"I've always liked flowers," she stated. "I worked in a florist shop in high school."

"So, you're just going to throw your medical career away?" he asked, his tone incredulous.

Zoey turned around and looked at him. If this were a cartoon instead of life, he'd have steam shooting from his ears.

Cooper continued his rant. "After all these years in school? After all the time and effort and money you invested. You'd quit your career before you even start it and declare you're going to sell posies for a living? I can't believe this!"

"Posies and daisies and roses and potted plants."

He made a gurgling, growling noise and glared at her. "I guess that fits. You've become a potted plant. When was the last time you left the house?"

"I'm relaxing." She sauntered over to the sofa and dropped

into it, stretching out her legs. "I'm due. I all but lived at the hospital in June."

"You were too relaxed to go see Dr. Rios?"

Enough. That's enough. Zoey folded her arms. "I don't need to talk to Dr. Rios. I'm not going to see her again."

"Dammit, Zoey." Cooper threw out his hands. "Two visits are not adequate for treatment for depression."

"Oh, so you've diagnosed me now, Dr. MacKenzie? Isn't that special. So, do I need to whip out my HSA card and let you run it?"

He set his mouth in a firm line and slowly rubbed the back of his neck.

Say it, Zoey thought. *Say you want to end the engagement.*

Silence stretched between them like a big old brittle rubber band about to break. As it had for most of the past month, a heavy sense of despair rolled through her. She closed her eyes and fought it back for a moment before meeting his gaze and speaking with sincerity. "That was snarky. I apologize. Listen, Cooper. Dr. Rios and I are not a good fit. I'll look for someone else. I know I need to talk to someone."

He visibly relaxed.

"But I'm still not going to take the job at TCH." Texas Children's Hospital had made her a lucrative offer, but she just couldn't do it.

"Zoey—"

She hastened to add, "You don't need to worry about the money because after mom's will is probated and I'm able to sell her house, I'll have seed money for the business."

He closed his eyes. "I don't know what to say to you, Zoey."

Ask me to come with you to Boston.

That's where this discussion had begun half an hour ago.

At a dinner last night with a former colleague, Cooper had

been offered the opportunity to join a prestigious research group on a three-month project based out of Massachusetts General Hospital. This morning, he'd requested an emergency breakfast meeting with his own partners, during which he secured an extended leave of absence.

Then he came home and told Zoey he was moving to Boston early next week. An invitation to join him had been conspicuously absent.

So, Zoey had rolled out the idea she'd been nursing about owning a flower shop because it had seemed like the thing to do at the time. She knew she was lashing out, but she couldn't seem to help it. Zoey was burned out and frustrated with her job. With her life. And here they were—with a great big elephant in the room that neither of them seemed to want to mention.

Well, screw it.

"What about the wedding?" Had she not been watching Cooper closely, she'd have missed his slight hesitation before he said, "It goes on as scheduled. I already told Larry I needed to take off that Friday. I'll fly to Colorado Thursday night and back to Boston on Sunday."

I won't cry. I will not! She couldn't keep the bitter note from her voice as she asked, "So, what? You'll attend the honeymoon over Zoom?"

"There's that snark again." Cooper's brown eyes sparked temper as he crossed to the accent table beside the front door. He scooped his keys and wallet from the wooden tray where he habitually left them and deposited them in his pocket. "We push the honeymoon to October after the project is done. I'll still have my two weeks of vacation, and it sounds like your schedule is flexible."

Now who was tossing snark?

"Lovely."

Temper stormed across his expression, though he kept his tone calm and only the slightest bit accusatory. "This is an amazing opportunity for me. I thought that you, of all people, would understand and be supportive."

It was a verbal throwdown. Of course, he would play that card. He'd been holding the marker for three years, ever since she'd received the fellowship match and asked him to move to Houston. The surgical booties were on the other feet this time, and they both knew it.

"I do understand, Cooper."

She understood that she needed to do some serious thinking. Perhaps so did he. Their relationship road had grown downright rocky, and for the first time in years, she nurtured uncertainty as to just where their road led.

Zoey reached deep down inside herself for a smile. She pasted it on her lips and strained to lift it into her eyes. Her results were mixed. "And I support you. Congratulations. It's exciting research, and you'll be a valuable member of the team."

He squared his shoulders, lifted his chin, and nodded. "Look, I need to get to the clinic. We can talk more about this tonight."

"Sure." Though, they probably wouldn't. That was their pattern of late, wasn't it? They hadn't had a real honest discussion since her mother's funeral.

She listened to the squeak of his sneakers against the steps' wooden tread as he headed downstairs. She heard the kitchen door close with a louder-than-necessary *thunk.* Walking to the window, she watched him back his gray BMW from the garage and into the street. She wasn't surprised when he punched the gas, spun the tires, and sped away.

Only then did Zoey allow the tears to fill her eyes and overflow. She'd cried more in the past six months than she'd cried in her entire life.

They were off the rails, she and Cooper. Their boat was taking on water. Their plane was losing altitude and, well, whatever other bad metaphors she couldn't bring to mind at the moment.

It wasn't his fault. She could admit that. Well, except for this Boston business. That was definitely his fault. However, she'd been a basket case for months, even before Jennifer came to Houston. These weeks since her mother's death and the frantic efforts to complete her fellowship requirements, Zoey had drained her tanks dry.

Except for little puddles of crazy.

She lifted her hand to swipe the moisture from her cheeks and noticed the glint of sunshine on the window glass reflecting off the diamond on her left hand. Turning away from the window, she studied her engagement ring. It was beautiful, a simple and elegant solitaire on a platinum band. The stone was big enough to suggest good times ahead but appropriate for a relationship where student loans ate a big chunk of their paychecks. Zoey had loved it when Cooper gave it to her on Christmas Eve. She'd loved Cooper on Christmas Eve. She believed that Cooper loved her in return.

So how had everything fallen apart six months later? How had the scratch on the skin of their relationship become a seeping wound?

An infection had set in, that's how. Little uglies of grief, self-doubt, simmering resentment, and neglect penetrated and poisoned. After this morning's exchange, Zoey wondered if either she or Cooper had the skills to stop the bleeding.

She tugged at the engagement ring. It wouldn't slide over her knuckle. *He's going to fly in for the wedding. For the weekend. And fly out again. Alone. To Boston.*

Forget Tahiti. Forget their plans. Their dreams.

He hadn't asked her to go to Boston with him.

Zoey's ring finger began to throb. She yanked hard, and the ring slid off. She threw it at Cooper's pillow.

Zoey was breathing hard. Her heart was breaking. She needed to talk to someone. She needed a good therapist. She needed a friend.

She needed a mother. She giggle-snorted aloud at that. The story of her life.

If Mimi were still alive, Zoey would call her, but her beloved grandmother had died a decade ago. Dad had tried to fill the void. He was a good father, and he'd done his best when Zoey had wanted mothering, but he'd never been truly comfortable in the role.

Nevertheless, he was who she had.

She grabbed her phone off the bedside charger and dialed her father. He answered on the second ring. "Hey there, pookie. What's up?"

"Are you busy, Dad?"

"Nope. I'm just heading out to take a walk. What's up?"

Exercise was always good medicine. There was a nice little neighborhood park about halfway between their homes that they'd used for their meet-ups in the past. "Want to join me at our usual spot in a little bit? Say, half an hour? I could use..." What? Advice? A shoulder to cry on? "...my dad."

He responded with a mix of delight and concern in his tone. "I'd love to meet you."

After ending the call, Zoey quickly dressed in running clothes and left the condo. She took the long route, running at a fast clip. Maybe she'd get lucky, and the sunshine and physical exertion would clear her mind, so she wouldn't need to humiliate herself by pouring out her heart to her father.

She made an effort not to think about Cooper and his research opportunity as she ran, and slowly, her tension eased. She was able to greet her father with a smile when they met.

At fifty, Adam looked the part of a distinguished physician, even in running shorts and a Houston Astros tee. And today, he had a dog with him.

"What's this?" Zoey asked as she knelt and scratched the darling black-and-white schnauzer beneath his snout.

"I've been dog-sitting while his person is at the hospital."

"Your hospital?" she asked, knowing that would mean a cancer patient.

"Yes. A friend from church. Jack fought the good fight, but he'll be moving into hospice today."

"I'm sorry, Dad."

"Me, too. He's a good man. However, he's lived a long and fruitful life and says he's ready to go. Honestly, his only concern is for Freeway." Adam gestured toward the dog, whose ears twitched at the sound of his name. "He needs a home. I can't take him. He'd end up dying of thirst or starving to death like I almost killed you."

Zoey laughed. "Oh, Dad. It wasn't that bad. You only *totally* forgot about me a time or two."

When her father was deep into research mode, he tended to forget about everything. And upon occasion, everyone. Twenty years later, he still felt horribly guilty about the time he forgot her elementary school Christmas program, missing her voice solo, and leaving her to find her own way home. At night.

Zoey didn't hold it against him. The man was a brilliant researcher whose efforts had made a significant contribution to humanity. What was one grade-school performance compared to that?

Love welled up inside Zoey, and she stood and kissed her father's cheek. The dog demanded her attention when he plopped himself down atop her left sneaker. Zoey grinned down at him. "Freeway is an interesting name."

"He was a stray who my friend rescued from the middle lane of a freeway."

"Oh wow."

"I think he should have been named Lucky."

Adam and Zoey both turned to watch a man hitting pop flies to a mitt-wearing boy on the baseball diamond. Beyond the pair, a silver-haired woman walked a black Labrador retriever. "What are you going to do with Freeway the Lucky?"

"I don't know." He paused a beat, then asked, "You want a dog?"

Zoey shocked them both when she said, "Maybe."

At that point, Adam Hillcrest turned toward his daughter, concern lighting his blue eyes. "Ready to tell me what's wrong?"

"Maybe," she repeated. She eyed a nearby park bench, intending to sit down, but then veered toward the swing set and sat in one of the black saddle seats. Her father and Freeway followed her. Dad leaned against the swing's metal frame, folded his arms, and waited. He always did have the patience of Job.

So she let him wait.

It had been years since she'd sat in a swing, but muscle memory kicked in. Zoey swayed back and forth, back and forth. As thoughts of Cooper threatened to intrude, she felt her father's hands at her back, giving her a push. Suddenly, she was a girl again, swinging higher and higher. She told herself the wetness streaming from the corner of her eyes wasn't emotional tears but nature's reaction to the breeze on her face.

Adam pushed her for a good five minutes before Freeway darted away after a squirrel, trailing the leash behind him. Adam went after him, and Zoey allowed the swing to slow and stop. She unwrapped her fists from around the chains, and her gaze settled on her left hand. Her finger looked naked without Cooper's ring on it. She wondered how long it would take her to get accustomed to the change.

Whoa. Are you really going there?

"Maybe," she murmured. She twisted full circle in the swing three times, winding the chains, then letting go. She spun like a top and murmured, "Maybe I am."

Apparently, she'd been doing some thinking when she wasn't thinking.

The schnauzer and her father returned. Zoey spun herself a second time, then when she finished, her father quietly asked, "What did you and Cooper fight about?" She drew in a deep, shaky breath, then exhaled in a rush. "Cooper accepted a three-month-long research position with the Perry Group."

"Huh." Adam took a seat atop the picnic bench nearby. "Out of Harvard?"

"The very ones."

Adam gave a slow whistle. "That'll be a feather in his cap."

"Yes, so I understand. He starts next week."

With that tidbit of information, her father's eyebrows winged up. "What about the job here?"

"His group gave him a leave of absence. Like you said, it's a feather in his cap."

"No." He folded his arms. "I meant *your* job."

Thank you, Daddy. He'd thought of her. Zoey had needed that little show of support more than she'd realized. She couldn't hold back the bitterness in her tone as she answered him. "His opportunity doesn't change my plans. I'm not going to Boston. I wasn't invited to join him. In fact, I was discouraged from joining him."

"What!"

She parroted off the points Cooper had made. "He'll be at

the lab all the time. No sense trying to juggle schedules and for me to be sitting around waiting on him all the time. It'd be too stressful for both of us."

"You'll be newly"—Zoey saw his gaze drift to her left hand—"weds. Ah, hell, Zoey."

Just now noticed that, did you, Dad? As tears flooded her eyes once again, he snapped, "Did he break up with you?"

"No. The wedding is still on." For now. "This *is* a good opportunity for Cooper, Dad. I'm happy for him. Had he discussed it with me, I would have encouraged him to take it."

South Pacific honeymoon notwithstanding.

"But he didn't discuss it with me. He made the decision all on his own."

"Ah, hell, honey."

"And then I told him I was quitting medicine and opening a flower shop."

"You what? You're kidding me. Right? You're kidding me?"

"I'm a mess, Daddy. I haven't been happy for a while. Cooper insisted I talk to a shrink, but the doctor and I didn't sync."

"So, the flower shop is just a metaphor."

"No. I don't know. Maybe not. I love flowers."

"Oh, Zoey." He pulled her into his arms and hugged her tight. "You've had a lot on your plate. You don't need to quit medicine. You need a vacation."

"I agree with that. In a few weeks, I could go on my honeymoon. All by myself."

"Maybe somewhere other than the South Pacific would be good. Rome? Paris?"

"Maybe I should go to a NASCAR race."

Adam did a double take, releasing her and stepping back. "You've lost me."

"Don't they have red flags at car races? I'm all about the red flags right now. My whole relationship with Cooper is one great big red flag, don't you think?"

"Uh, honey..."

Zoey continued. "You're right. It's not a red flag. It's a ball. It's Cooper putting the breakup ball in my court. That's what this is."

"Now, Zoey." Adam awkwardly patted her arm.

She gazed up at her father imploringly. "He didn't ask me to go with him, Daddy. He'd played the 'you owe me one' card instead."

Adam sighed heavily. He leaned forward with his elbows on his knees and his hands clasped between his legs. "In Cooper's defense—"

"I do owe him," she interrupted. "He moved to Houston to be with me after he finished his residency instead of going home to Michigan as he'd always planned."

It was true. Because Zoey's pediatric residency was two years shorter than Cooper's orthopedic program, she'd finished her residency a year before he did. She'd planned to remain in Southern California and work until Cooper finished up at Cedars-Sinai. But then she'd won the three-year fellowship in Houston. She'd moved to Houston, and he'd remained in California.

That year apart trying to juggle their professional and personal lives almost killed them both, but they'd made it work. Cooper changed his career plans and shifted his goals in order to be with her. He'd moved to Houston and gone to work with a group of doctors here with the understanding that they'd consider relocating somewhere north sometime in the future.

She'd always felt a little bit guilty about it. He was a northern boy at heart, and he'd spent nine years in Southern California and now two years in Houston when he'd dreamed of returning home. The man had a thing for winter. For snow. Zoey didn't get it, but she accepted it.

And apparently, the frustrations of the past six months had breathed life back into Cooper's simmering relocation-north dreams.

"He has to know that I would have said yes and gone to Boston if he'd asked me. It would have been easily doable for me. The start date on the job at TCH isn't until October, and he didn't know I was thinking about turning it down until today."

"Wait. Did you talk flower shop with him? No wonder he's spooked."

"He didn't ask, Dad," she replied, ignoring the question. "Cooper didn't ask me to come with him."

It broke her heart. Her thoughts spun in that constant whirlwind. He hadn't asked her to go to Boston. She guessed she shouldn't be surprised. The two of them didn't talk anymore. They hadn't really talked—well, except to snipe or argue—since her mother came to town. Zoey shut her eyes against that remembered pain.

Because her eyes were shut, she didn't see what was coming. Before she quite knew what had happened, her father had deposited Freeway into her arms, saying, "Hug a puppy, Zoey. It's guaranteed to make you feel better."

Staring down into the schnauzer's big brown eyes, Zoey couldn't help but smile.

"Do you love him?" Adam asked.

The dog licked her face. "He's a really cute pup, but—"

"Not the dog. Cooper. Do you love Cooper?"

The answer came instantaneously. "Yes, but—"

"No. No 'buts.' As a rule, I try to keep my lips zipped when it comes to you and your love life, but you came to me today. So, I'm going to offer you a bit of advice. You gonna listen?"

Zoey nodded.

"You need to stop at the yes. I know that your feelings are hurt, but you didn't hesitate when you declared your love for Cooper. That is your bottom line, Zoey."

It wasn't *her* bottom line that worried her. It was Cooper's. He wanted out. Otherwise, he'd have invited her to Boston.

Freeway snuggled into her arms and buried his snout in her armpit. Zoey absently scratched him behind his ears. Maybe she *should* get a dog. It would keep her company when Cooper was gone.

"Back to this flower shop thing. I'm not a psyche doc, but this one is pretty easy to psychoanalyze. Your education has been your focus for a long time, and now you're facing an actual career. That's scary. The thought of running away is appealing to you. That's scary to Cooper."

"I won't argue that point."

"In that case, I think you need to think about Cooper's upbringing," her father advised. "Remember all that he overcame in order to be at that wedding where the two of you met."

Zoey thought back to that night. She'd been in medical school at UCLA. He'd been a year into his residency at Cedars-Sinai and stood up as best man for a colleague who'd married a friend of Zoey's. She'd thought him the most handsome man at the wedding, and she'd been flattered when he'd paid her particular attention. When he'd asked for her number at the after-party and called her Sunday and asked her out, she'd floated on air.

Adam continued. "Growing up poor, scrambling for scholarships, taking on the kind of debt that his education required put him in a different spot than you, who came from a privileged background."

"I know that," Zoey replied, her tone defensive. She'd always been sensitive to Cooper's financial concerns. Plus, while she'd never say it, her father had touched on one of Zoey's triggers. It was true that she'd been blessed to grow up with wealth, but Cooper had been born into a family with brothers and sisters and two loving, married parents who were married still today. That was a privilege, too.

"I know you weren't married yet when he followed you to Houston, but y'all were together in a committed relationship. You changed your mind about continuing your education with this fellowship. He moved to be with you. That was a big deal for him."

"I know that," Zoey repeated.

"I just think you need to look at this situation from his point of view. He's put you first. He's waited on you. Even strong men have vulnerable spots, honey. Maybe he needs you to return the favor."

"Maybe he does. I wouldn't know because for the most part, we don't talk to each other anymore, Daddy."

Agitated now, Zoey pushed out of the swing and set the dog down. She paced as she explained. "Things have been weird at home ever since I had pneumonia. We just haven't had any quality time together. I was swamped at the hospital trying to make up for everything I'd missed, and then Jennifer arrived. Now that I finally have time, he's leaving, and he didn't ask me to come along. He's putting off the honeymoon, so we won't even have that time alone together to reconnect then. And yet, if it takes a honeymoon for us to talk to one another, maybe we're making a mistake having a wedding at all."

"You don't think that."

"I don't know what I think, Dad. I—"

The ringing of his cell phone interrupted them. Adam checked the number and grimaced. "It's the hospital."

"Take it. I understand."

Adam connected the call, listened a moment, and then said, "Thank you for the heads-up. I'll be there as soon as possible."

Having ended the call, he gave Zoey a sad smile. "My church friend has had a stroke. He's in his final hours."

"I'm sorry, Dad."

"Thanks. I'm headed for the hospital. I don't want him to be alone." Adam stared at Freeway with dismay. "I hate to ask, but could you help me out with ol' lucky Mr. Freeway here? I could call an Uber and go straight there from here."

"Of course. I'll take him back to our townhome. Honestly, I can use the company."

"Great." He ordered the car and sounded relieved when he shared, "My ride is two minutes away. Look, if something comes up for you or this takes longer than I expect, feel free to leave Freeway at my house. You have a key. He has food and water."

"That'll work."

"And if you think of anyone who would be willing to give him a permanent home, I'd be forever grateful."

"I'll definitely put on my thinking cap." Zoey saw the Uber approaching, and she waved at the driver.

Adam scratched Freeway behind the ears and murmured, "I'm glad I sneaked you into the hospital yesterday for a visit. The way Jack teared up and you whined when we left, I wonder if both of you sensed that it might have been the last one."

"I wouldn't be surprised," Zoey observed. "The bond between a dog and his human can be an amazing thing."

A few moments later, her dad departed, and Zoey turned toward home with her new four-legged pal.

When her thoughts returned to Cooper, she felt stronger. He'd said they'd talk tonight. She would hold him to it. They hadn't talked—really talked—in months. That was over.

He'd lobbed the break-up ball to her, hadn't he? Well, she planned to return it with an overhead smash.

It was almost noon when she finally returned home, found an old pillow for Freeway to use as a bed, set out a bowl of water, and then hit the shower. She'd just finished blow-drying her hair when she heard the sound of activity coming from the kitchen. "That dog had better not have gotten into something he shouldn't," she grumbled as she set down the dryer and hurried toward the kitchen.

She discovered that Freeway wasn't making the noise. Cooper was making a grilled cheese sandwich. Actually, he was making two grilled cheese sandwiches. He'd set out placemats, plates, silverware, and glasses of iced tea in front of their usual spots on the bar. When was the last time they'd sat down together to eat? Zoey couldn't recall.

"This is a surprise," she said, taking her seat at the bar. A nice one? She couldn't tell.

He gestured toward the dog, who was asleep on his pillow. "Who's your friend?"

"His name is Freeway." She gave Cooper a brief synopsis of how the schnauzer had come to be in their kitchen.

He nodded and used a spatula to check the bottom of the sandwiches. "Adam shouldn't have a hard time finding a home for him. He's a cute dog."

"Yes," Zoey agreed as he slid a sandwich onto her plate. "Thank you. This looks good."

"You're welcome. I saw your running shoes were missing. I figured you haven't had lunch yet."

"I haven't." Zoey didn't have much of an appetite, but she wasn't about to mention that. This was Cooper's show.

He placed a sandwich on his plate and then returned the pan to the stovetop. While he opened the refrigerator in search of sweet pickles, Zoey figured, she picked up her glass. She sipped her tea, and her gaze drifted across their living room.

That's when she spied his suitcase sitting beside the door. She almost dropped her glass. "You're leaving now?"

Simultaneously, he set the pickle jar on the bar and said accusingly, "You took off your ring."

They both looked a bit guilty. Zoey sucked in a shaky breath, then explained, "I had a fit of temper. Then I went running."

Cooper said, "My dad fell this morning and broke his hip. I'm flying home later today."

"Oh no. Poor Pat. I'm so sorry."

"I'll fly from there to Boston."

Zoey shut her eyes and nodded. *I'll get through this. I'll do it. I can do it.*

Cooper shoved his fingers through his hair. "Before I got the call about Dad, I figured I could come home tonight, and we could hash out why we've been... um..."

Um. Cooper was one of the most eloquent people she'd ever met, but he couldn't find the words to define their relationship. *Oh, joy.*

"I'll take a stab at it. In the midst of a cold war?"

He grimaced but didn't disagree. "I know your world has been stupid hard this year. I've been at a loss on what to do or how to help."

"You held me when I needed holding."

"You didn't let me in, Zoey. And you wouldn't get help. Won't get help."

Anger stirred. "Dr. Rios is a class-A bitch. It's not a good fit. I haven't exactly had a ton of time here, Cooper. We're barely into July."

"I know. I know." He opened his sandwich and placed a layer of pickles inside it. "But it seems to me that I'm only making it worse. I've known you've been unhappy at the hospital. You're grieving your mother, who was awful to you, but she was still your mother. You're recovering from the insanity that is finishing medical school. You're working through it all, but you seem to be wanting to do it all on your own."

"Is that why you didn't ask me to go to Boston with you?"

"Yes. I thought if I wasn't around, it might be easier for you. I didn't think throwing another big change on top of everything else would be good for your mental health. I thought if we had some time apart, it might be healthier for us both."

He glanced up from his sandwich. "I didn't anticipate the florist thing. If you are seriously considering quitting medicine, then I don't understand you at all."

"And I have never understood how 'time apart' helps anything."

He glanced away from her. "I should have talked to you before I accepted the position."

Yes, you should have. Zoey squared her shoulders. "I wish you had talked with me. I would have told you that I recognize that it's a wonderful opportunity. I absolutely think you should take advantage of it."

"Thank you." He picked up his sandwich and took a bite. Zoey's mouth twisted with an unhappy grin. Cooper and his comfort food.

Comfort. She could use some comfort. Some peace. Zoey continued. "If you had talked to me, we could have discussed my going with you."

"We can discuss it now."

"No. No, I think that ship has sailed, Cooper."

"What are you saying?

Yep, he's a pro at getting the ball back into her court. *Does he want me to call off the wedding?*

Well, she wasn't ready to do that. Not today.

"Like you said, I have things to work through. Your instincts were for me to do it by myself. We will go with that."

He nodded, then picked up his plate and threw his barely tasted sandwich away. Zoey watched him and considered that she could make a metaphor out of that action if she wanted.

They had little else to say to each other as he prepared to leave for the airport. His good-bye kiss was hesitant and without passion. "I'll call you when I've seen Dad. Let you know how he's doing."

She nodded. "Please do. Safe travels."

When the door shut behind Cooper, Zoey's knees gave out. She sank down onto the ground, and a black cloud of silence surrounded her. At what point Freeway came out from under the bed and crawled to cuddle in her lap, she didn't know. How long she sat there, she hadn't a clue.

The first two times her watch vibrated, signaling an incoming call, she ignored it. The third time, she looked. She'd had two spam calls and an appointment reminder robocall from her dentist.

When the watch vibrated again, this time with a text, she looked at it without checking the number. **Zoey, you have a DNA match to explore.**

Zoey's arm started shaking. Her stomach took a roll. Oh wow. Did she really want to do this?

She hadn't given this much thought since her mother died. She'd pretty much blocked the whole thing out. She'd been stupid busy at the hospital up until two weeks ago, and since then, she'd been obsessing about flower shops. And looking forward to her life with Cooper. She'd been in the process of shutting the door on the past and looking to the future.

Look where that had gotten her.

She tapped the face of her watch. The message came up. *Hmm.* Reading it required that she follow links. Better she did this at the computer.

Zoey rose and walked to the desktop in the condo's second bedroom. Her chest was tight. Her mouth was dry. She wiggled the mouse, and her screensaver came up.

Moments later, her world changed with a click.

Brooke Prentice. 1st cousin, once removed. 12.5% DNA shared. Parent 1's side.

Parent 1. Dad, not Jennifer.

The notice came with photos. Zoey's breath caught. So, those nagging suspicions had something to them. She had seen photos of Brooke Prentice back in January on Willow Eldridge's desk and office wall. She'd been a bridesmaid at her brother's wedding.

Zoey dragged her hand down her face. So, Willow was not Zoey's doppelgänger. She was a cousin. Zoey and Willow looked so much alike because they were cousins. Once removed, but whatever. Cousins.

How appropriate was that?

The Prentice family, who had been so lovely to work with these past months, shared history with her warm, wonderful father, who had been placed with a warm, wonderful family in a private adoption. Willow had been nothing but warm and wonderful while Zoey worked with her on wedding plans. Her mother and aunt had been nothing but warm and wonderful when she'd met them in January.

Warm, wonderful women. Zoey knew a surge of yearning as strong as any biological urge she'd ever experienced. She picked up her phone and, without giving it a moment's thought, placed a call to Willow. She answered on the second ring, saying,

"Zoey! You and I must be on the same wavelength. I have you on my list to call today."

"Oh?"

"I have something important I need to run past you. Do you want me to share it, or would you rather discuss whatever you're calling about first?"

Zoey didn't really want to talk about the wedding. However, she didn't know exactly why she'd made the call to Colorado. She could listen. Listening was easy.

She didn't have to share any DNA bombshells with her wedding planner. Not yet. "Sure. What do you have to tell me?"

"I know it's awfully late in the day to make changes, but we've had an exciting development, and I want you to know about it. Our contractor will have our new Glass Chapel in the woods finished ahead of schedule. If you and Cooper would like to have your ceremony there, we'll be happy to change the arrangements."

The yearning still humming through Zoey's blood intensified. That spot in the woods had been so peaceful and beautiful.

Willow continued. "I can send you pictures—"

"No," Zoey interrupted, her heart beginning to pound. "I want to see it. My schedule is free right now. I know it's tourist season. Does the inn have any open rooms? Or if not, do you know of a place where I could stay? I can probably get there tomorrow. It'll be just me."

"I'm sure we can find something for you, Zoey. It'll be wonderful to be able to go over the wedding arrangements in person instead of doing everything over Zoom."

Zoey shifted Freeway off her lap and rose. Her gaze focused on the dog, she added, "Actually, it will be more than just me. Any chance it can be a pet-friendly room? I seem to have a small dog. He's a schnauzer, around fourteen pounds. He's very well-behaved. Honestly, I think he may be a bit depressed because his owner went into hospice."

"Of course. We are a pet-friendly facility. If worse comes to worst, I'll take him out to my place. He can pal around with our pups. How long do you think you'll stay?"

The question stumped Zoey. "Well, today is Tuesday. If I can get there tomorrow, maybe until Sunday? I'll send you a text when I have a better idea about arrival time."

"Sounds perfect. I'll get everything arranged on this end. I'm looking forward to seeing you, Zoey. I'm so excited to show you everything we have ready for your wedding. It won't be long, now."

Maybe. Maybe not. That remains to be seen.

Willow continued, "So, that's my news. What did you need to ask me?"

"Oh." Zoey winced and fumbled for something to say. Finally, she settled on, "It's nothing that won't keep until I see you. I'll shoot you a text when I have a better sense of my ETA."

They exchanged good-byes and ended the call. Zoey's heart continued to pound as she stared down at Freeway. "Would you rather fly or drive?"

The dog's tail thumped against the hardwood floor. Zoey pulled up the airline app and checked available flights. Her choices weren't appealing. The earliest she could get to Durango was midnight, and then she'd have to drive those high mountain roads to Lake in the Clouds in the middle of the night. That wasn't happening. She might be unsettled, but she wasn't suicidal.

"Driving it is."

Twenty minutes later, she loaded her suitcase and Freeway into her car. Headed north on I-45, she called and left her father a voice mail telling him simply that she was taking a few days of vacation and she'd call him when she returned. She thought about calling Cooper, too, but decided to send a text when she stopped to get gas.

She forgot to send the text when she bought gas.

She forgot to put her engagement ring back on before leaving the house.

Not entirely on purpose.

Maybe a little bit on purpose.

Unfortunately, being a physician specializing in pediatric emergency medicine didn't mean Zoey knew how to treat emotional wounds worth a damn.

Chapter Eight

GENEVIEVE'S PACE WAS BRISK as she followed the winding trail through the woods toward the Glass Chapel. Willow had called her first thing that morning with the exciting news that the chapel was wedding-ready, and they'd arranged to meet there at ten. Genevieve was excited to see the final product. She hadn't been out to check on progress for more than a month.

She'd been a busy little beaver ever since Founder's Day. Her youngest, Brooke, had spent ten days in June with Genevieve in Lake in the Clouds. She and her daughter had split their time between playing tourist and enjoying family activities with Helen, Willow, Noah, and the kids. After Brooke departed, Genevieve and Helen spent a few days prepping for their booth at the town's upcoming Christmas in July market. Genevieve had scheduled to spend part of the last week of June up at the Triple T, tackling the redecorating project Gage had requested. Unfortunately, she'd come down with a summer virus and spent three days at home in bed instead of up at the ranch with Gage. By the time she'd recovered, he'd been off on a cattle-buying trip. She'd then traveled to Texas to visit with her sons prior to the family's traditional July Fourth gathering at the Prentice family lake house.

She did have a lunch date with Gage today. He was supposed to call her sometime this morning to arrange when and where they'd meet.

The path made a turn, and Genevieve spied the chapel. Her breath caught.

Nestled among the white-barked stand of aspens and built in the long, narrow style of a small country church, the Glass Chapel was an enchanting blend of tradition and modern design. Genevieve approached smiling, enchanted by the way the sunlight filtered through the towering trees, danced and refracted through the transparent walls.

Willow and Zach Throckmorton, Gage's eldest son, spied her approach and exited the building. Genevieve called to her daughter. "Oh, Willow. It's fabulous. Truly fabulous. Congratulations. This is wonderful."

"Zach is the guy who made it happen," her daughter responded. "Zach and our architect."

"It was your vision, Willow," Zach said as he joined them, a toolbox in hand. "Punch list is completed, boss. I think we're officially done."

"Excellent," Willow said. "If you'd like, after I give Mom a tour, we can meet up at the office, and I'll write you a check."

"Works for me. Although, I'm expecting a tourist, myself, shortly. I invited Dad to come see the finished product."

"He and I have lunch plans for today," Genevieve said. "I was going to suggest Cloudwiches, but maybe we'll eat up at the lodge's restaurant. Helen tells me the new salads Kelly has added to the menu are excellent."

Willow nodded. "They are wonderful. If you have lunch at the inn, you'll likely be there when our bride arrives."

Genevieve frowned. "We don't have a wedding this weekend, do we?"

"No. Zoey Hillcrest is on her way to town. She's making a special trip to see the Glass Chapel, and she's due to arrive sometime this morning. I offered the chapel to her and Cooper for their wedding if they'd like it. They'd be our first."

"Oh, I love that. They're the sweetest couple. Will her fiancé be with her?"

"No. It's just her and her dog." She glanced toward the path and added, "Shall we wait for Gage to begin the tour?"

Zach shook his head. "Y'all go on. Dad will be interested in different things than you, Genevieve. He'll want to see nuts and bolts, and you are all about aesthetics."

"True," Genevieve said with a laugh. "You've built enough things for me by now that you know how I think."

Willow looped her arm through her mother's. "C'mon, Mom. Let me show off my summer baby."

"As opposed to your winter baby," Genevieve observed, nodding toward her daughter's little baby bump. Both women were smiling when Willow led Genevieve to the chapel's front doors, opened them, and stepped inside with her mother. Although truth be told, it felt like they remained outside.

The minimalist design allowed the interior to flow to the exterior. The gently bowed roof mimicked the arch of tree branches. The woods provided art for the walls. Simple wooden pews sat on a hardwood floor, and at the front of the chapel, a plain wooden altar stood on a raised stone section. Genevieve's gaze settled on the pair of clear glass vases on the altar that contained wildflowers likely picked from the field at Willow's home. Genevieve recognized the glass artist's work. "Those vases are a Cicero design, aren't they?"

"Good eye." Willow pointed upward, calling Genevieve's

attention to the light fixtures. "He did those, too. They sparkle like fairy lights."

"This is just spectacular, sweetheart. I'm so proud of you. The Glass Chapel will be one of the most beautiful wedding venues in Colorado. I can't wait to see a wedding here. I hope Zoey chooses to move their ceremony."

"Me, too." Willow next showed Genevieve the bridal party prep suites hidden from the view of the chapel by a stand of trees. When they returned from exploring those, Genevieve discovered that Gage had arrived and toured the chapel.

He was dressed in jeans and a blue chambray shirt that complemented and deepened the color of his crystalline blue eyes. He wore a white straw Resistol cowboy hat and a pair of snakeskin boots. Upon seeing Genevieve, he gave that slow, sexy smile that always made her heart go *pit-a-pat.* "Hello, Genevieve. You are a sight for sore eyes. Welcome home. How was Texas?"

"Thank you. I'm glad to be back. Texas was hot, but good family time."

He strode over to her, took her hand, then leaned down and kissed her cheek. "Looks like our kiddos hit a home run with this chapel. It's a special place."

"Isn't it?"

Willow glanced down at her watch, and Genevieve watched her read a text. "Zoey is half an hour away. I need to go. We're totally booked for the week, and I'm praying for a last-minute cancellation. Otherwise, I'm going to have to put her in the Honeymoon Cottage, and I hate to do that. The first time she stays there should be their wedding night."

Genevieve frowned. "Oh, I agree."

"I called around town, and there's not a room to be had for tomorrow."

Genevieve tilted her head and thought about it. "Why don't

you check with Helen? The visitor's apartment at her condo complex might be open."

"Ooh, good idea, Mom." Willow gave Genevieve a hug, then said, "I should second Gage's comment. Welcome home. We missed you. Gage, nice to see you this morning."

"Right back at you, sweetheart."

"I'll come with you," Zach said. "I promised Kelly I'd take a look at a door that's sticking." He picked up his toolbox and a jacket he'd left at the base of a tree, then followed Willow on the trail into the woods that led back toward the inn.

Gage grinned down at Genevieve. "Finally alone."

As she smiled back up at him, his gaze locked on hers, and the light in them intensified. In response, Genevieve's heart began to pound. Time slowed, and the aspen grove and birdsong faded away. The world existed of only the two of them.

Gage brushed his thumb lightly along her cheek. Genevieve instinctively turned toward his touch, and she wallowed in the faint, familiar scent of man, leather, and the clean fragrance of soap. He moved closer. He slid his arms around her waist and pulled her against him. Genevieve's breath caught as he slowly, deliberately lowered his mouth to hers.

Genevieve melted against him as sensation bloomed through her. The man knew how to kiss. He was gentle and yet insistent, coaxing her with his touch, his tongue, and soft sounds that sent shudders of desire skittering along her nerves. Gage stoked the embers of yearning into a heated flame of need.

Gage made Genevieve feel young again. Hormones were a part of it, that was true. However, as important as the sexual hunger he stirred to life within her was the unspoken offer of intimacy, affection, and trust that he laid before her. Gage Throckmorton tempted her with the promise of possibilities.

If she were courageous enough to accept.

When they broke apart, he gazed down at her with tenderness and perhaps a hint of vulnerability. "I missed you."

"I've missed you, too."

"How about we go inside and sit a spell? I like the mood of your Glass Chapel."

"I do, too. That sounds like a great idea, Gage."

Holding hands, they approached the entrance to the building and stepped inside. "Here's something I don't know about you, Genevieve. I know you attend St. Vincent's in town. Are you somebody who likes to go early to get one of the good seats in the back, or are you a front-of-the-church kind of girl?"

Genevieve laughed. "I'm a middle-of-the-roader, as a rule."

"Right side or left?"

"I'm flexible."

He led her to a pew halfway up the aisle, then gestured for her to choose a seat. She slipped into a seat on the right side of the chapel. Gage sat beside her, and for a time, they sat together in peaceful, harmonious silence.

Genevieve lifted her gaze to watch the summer green leaves of the aspen flutter in the gentle breeze. This was such a tranquil spot. In the past half hour, clouds had drifted across the bright blue sky, and now, a soft patter of raindrops added nature's music to the scene. Happy, she leaned her head against Gage's shoulder and soaked in the serenity of the space.

She was totally unprepared for the bomb he lobbed. "Genevieve, I think we should get married."

Her serenity evaporated instantaneously. She pulled away from Gage and stared at him in shock. "Married! We never talked about marriage."

"It's time we did."

Panic rolled through her. "Why?"

"Because I want to marry you."

"Why?"

He chuckled softly. "You should see your face, Genevieve. You're a green-eyed Bambi in my pickup truck's headlights."

"That doesn't address my question."

"The answer is simple. I'm in love with you. I want to share my life with you."

Genevieve's mouth dropped open. He'd never used the word "love" before. "When did this happen? One would think you would have mentioned it."

"I'm mentioning it now."

Genevieve blinked. "Ordinarily, one would mention the L-word prior to a proposal."

"Oh, I'm not proposing. I'll do something a lot more romantic than this when I officially propose."

I think we should get married. I'm in love with you. I want to share my life with you. Genevieve couldn't disguise the panic fluttering through her as she asked, "Then what is this?"

His mouth twisted ruefully. "I was hoping for a discussion, but judging by your reaction, I'm thinking maybe it should be classified as a warning. Your reaction isn't giving me the warm fuzzies, Genevieve."

"I'm sorry." She shoved to her feet and fled to the aisle, then paced at the front of the chapel. She laced her fingers behind her neck. "This is coming out of left field. I'm not prepared."

Gage rose to his feet, walked to the center aisle, and folded his arms. "This shouldn't be so hard."

"Well, it is!"

"Why?"

"A million reasons."

"Give me one."

"All right. Lindsay."

He pursed his lips. "Okay, that's a fair one."

"Your daughter hates me."

"Now, that's not true. She'd be this way about anyone I decided to see. I've talked to her about her attitude, and I've told her I won't tolerate her being disrespectful to you."

"She moved back to Lake in the Clouds to protect you from me."

"Now, Genevieve."

"Don't 'now, Genevieve' me! She admitted as much at the nail salon. She thinks I'm a gold-digger out to steal your ranch."

"What are you talking about?"

"Her pedicure! She was choosing between Tickle My France-y and Yank My Doodle and—"

"Pardon me?"

"Colors. Lindsay was standing at the color rack and talking on her phone. She didn't notice that Marsha Watkins walked into the salon and could hear everything she said."

"Marsha Watkins is the biggest gossip in town."

"Tell me about it! I heard the news before Lindsay got her topcoat on, and that was fourth-hand news from my sister."

Gage grimaced. "Okay, that's not good. However, that happened before you left for Texas, right?"

"Yes, but—"

"That's before she and I had our Come-to-Jesus meeting," Gage said. "We talked it out. I recognize that it's natural for my daughter to feel threatened that her mother's memory is somehow going to be usurped when I remarry. I explained that it wasn't going to happen. You're not trying to take Emily's place any more than I'm trying to take David's. Lindsay won't talk that way again."

Genevieve lifted her gaze toward the heavens in supplication. "Gage, you need to understand. She might not say it anymore, but that is still what she thinks."

"Well, what she thinks is wrong and frankly, stupid. I've tried to be sensitive to her grief and her feelings, but this is my life to live, and I'm not getting any younger. I'm not going to let my daughter's hissy fits dictate my actions. She needs to grow up, and she will. She's a good girl. So, what else? What's your number two?"

Genevieve shot him a confused look.

"Your second out of a million reasons why my suggestion has you so freaked out. Is it because you don't return my affection? Have you been leading me on, Genevieve?"

"No! Absolutely not. I . . . I . . ." She fumbled for words.

He arched a mocking brow and waited.

This wasn't the way a person should go about this. Frustration sharpened into anger, and Genevieve snapped. "No. No, you don't. I own my own feelings." She poked her chest with her thumb. "*I* will decide when and how I tell you that I've fallen in love with you. Love, by definition, is freely given. You will not force my hand. This is happening way too fast. Honestly, I'm still trying to figure out what love is at our age. We only have been officially dating for six months."

"So, you *have* fallen in love with me?" Gage's lips twitched, and satisfaction gleamed in his eyes.

Genevieve let out a shriek of frustration.

"You really are pretty when you're riled, Genevieve." He leaned in and stole a quick kiss. "Look, they say sixty is the new forty. Personally, I tend to think that at our age, six months is the new six years."

Genevieve covered her face with her hands. "You're not listening to me."

"Sure I am." Gage strode toward her, took hold of her hands, and lowered them, keeping hold. He met her gaze and held it. "I want to spend time with you. I've hardly seen you in the past couple of months. I want you in my bed, Genevieve. I desire you."

Oh wow. Okay, she'd known this was coming. Truth be told, she'd fantasized about it more than once. It was a huge step. She hadn't made love with a man in more than a decade. Which meant she hadn't been naked in front of a man for more than a decade. Not even a doctor, since she'd switched to female physicians years ago.

It was a big step. A huge step.

Not as huge as getting married, though.

Genevieve sucked in a deep breath, then said, "Okay, well, I'm not against the idea of making love with you. I admit I'm a bit nervous about it. It's been a long time for me, but I desire you, too, Gage. We don't need to get married to sleep together."

"See, that's the thing. I do. I don't shack up."

Genevieve drew back. "Seriously?"

"Seriously. Haven't you wondered why I haven't asked you to go to bed with me?"

Well, yes. "I haven't fretted about it. You and I were getting to know each other. We've been becoming friends."

"Yes, we have. And I don't have sex with my friends. Why would I risk burning a relationship that's become important to me by having sex without commitment? Now, I want more than friendship. I want intimacy, and for me, that means commitment. I know it's old-fashioned, but that's who I am."

"I like who you are," Genevieve said softly.

He brought her right hand up to his mouth and gave it a gallant kiss. "I'm glad to know that. Also, I was listening when you said that you own your own feelings. I hear you. I'm not trying to pressure you." He paused, his brow creasing as he considered. "Okay, maybe I was trying to pressure you a little bit. This whole dating thing isn't easy for me. I'm really rusty."

"You do it pretty darn well."

"I'm trying. So, why don't you hit me with number three?"

Genevieve sighed. "You are persistent, I'll give you that. Gage, I've been a widow for a long time. I've dated some, but not a lot. I'm pretty rusty myself. Seeing you these past few months has been wonderful. I've enjoyed the experience tremendously. But I need to tell you that I haven't given any thought to remarrying. To be perfectly honest, I've shied away from thinking about it."

"Which brings us back to reason number three. That's it? You've been a widow for too long?"

"Well, yes. I'm set in my ways, Gage. Marriage would be a huge change. Bigger even than selling all my belongings and running away from home."

"That one turned out well, though, didn't it?"

"Yes, it did. I love my life right now. You talk about risk. Well, marriage is a huge risk. Nothing hurt me so much as losing David. You understand that. I know you do."

"Yes, I do."

"In all the years since then, I have protected my heart. I have armor around it that's a foot thick. I can love you, Gage, but I don't know if I can allow myself to be in love again. All these years, I haven't been able to do it."

"Well, that's understandable. You haven't been falling in love with me." When Genevieve sputtered a laugh, Gage pulled her against him and held her tight, nuzzling her hair. "You're afraid. I get that. Believe it or not, I'm trembling in my boots here, myself."

Genevieve sighed. "Not you."

"Yeah, me.

"I still need more time."

"Don't take too long. We're not getting any younger. When I finally get you in my bed, I'll need my stamina to fulfill all these fantasies about you that have been running through my mind."

She lifted her mouth for a kiss, and he accommodated her. When he lifted his head long moments later, she could have purred. "Oh, Gage. I do want you. However, the thought of you seeing me naked scares me witless." He blinked at her in confusion. "It's one of the numbers. I've lost track of where we're at."

When he pulled back, obviously shocked, she gave him a sheepish look. "It's been a long time."

He rolled his eyes. "That's the silliest thing I've ever heard."

"I'm in my sixties, Gage."

"So am I."

"But you're a man."

"I'm glad you noticed. However, I don't see what that has to do with anything."

"Men get more attractive as they age. Women... sag."

His amazing blue eyes took on a twinkle. "I've always had a fantasy that involves a high-necked, long-sleeved cotton nightgown. We'll get you one, and you can leave it on."

"Gage, I'm being serious."

"I am, too! I seriously like the idea of having a little adventure in the bedroom. We're not too old for that, you know."

"I know that." She paused a moment and added, "How much adventure are we talking about here?"

"I'm not suggesting hanging an upside-down pineapple on the front door at the Triple T, but—"

"That's an urban legend," Genevieve fired back. "People don't really do that to indicate they're swingers."

He gave a smirk, then a shrug. "Maybe you should take a closer look next time you visit your sister."

Genevieve's eyes rounded, and her chin dropped in shock. Gage hastened to say, "Not Helen's doors. Check out some of the doors at the Mountain Vista condos."

"No. I don't believe that. Helen would know if that was true, and she would have told me."

"We're getting off track, honey. Let's take a moment and take advantage of where we're at." He guided her toward the front pew, sat her down, and took a seat beside her. "Let's peace out for a few minutes, shall we? It looks like the rain is finished. Watch the woods. Clear your mind. Let this place do its thing the way y'all intended it. Deal?"

"I'll try."

"Look there at about two o'clock. See that cardinal tucked underneath a leafy bough?"

Genevieve spied the bright red bird, nodded, and took a deep, cleansing breath. Attempting to rid herself of agitation, she focused on the cardinal. She studied how the dappled sunshine painted the foliage around it and how raindrops slowly released their cling on the tips of aspen leaves and fell in big fat plops to the forest floor. She gradually began to relax.

Attuned to her, Gage obviously sensed it because he said, "That's better. This place is good medicine. Is the Glass Chapel up on Yelp yet? I might need to leave a review."

Genevieve briefly rested her head on his shoulder. "You are a good man, Gage Throckmorton."

"I do try. But I'm also a man who prefers confrontation to avoidance. That brings us back to the subject at hand. Do you have another number to bring up?"

"Persistency can be a flaw, you know." Genevieve wrinkled her nose.

"Avoidance doesn't solve anything, you understand." He

waited until she'd finished her sigh to ask, "What other concerns do you have, Genevieve?"

"I think I've hit the top ten."

"I thought we're on four or maybe five?"

Dryly, Genevieve said, "Lindsay counts for five all by herself. Let's circle back in that direction and add the rest of our progeny to the discussion. My kids are happy to see me dating, and while I'd expect them to support me if I decided to remarry, they'd still have some twinges. And it's been over twenty years since they lost their dad. Gage, Lindsay's grief is still raw. And I don't doubt your boys will have those twinges, too."

"I hear you, but Emily has been gone for three years, not three months. Three years isn't rushing."

"No, it's not. However, the anniversary of her death was only a few days ago. I have experience with anniversaries, Gage. They're a ticket to Six Flags with a Fast Pass on all the roller coasters. Frankly, your decision to bring this up today, which is so close to the anniversary of Emily's death, raises all sorts of red flags."

"Wait a minute." Now it was Gage's turn to shove to his feet and begin pacing the front of the chapel. "I don't think it is deserving of a penalty flag. I've been thinking about this for months."

"But why did you bring it up *today?*"

He halted and faced her and folded his arms across his chest. "Not because of Emily. Because of you. I want to be with you. Next time that you go to Texas or I go to Alaska, I want us to go together. I talked to my kids about the possibility of my marrying you months ago. And yes, that probably contributed to Lindsay's decision to move back to Lake in the Clouds. I'm bringing it up today because I missed you these past weeks, Genevieve. You. I want you to be my wife."

Genevieve gave him a long, searching look. "I need to think about it, Gage."

"That's why I brought the subject up. You think about it. Think hard."

"I will. I promise. However, I'll ask a favor of you."

"What's that?"

"Don't blindside me with a proposal. Let's you and I talk about this again before you run off and make plans for some grand gesture that I don't want to be part of."

His tone droll, Gage said, "I wasn't planning to do a live TikTok, Genevieve."

"Just so we understand each other," she replied. He nodded, and she continued. "Also, I'm giving you fair warning. I'll probably talk to Lindsay, too. And your boys."

"Whatever trips your trigger."

She nodded once. "Okay, then. Final question."

"Yes?"

She smiled warmly as she asked, "Where are you taking me to lunch?"

Chapter Nine

AT HALF PAST TEN, Helen entered the visitor's apartment at Mountain Vista Retirement Community carrying a tray of goodies for the pantry and refrigerator. In a moment of good timing, the housekeepers had visited yesterday, so she expected to find the place guest-ready. A quick perusal assured her that all was well and ready for the bride-to-be.

She'd just finished loading a wooden bowl with a selection of fresh fruit when she heard a knock at the front door. She set the bowl at the center of the kitchen table, then went to greet the visitor.

Helen opened the door and couldn't help but laugh. Zoey Hillcrest stood holding a black-and-white schnauzer in her arms. The bride-to-be's hair was a tangled mess. Her shirt was streaked with what appeared to be ketchup. Helen hoped it was ketchup and not blood. The look in the young woman's eyes bordered on wild. "Oh my. Difficult trip?"

"Like nothing I ever imagined," Zoey fervently replied.

Helen motioned her inside, and as the young woman glanced curiously around the apartment, she continued, "I've been on a transatlantic trip seated next to a mom traveling with a set of eighteen-month-old triplets. That wasn't nearly as chaotic as a road trip with Freeway."

"Freeway?" Helen reached out and scratched the dog beneath his muzzle. "That's a fun name."

"His former owner named him. Apparently, he was found on the freeway. Please don't report me to PETA, but after traveling with him from Houston to Lake in the Clouds, I totally get why he might have been abandoned on a roadside."

Helen made kissing sounds at the dog. "Poor abandoned baby. You obviously have a good reason for hating car rides."

"I promise he was perfectly well-behaved when I had him at my home and last night in our hotel," Zoey assured her. Her brow creased with concern as she added, "He's house-trained. He didn't chew or tear anything up. He didn't bark all night long. I'll do everything possible to ensure that Freeway and I are good neighbors for you here at Mountain Vista. If he doesn't calm down and behave now that I have him out of the car, then you have my word that I'll pack up his crate and my toothbrush, and we'll go sleep in the car."

"Oh, honey, don't you fret. Chances are the poor little guy gets carsick. I had a dog with that problem once upon a time."

"I hope that's all it is," Zoey said fervently.

"Now, let me show you around. First, I put water and kibble bowls down in the kitchen for Freeway. Through here."

The schnauzer's stomach wasn't too upset because he all but dove for the kibble.

While Freeway ate, Helen gave Zoey the rest of the nickel tour. The wild look in the young woman's eyes faded, and exhaustion took its place. Taking pity on her, Helen offered to dog sit while Zoey took a nap.

The bride-to-be all but wept in gratitude.

"I've already told Willow I want to wait until tomorrow to visit her chapel. I am too tired to appreciate anything today."

"You sleep as long as you want," Helen told her. "I have nothing on my calendar until later this afternoon when I'm supposed to meet Genevieve downtown. We have a vendor booth in the Lake in the Clouds' Christmas in July Festival that opens tomorrow. We need to put the finishing touches on our booth."

"A Christmas market! How cool. I love Christmas markets."

"Genevieve and I have a family-themed booth. You'll have to come to check us out."

"I'll do that. Maybe I'll find a Christmas gift for my dad."

"Well, first, you go get your nap. I might take Freeway and my pup to the dog park here on the property, so text me when you wake up, and I'll tell you where to find us. My number is on the pad in the kitchen."

"Thank you so much, Helen."

The girl was swaying on her feet. Helen reached out and gave Zoey a quick hug, and then Helen and the schnauzer retreated to Helen's condo. There, she introduced him to her dog Cookie, short for Cookie Monster, whom Genevieve's son-in-law Noah had convinced Helen to adopt. The two dogs took to each other immediately, and Helen followed through on her idea to take them to the dog park to play. She threw a ball for a bit, then sat on a bench to read a few chapters of her current murder mystery while the dogs ran wild and wore themselves out. Upon returning to the condo, they plopped down in front of the living room picture window and watched the squirrels, birds, and bicyclists go by.

Zoey texted Helen when she awoke after a nearly two-hour nap. Helen called her, told her the dogs were doing fine, and assured her that she had time to shower before picking up Freeway. "Why don't you take a little more time for yourself, then pop over to my place in about an hour for a late lunch? I haven't eaten yet. It's salad day for me, and it won't be any trouble at all to throw in a little extra lettuce."

"That sounds wonderful," Zoey said. "Thank you."

Helen shared her condo number and location, and exactly thirty minutes later, she heard a knock at the door, and invited the young woman inside. Helen was once again struck by Zoey's resemblance to Willow. "You look like a new woman. Feel better?"

"I do. That steam shower is beyond awesome."

"I have one of those here, too. They are awesome." After Zoey stopped to meet Cookie and give both dogs a scratch and a pet, Helen led her through the condo, saying, "I thought we'd eat on the patio if that's all right with you? We had rain earlier this morning, but that's cleared off, and it's a bright, beautiful summer afternoon."

"I'm thrilled to do anything outside this time of year. It's hot and humid at home, so this Lake in the Clouds weather is a treat for me."

Helen showed Zoey to a bistro table set for two on her patio. They discussed the gorgeous view for a moment before Helen went inside for the salad and fresh croissants that she'd picked up at the bakery on her way home from yoga class that morning. They made small talk while they ate, discussing Zoey's drive from Texas and the potted rose bushes that decorated Helen's patio.

It was when Zoey picked up a knife to butter her roll that Helen noticed what was missing. *No engagement ring?*

Helen remembered the ring. It had been a lovely square-cut diamond on a platinum band and had reminded her of the ring her second husband had given her. They'd picked out the ring together in the jewelry store. Helen had always loved square-cut gems.

She debated whether to ask about Zoey's ring or not. There could be a perfectly harmless reason why the bride-to-be wasn't wearing her engagement ring. She might have taken it off to shower and forgotten to put it back on. But what if she'd left it in a gas station bathroom somewhere? Helen's next-door neighbor had done that exact same thing during a trip to visit her daughter in April. Luckily, an honest traveler had found it in a ladies' room in Raton and turned it in. So, when Helen's neighbor inquired at the station and identified the ring, she was able to get it back.

Of course, another reason why Zoey wasn't wearing her engagement ring could be because there was trouble in paradise. If that were the case, Willow should know. Right?

Helen should explore this mystery.

She took a sip of her iced tea, then said, "Zoey, I can't help but notice that you're not wearing your engagement ring. Is everything okay?"

Zoey slowly and carefully set down her croissant. She flexed her fingers and stared down at her left hand. Her voice sounded a little tight as she said, "I haven't come to Lake in the Clouds to cancel the wedding."

Oh dear. Definitely trouble in paradise. "I'm sure Willow will be relieved to hear that."

"It's pre-wedding jitters, I'm sure. It's been a difficult few months." She looked away from Helen and focused on her view of Granite Mountain. "My mother died recently."

"Oh, honey. I'm so sorry to hear that."

"It's caused me to think a lot about family, especially siblings." She shifted her gaze back to Helen and asked, "I know that you and Genevieve are sisters. Do you have any other siblings?"

"We had three brothers. Sadly, they've all passed."

"Oh." Zoey sat back hard in her seat, her expression crestfallen.

Curious reaction, Helen thought. Although, she did just lose her mother. Grief affected everyone differently, so it was understandable why she might wear her feelings on her sleeve.

Zoey cleared her throat. "Losing a sibling must be so hard. Were your brothers older or younger than you?"

"I had two older brothers, and then our brother Mark was the baby of the family. I'm older than Genevieve."

"Wow. There were five of you," Zoey blinked away a sheen in her eyes. "That's a big family. I would have loved to be part of a big family."

"Do you have any siblings?"

"No. I was an only child. I always wanted siblings. I thought it would be nice to have a sister, but what I really wanted was a brother. Brothers, plural. My biggest want was to have big brothers, to be precise."

"Oh?" Helen resisted the urge to reach over and give Zoey's hand a comforting pat. "Why is that?"

Zoey shrugged. "My dad was pretty wonderful, but he worked a lot. I thought brothers would be like Dad, only more available. A girl in my class had two big brothers, and they were always her champions at school and in the neighborhood. They were her protectors. I thought that was awesome."

Helen nodded and offered her a rueful grin. "My brother John was that way. Paul, not so much."

"I also wanted brothers who would play ball with me. I was a real sports fanatic. Football. Basketball. Baseball and soccer. I wanted to be the first female pitcher in our district. Dad would play catch with me when he had time, but that didn't happen often."

"What does your father do for a living?"

"He's a scientist. A cancer researcher. His work is vitally important, so I tried not to complain when he didn't have time to play ball with me. Don't get me wrong. He's a great dad, and he always made the time we did have together count."

"Balancing family and career life is a challenging thing for a parent. Especially a single parent. If your dad is working toward curing cancer, wow. I'm sure that he appreciated having your support."

"I grew up knowing how important his work is, so I tried to be supportive. I admit I slipped sometimes, but we soldiered through." Zoey diverted the conversation away from her family and back toward Helen's by asking, "Were your brothers into sports? Did they play with you?"

Helen sat back in her chair and considered the question. "My elder brother, John, played football in high school. However, he was ten years older than me, so he didn't have much to do with me."

"That's a big age difference."

Helen nodded. "Our entire family was spread out, age-wise. My brother Paul was four years older than me, and he wasn't into sports. He was all about machines. My most vivid and frequent memories of Paul during our childhood were of him lying on the driveway beneath Dad's car. All you could see of Paul were his legs."

"What about your younger brother?"

"I do recall playing ball with Mark." Helen remembered her baby brother running across the front yard chasing a baseball with their dog, Blackie, nipping at his heels. "However, he was ten years younger than me, so once again, we were at different life stages. Our parents basically had two families—I was the baby of one, the eldest of the other. I think the siblings in family number two were closer to one another. Mark used to accuse Genevieve and me of being his 'smothers.'"

At Zoey's curious look, she clarified. "Smothering mothers. We tended to practice our mothering on him." Shrugging, she added, "That's the lot of being the baby of the family, I think. And Genevieve and I did have quite a maternal way about us. Genevieve is still a Mama Bear with her kids and grands."

"That is a gift to your children. My mother had rare bursts of maternal feelings." Zoey's rueful gaze met Helen's. Casually, she asked, "What about you? Do you have children?"

"No," Helen replied with a sad smile. As always, the question gave her a twinge. "Unfortunately, I suffered multiple miscarriages. Not having children is the biggest regret of my life."

Zoey reached across the small table and gave Helen's hand a squeeze. "I'm so sorry."

I like this girl, Helen thought. *She has a compassionate heart. Bet she's an excellent physician.* "Me, too. Luckily, I had lots of nephews and nieces to smother with love." She winked and added, "All that practice I had with my little brother."

"So, how many nieces and nephews do you have? I recall that Willow is one of four?"

"Yes. She has two brothers and a sister. Plus, we have a bunch of Bennetts running around. John had three, Paul had six, and Mark had three."

Zoey pursed her lips thoughtfully. "So, twelve."

"Sixteen, counting Genevieve's."

"That's a big family. Do you see your brothers' children often?"

Something about the oh-so-casual way in which she asked the question had Helen studying her with a suspicious eye. "Okay, spill the tea, Dr. Hillcrest. Why all the questions about my family?"

Zoey's cheeks stained pink. "I'm sorry. I didn't mean to be rude."

"You're not being rude. You're being inquisitive. I recognize inquisitiveness because I share that trait, myself." Helen leaned back in her chair, folded her arms, and considered her guest.

Something was happening here. This wasn't a general lunch conversation. Zoey was digging for nuggets. Why?

The answer was staring her in the face. Literally. Helen never was one to beat about the proverbial bush, so she challenged Zoey head-on. "This is about your resemblance to Willow, isn't it? You think there's some sort of family relationship between you and Willow, don't you?"

Zoey opened her mouth, then shut it without saying a word. It didn't matter. Helen could read the answer in her expression, and her analytical mind went to work.

Zoey had said her mother had recently died. Had she made some sort of deathbed confession? The resemblance between Zoey and Willow was striking, and Willow did take after her mother's side of the family. Helen snapped her fingers as she figured it out. "You suspect one of my brothers was your father! You're what, thirty-two? Thirty-three? Mark would be the logical suspect due to your age, but I guess we shouldn't rule out—"

"No!" Zoey interrupted, the denial so fierce that Helen was taken aback. "That's not it at all. I know that my dad is my dad. And my mom was my mom, too, for that matter."

"Then I don't understand. What…oh, wait." Helen pursed her lips and then reasoned aloud. "If not your parents, then…"

Helen's eyes rounded in surprise. She sat up tall. "You're thinking grandfather? One of my older brothers, then. Whoa."

She drummed her fingers against the table. "I'll put my money on Paul. He was a ladies' man when he was young, though I believed he was faithful to his wife. His children won't like learning otherwise if it's true."

"Wait a minute." Zoey held up her hand, palm out. "I don't want to destroy anyone's memory of their father. That's not why I'm here. I wasn't even sure I was going to say anything. This trip is as much about my bridal cold feet and my career doubts as it is the DNA results."

Helen alerted like a bloodhound on a scent. "DNA results? What DNA results?"

Zoey delayed her response by taking a sip of tea. A long sip. Helen wanted to reach across the bistro table and swipe the glass from her hands so she'd get on with her story.

Finally, Zoey set down her drink and met Helen's gaze. "I went looking for answers about my mother and registered with an ancestry database company. Instead of discovering something about Mom, I found out why I happened to look so much like my wedding planner."

"Wait…wait…wait." Helen was confused. "You did a DNA test, and it matched Willow?"

"No. Willow isn't in the database. Her sister Brooke is. I am Brooke Prentice's first cousin once removed."

Helen sat back in her chair, her thoughts whirling as she tried to put the pieces together. She wasn't exactly sure about the whole once-removed thing. She'd never paid attention to it. Family was family as far as she was concerned. "So, let me get this straight. Brooke has done one of those ancestry kits, and your mother matched her. Was she related to Brooke through her father or through her mother?"

"No, that's not right. I didn't submit my mother's DNA. I submitted my own to a couple of different databases. The match hit on my dad's side."

"I'm still confused."

"We've always known he was adopted, but he never tried to find his birth parents. He never cared about knowing. My grandparents were wonderful people, and they were his family. Our family. It didn't matter that we weren't genetically related. But they're gone now, and my mother was a great big mystery because she was a liar, and she was dying, so—"

Zoey broke off abruptly and shook her head. "Her story isn't pertinent. She's the reason why I tested, but she's not part of these results."

"Okay, remind me. First cousin, once removed means . . . ?"

"Brooke is my father's first cousin."

"So, your father is my nephew. He's one of my sibling's offspring."

"Correct. Dad and Brooke share the same grandparent."

"And your father is how old? What's his name?"

"Adam. Adam Hillcrest. He's almost fifty."

"He can't be Mark's," Helen surmised. "Then he must be either Paul's or John's."

Helen gave Zoey a measuring look. "I knew you were related to us when I saw you in January. The resemblance is too stunning to be coincidental. Well, then." She smiled brightly, leaned across the small table, and gave Zoey a hug. "Welcome to the family, Zoey. This is exciting."

Tears misted the young woman's eyes, though they did not fall. "Thank you. Oh, thank you so much, Helen. That means the world to me."

"Auntie. Call me Auntie from now on like Willow does. And none of that great-aunt stuff. I am great, but I'm not old. So, we're sticking with Auntie. Got it?"

"Yes, ma'am," Zoey said with a little giggle.

"I'd open a bottle of champagne if I didn't have to drive later." Helen sat back in her chair and studied Zoey. "So, what do you want to do with this information? We gonna whittle it down and find out exactly which branch of the family is yours?"

"I don't know. I need to think this through. I don't want to cause anyone grief, especially since neither of your brothers is able to offer information or an explanation. Are their wives still living?"

"Yes, both of them."

Zoey winced, and Helen added, "We're not close. We exchange Christmas cards and show up for weddings and funerals, but it's that first and second family thing. Also, Paul had so many children that they didn't really have room in their lives for extended family."

"I see." Zoey sat back in her chair, lost in thought.

"This isn't information I can keep to myself," Helen warned. "We will have to share the news with Genevieve and Willow. My sister would never forgive me if I tried to keep something this momentous to our family to myself. She'll want to welcome you to her brood, too."

Zoey's eyes grew misty once again, and she smiled crookedly. "I didn't expect this to be this easy. I had planned to try to weasel information from Willow. Didn't expect to hit the motherlode with you."

"So, this is the real reason you've come to Colorado? You didn't drive a thousand miles to look at the glass chapel?"

"Oh, I do want to see it. When Willow first told me about

it, I thought it sounded fabulous. That spot in the woods is so peaceful."

"So, you're thinking about moving the ceremony from lakeside to the chapel?"

Zoey froze. The smile melted from her face and she closed her eyes. When she spoke, her voice trembled. "Actually, maybe I have come to Lake in the Clouds to cancel the wedding."

With that, Zoey burst into tears.

Two hours later, Zoey had decided that calling Helen Auntie wasn't appropriate. A better name was General Auntie.

Helen took charge.

After Zoey had sobbed out her relationship woes, Helen marshaled her troops. First, she declared that Zoey wasn't to visit Reflections Inn at Mirror Lake at all today. "Not even to have a nightcap on the deck to watch the sun go down. You need a nice long session of good old-fashioned girl talk, but it shouldn't happen at your wedding venue. No sense harshing the vibe there in case you decide to continue with your wedding plans as they are now. Wait until you are in a better frame of mind to make that visit."

Zoey didn't argue with Helen. It would have been wasted breath.

At so it was that instead of spending the afternoon attempting to find her peace beside a picturesque mountain lake, Zoey found herself seated on a cardboard box on a sidewalk in downtown Lake in the Clouds, sorting Christmas ornaments while Helen and Genevieve talked over her head.

Helen started with the reason why Zoey wasn't going out to the inn that afternoon. She summed up the story about Zoey's rocky romance road in a clear, concise manner that put her former attorney skills on display. She ended the recitation by saying, "Her feet are a little chilly right at the moment."

"Completely understandable." Genevieve gave Zoey's shoulder a supportive squeeze. "You've gone through a lot since you visited us in January. What you need is a little R&R and TLC. You've come to the right place for that."

Helen used a box cutter to slit the cellophane tape sealing a box. "Genevieve is a world-champion TLC giver. You've caught her at a good time at the moment because she has some new grandbabies on the way, and she's in training for them."

"Congratulations," Zoey told her.

"That reminds me. If one of you stumbles across the 'Baby's First Christmas' ornaments before I do, give a shout-out. I want to put a few of them away. I think they're going to be big sellers."

Zoey pulled a "World's Best Sister" ornament from her box and held it up. "Which one of you is this?"

"Me," the two women chimed simultaneously.

Zoey laughed, her heart lighter than it had been in weeks. Maybe even months. *These women are my family.*

"Genevieve," Helen said. "I think you should share the story about how you broke up with David three weeks before your wedding."

The suggestion obviously shocked Genevieve. "Well, now, there's a blast from the past. I don't believe I've even shared this story with my children."

Helen met Zoey's gaze. "It was all our brother Paul's fault."

"Most problems usually were," Genevieve said. "That said, David and I did more fighting in those last couple months before our wedding than we did our entire marriage."

"You did?" Zoey's interest was caught.

"We bickered all the time. We were young. Our families tried to tell us we were too young to get married, but—"

Helen interrupted. "I never said that."

"—true. I stand corrected. Helen actually encouraged us." Gen tossed her sister a smile as she added, "I've always loved her for that, especially after David was taken from us so young. I'll never forget my sister leaning against the threshold of my bedroom with her arms folded and saying, 'Life is too short. Don't waste a minute of it.'"

"I've always been a particularly wise woman."

"Anyway, back to our story. It just so happened that the biannual Bennett family reunion was being held in Estes Park, Colorado, a month before our wedding. Since not everyone was going to be able to make it to Texas for the ceremony, my parents invited David to make the trip with us so that they would get an opportunity to meet him. They had a little reception for us. It really was quite lovely."

"Until our great-aunt Dutz had a little visit with him," Helen added, her eyes twinkling. "She was Irish, don't you know? Claimed to have a touch of the Sight."

Genevieve shook her head in bafflement. "I was so gullible. She talked a good story, you have to admit."

"Woman should have been on Broadway," Helen agreed. "As playwright, director, and actor. In Genevieve's defense, we all believed her. So, when she sat David down and read his tea leaves, we all hung on her every word as if it were gospel."

"What did she say?" Zoey asked.

"She said that David would decide to pursue a career as a musician. He would write and perform a hit song and become famous—then leave her for a pop star."

"Oh dear."

"When"—Helen lifted her pointing finger and quoted dramatically—"she was *heavy* with his children."

"Heavy!" Genevieve repeated.

A smile flirted on Zoey's lips. "Children? Twins?"

"Triplets." Helen laugh-snorted. "Three boys."

Genevieve rolled her eyes toward heaven. "It didn't help anything that David took it all as a joke. I was so upset. I could see it happening. Not the triplets part, but him becoming a famous singer. The man had a gorgeous voice. Plus, two of our cousins made it their purpose in life to remind me of all the times Great-Aunt Dutz's predictions had come true."

Helen nodded. "They had a point about that. She did have an impressive record."

"True. That's part of the reason I called off the wedding."

"What was the other part?"

Simultaneously, Genevieve and Helen said, "The serenade."

Helen shook her head as she continued the story. "Allow me to set up the scene. It's after midnight, long after the official lights-out. Genevieve and I were in a bunkhouse with a bunch of female relatives. Then, out of the darkness comes the strum of a guitar and a deep, velvety voice." She glanced at her sister and gave an aside observation. "Gave us all girly shivers, it did."

"What did he sing?" Zoey asked.

Genevieve snorted. "His own rendition of an old song that Neil Diamond made a hit in the '70s called 'He Ain't Heavy… He's My Brother.' He rewrote the lyrics."

Helen sang, "She's so heavy, she's a mother."

Her eyes widened in surprise, and Zoey giggled softly.

Genevieve continued. "David didn't often read the room wrong, but in this instance, he totally blew it. His lyrics basically took Great-Aunt Dutz's prophecy and made fun of it. It hit me wrong on so many levels."

She pulled a mug from a box and silently displayed it to her sister and Zoey. Zoey read: *Insanity runs in my family. It practically gallops.*

"How appropriate," Helen observed.

Genevieve set the mug on a display shelf. "I was angry because a tiny little part of me believed the prophecy. I was angry because he didn't take it seriously. I was angry that he'd joked about me being fat three weeks before our wedding! My nerves were a little stretched."

"Just a little," Helen agreed. "She marched out of the cabin and grabbed the guitar away from David, and hit him with it."

"Oh no!" Zoey said. "You didn't!"

"I did." Gazing blindly into the distance as she remembered the moment, Genevieve laughed.

Helen added, "Before you ding her for domestic abuse, you should know that her husband was a big guy. Almost six feet four. Strong and broad. She was even tinier then than she is now."

"I think I only landed that first blow," Genevieve said. "I was too busy screaming at him to concentrate on swinging the guitar. I told him the wedding was off, and I demanded he leave the family reunion because he wasn't my family and never would be my family, and he should just go find his mistress and get her pregnant with triplets."

"At the top of her lungs," Helen added. "It embarrassed David, and he got furious and stormed off."

"By morning, I had calmed down and was filled with regret, but he was gone. Those were the days before cell phones. I waited and waited, but he never came back. I was devastated."

"Did he go home?"

"No, not at first. That was my hope, but when he didn't return to the camp, I talked Helen into leaving a day early, and we headed home. He wasn't there, either. His parents hadn't heard from him.

"I was so distraught. I cried buckets of tears and didn't breathe an easy breath until our doorbell rang three days after we got home. We hadn't spoken for five days at that point. Obviously, we made up. It turned out that the time apart was good for both of us. We each spent that time searching our hearts so that when he finally came home, we were able to talk honestly about the fears and insecurities that bothered both of us. That silly song turned out to be a good thing for our marriage."

Zoey lifted an "Our First Christmas Together" ornament from the box. Shaped like a heart and three-dimensional, it featured two lovebirds perched on a tree branch, and the date. She traced her index finger over the birds, her smile wistful and bittersweet. "I hear the message. I just don't know if it's applicable to my situation."

"I would say time will tell," Helen said.

"Have you spoken to Cooper since you left Houston?"

Zoey shook her head. "We exchanged texts about his father's injury. Nothing personal." After a moment's hesitation, she added, "I haven't told him where I am."

She'd actually turned off her phone.

She didn't want to have any contact with him right now. She didn't want to be listening for the phone to ring or ding with a text. She didn't want to obsess about whether or not he'd tried to call.

Genevieve and Helen shared a look. Genevieve said, "Sometimes it's a challenge to find a balance between needing space and being considerate of other's worries."

Zoey shrugged and set aside the ornament. She'd reached the bottom of the box. "I have these all unpacked and separated. What should I do with them now?"

Helen rummaged through the stack of boxes they'd yet to open. She found a tabletop Christmas tree and asked, "Where do we plan to put this, Genevieve?"

Genevieve checked their planning sheet and pointed to the appropriate spot. Helen set the tree down and then answered Zoey's question. "If you would hang one of each on this? The extra stock goes in one of the flat plastic tubs, which sits beneath the display table. We'll restock the tree as we sell from it."

"Sounds good. Are there hangers for these, or do I use the ribbon?"

"We have hangers. I think they're over here."

Helen found a box of decorative hangers and passed them to Zoey, who accepted them, saying, "Thanks, Auntie."

Genevieve caught the reference and gave Zoey a curious look. Helen met Zoey's gaze and asked, "Do you want to tell her, or shall I?"

"You did a good job summarizing my romantic troubles. Please, be my guest."

Helen met her sister's gaze. "Don't unpack anything fragile while I share this story, Genevieve. We don't want to lose potential sales to breakage."

Seated on top of a box, Genevieve clasped her hands and leaned forward. "Tell me."

Helen began. "I'll start with the money shot. Zoey sent her DNA to an ancestry database, and she discovered that she is either Paul's granddaughter or John's. That makes you and me her great-aunts, but I've told you before I'm not doing the 'great-anything.'"

"Oh my heavens," Genevieve breathed. Her gaze flew to Zoey, who smiled and shrugged.

Helen continued, encapsulating the story as efficiently as she had Zoey's wedding woes. While she spoke, Zoey finished hanging the ornaments on the tree and stacking the extra stock in the plastic storage tub. Once Helen finished the tale, Genevieve remained quiet for a time, silently tapping her foot as she considered what her sister had told her. Finally, she said, "Willow gave Brooke the ancestry kit for her birthday a few years ago. I don't recall her ever mentioning having received any results from it. Will she be notified of the match?"

"I believe so, yes. She needed to have checked the box for her results to show up for me."

Helen gave her sister a keen-eyed look. "So, who would you put your money on? Paul or John?"

"Paul," Genevieve said without hesitation. "I'm pretty sure he was having an affair when David died."

Helen was in the process of tearing tissue paper away from a wooden plaque that read: *Happiness is having a large, loving, caring, close-knit family in another city ~ George Burns.* She glanced at Genevieve. "What? You've never told me that. How come you never told me that? Why do you think that?"

"It was a little crack I overheard his wife say to him at David's wake. I can't recall now what it was. I do remember being shocked, though."

"Interesting. I can't believe you never mentioned it." Helen hung the plaque on the pegboard that stretched across the back of the sisters' vendor booth.

"I can't believe I remember it. So much of the time between David's death and his funeral is a blur for me." Genevieve focused her attention on Zoey. "I can't have you calling me 'Genevieve' when you're referring to my sister as 'Auntie.' We need a name for you to use with me. I tend to agree with Helen that being a great-aunt is not all that great. My brothers' children all call me '*Tía*,' which is Spanish for aunt. Would you like to use that?"

The warmth of acceptance washed through Zoey. "I'd love to

call you 'Tía.' Thank you." Zoey flashed a shy grin and added, "'Tía.' I love the name. How did it come to be yours?"

Genevieve and Helen shared a warm smile. Helen said, "Wednesday night Tex-Mex. Growing up, our family ate at a little hole-in-the-wall Mexican restaurant called Tía María's almost every Wednesday night because kids could eat for free and everyone loved their chiles rellenos. This was before Taco Tuesday was a thing. Years later, Genevieve brought chiles rellenos that she'd made to a family get-together and one of the boys declared them to be better than Tía María's. They started calling her 'Tía Gen,' it stuck, and the rest is history."

"Ooh, chiles rellenos are my fav," Zoey said, sending Genevieve a hopeful glance.

Her aunt laughed. "I'll be happy to make them for you one day soon. In the meantime, however, we should probably get to work unpacking these last half dozen boxes. While we prepare our family-themed booth for tonight's opening, I'd like to hear more about my nephew. Helen said he's a researcher at MD Anderson?"

"Yes."

"Tell us what you love the most about him."

"Hmm. That's both easy and difficult. He has a lot of exceptional qualities. It's difficult to choose."

In the process of hanging a plaque that read: *Families are like fudge. Mostly sweet with a few nuts,* Helen suggested, "Choose your top three."

Zoey considered a moment. "He always made me feel safe."

"That's a good one," Genevieve said.

"He's dependable with an asterisk. The asterisk is because he can get lost in his work, and time can get away from him. But in every other respect, he's as dependable as the sunrise. That one always counted a lot for me."

Because she'd never been able to count on her mom. Zoey gave her head a shake and brought her thoughts back to her father. "He always protected me enough without being overprotective."

"That's sweet," Helen said. "Give us an example."

She told a story about her first date with her second boyfriend. She'd been seventeen and attracted to the proverbial bad boy. The guy had a well-deserved bad reputation. Her dad hadn't forbidden Zoey from going out with him, but...

"The guy pulled up, and rather than coming to the door, my date honked his horn, expecting me to come out. Well, Dad wasn't having that. He walked me outside and went right up to the driver's side door. After gesturing for the guy to roll down his window, Dad leaned down, extended his hand, and introduced himself. When my date finally shook Dad's hand, Dad put a shark's smile on his face and told him to drive carefully and treat me with respect. Or else he'd invite him to the next autopsy Dad performed."

Genevieve and Helen laughed.

Zoey finished the story by saying, "Then he slapped the car door twice and told us to have fun."

"What a great story," Genevieve said. "I look forward to meeting him."

Zoey blinked. Crazy as it was, she hadn't thought about a potential meeting between her father and the family with whom she'd matched. In the midst of all the drama surrounding her mother's death, she'd failed to mention to her dad that she'd sent off the DNA test.

"Do you have a picture of him?" Genevieve asked. Zoey nodded as Genevieve glanced at her sister. She said, "He might look like Paul. Or like John."

In the process of removing something encased in bubble

wrap from a large box, Helen brightened with curiosity. "Well, I'm an idiot. I didn't think of asking to see a photo."

Zoey reached for her handbag and pulled out her phone. She hit the power button. While her device booted up, Helen unwrapped a beautiful glass bowl with the word *Family* etched repeatedly around the edge. "That's gorgeous," Zoey observed.

"Isn't it? It's from Whimsies in Eternity Springs. Our friend Gabby Cicero made it."

Zoey's phone flickered on, and she swiped to the photo app and then to one of her favorite photos of her dad, taken on a beach at sunset. She handed the phone to Genevieve, saying, "I took this during one of his visits to California when I was in med school."

"Oh my. He's so handsome. I love that smile." She studied it a moment, then shook her head. "I don't know that I see either John or Paul in him. What do you think, Helen?"

Genevieve held the phone out toward her sister. Helen looked down at the picture, and the smile on her face froze. The blood drained from her face.

Helen dropped the glass bowl, and it shattered.

Chapter Ten

HELEN'S HEAD SPUN. HER sight was reduced to a pinpoint. She saw only the face displayed on Zoey's phone. She swayed on her feet as her knees threatened to melt. She was seconds away from fainting.

"Honey?" Genevieve asked, concern in her voice. "What's wrong?"

Helen couldn't speak. She could barely think. Her mind was sluggish, every thought fighting its way through a thick fog of disbelief, devastation, and despair. Yet in her heart, a seed sprouted that was warm and hopeful and knowing.

Genevieve spoke more forcefully. "Helen! You're scaring me. Helen! Talk to me."

Her sister's voice seemed to come from far away as Helen focused on the photo. Knowing. Yes, knowing. She knew it in her marrow. She recognized him. "Oh my God."

"Helen!" She felt arms come around her as everything faded to black.

When she came to, she was lying on the grass, her legs

elevated. She heard Zoey speaking in a crisp, professional tone. "…an emergency physician licensed in Texas. Her airway is clear…"

Helen tuned Zoey out. The shock had faded, and thoughts that had been sluggish before began to careen around her head like pinballs. How had this happened? Why had this happened? Who was responsible for it having happened?

She knew, of course. It could only have been one person.

Helen opened her eyes and struggled to sit up. Hands reached toward her. "Easy, now," Zoey said.

"She's awake. Thank God." Genevieve's anxious voice asked, "Honey, are you okay?"

An EMT she vaguely recognized asked, "What's your name? Where are we?"

"I'm your mayor, and I'm done being laid out like a dead fish on the town square. Somebody help me up."

While Genevieve assisted her sister to her feet, Zoey had a brief, quiet conversation with the EMT. Helen gave a smile and a reassuring wave to the crowd that had gathered to watch the show. "I'm fine," she called. "Probably breathed in too much evergreen fragrance, and I got an overdose of Christmas. Y'all be sure to come to tonight's opening of the Lake in the Clouds Christmas in July Festival."

Softly to her sister, she said, "Get me out of here."

"Where do you want to go?"

Helen responded without thought. "Home. Take me home."

Luckily, Genevieve had parked her SUV close by in order to unload. Speaking to Zoey, she asked, "Will you ride with us? We can come back for the car later."

"Sure," Zoey replied. "Do we need to secure anything here in the booth?"

"No one will bother anything, and we haven't brought the cash box down yet." Genevieve gestured toward a bag in the corner and said, "Grab Helen's purse if you would, please."

Helen barely heard the conversation, so lost was she in the questions careening through her mind. She let herself be herded into the front passenger seat of Genevieve's car. Her sister climbed behind the wheel, and Zoey took a seat in the back.

Helen closed her eyes and dropped her head back against the headrest. "Zoey? When is your father's birthday?"

"June 8, 1974."

"The eighth? Not the sixth?"

Following a moment's pause, Zoey spoke quietly. "It was a private adoption through an attorney friend of my grandparents. He came to them on the tenth. From what Dad has told me in the past, they never saw an original birth certificate. The only information they were given was his birth date. Not a city or state."

"Hmm." Guess a two-day-old newborn and a four-day-old newborn didn't look all that different.

Genevieve said, "Helen, what is going on here? What do you know about Zoey's dad and his birthday?"

Helen didn't open her eyes. "Wait until we get home."

Genevieve gave a little huff of impatience, but she knew Helen well enough to let it go. They drove the rest of the way to the condo in silence. As Genevieve parked in her usual place, Helen removed her keys from her purse. She exited the car and hurried inside, where after briefly greeting Cookie, she went directly to her bedroom and into her large, walk-in closet. She pulled a stepstool from its storage space, climbed up, and reached for a shoebox tucked away on the highest shelf.

It was a sneaker box, size seven Adidas purchased her sophomore year in high school before the start of the spring tennis season. A thick layer of dust coated the lid. Helen had moved the box with her more than a dozen times over the years. She hadn't opened it since New Year's Eve 1973.

That had been a particularly bad night.

She exited the closet with the box and carried it into her living room, where her sister and Zoey waited. Genevieve was in her usual spot at one end of the sofa. Zoey sat cross-legged on the floor, Cookie draped over her lap, delirious to have her belly scratched. Rather than sit in her own favorite chair, Helen sat beside her sister.

"Pass me a tissue, please?" she asked Genevieve.

Genevieve pulled one from the decorative tissue dispenser on the end table and handed it to Helen. She dusted off the lid, inhaled a deep breath, and opened the box.

The black-and-white sonogram photo lay on the top of the pile. She picked it up and heard Genevieve gasp.

"I already knew that I was pregnant when I learned that Billy had died during a training accident during boot camp."

Genevieve's gaze locked on the photograph in Helen's hand, her heart pounding so hard she thought it might explode. What was she seeing and hearing here? Nothing made sense.

Helen continued. "I walked around in a state of shock for weeks. Then on New Year's Eve, I had a bit of a breakdown. I drove to the place where Billy took me parking, and I walked out onto that swinging bridge that stretched over the river."

Oh, Helen. Genevieve knew that bridge. It was a narrow, cable-supported footbridge that Genevieve had always hated. It scared her to death to use.

"It was bitter cold that night. The wind was blowing. A little sleet in it. I stood at the center of it, staring down at the water. I wanted to die. I truly wanted to die."

Genevieve lifted her gaze from the sonogram photo to her sister's face, and tears filled Genevieve's eyes. She'd never before seen Helen in such pain.

"I don't *think* I would have jumped, but I was pretty crazy that night. Somebody driving by on the highway saw me and reported it to the police. A patrolman came and escorted me off the bridge and down to the station. Mom came and got me. On the way home, I told her about the baby. She sent me to bed, and by the time I woke up in the morning, a plan was in place. I went to live with Uncle Ray and Aunt Grace."

Genevieve's mouth dropped open in surprise. "You didn't go to live with them until the next school year. You went to Paris for study abroad."

Helen quirked a sad smile. "Amazing how that came up at the last minute, isn't it? They needed a reason why you and our brothers wouldn't see me for six months. I wasn't studying abroad in the City of Lights. I was living in small-town Texas, being homeschooled by our father's sister-in-law. Had to keep the secret shame secret, you know."

While Genevieve reeled from the shock of the revelation, Zoey posed a question. "But that was the seventies, not the nineteen fifties. Unplanned pregnancies weren't so stigmatized."

"In small-town Texas, they were," Helen said. "And in our family..."

Grimacing, Genevieve nodded her agreement. "Dad must have gone postal."

"Actually, he went glacial. He didn't look me in the eyes for months."

"I remember that time," Genevieve said. "Your departure for Europe came out of the blue. One day, you were home, and the next, you were gone. I missed you dreadfully, and it seemed like every time I turned around, Mom was crying. When I asked why, she told me she was missing you."

Their parents had fought a lot during that time, too, Genevieve recalled. Home life had been tense. She remembered wondering if her parents would get a divorce. "I used to write you letters. You wrote me letters, too. They had a Paris postmark. How did they manage that?"

"I wrote them in bulk, and Dad mailed them to someone he knew who lived over there."

"You talked about all the places you visited. I was so jealous. I remember one letter about your trip to Versailles. It was filled with details. You wrote the best letters."

Helen laughed bitterly. "They were a class assignment given to me by Aunt Grace. History and English."

"Those letters were the reason why I asked David to take me to Paris on our honeymoon. I kept them for years." Genevieve thought for a moment, then added, "Actually, they might have survived the purge. I might have them in my keepsake tub that's stored in my attic."

"Keepsakes," Helen murmured softly. She set aside the photograph and picked up the next item from the box. Miniature cowbells jangled as a jumble of black and gold ribbons unfurled.

It was a football mum, Genevieve realized. On two of the ribbons, glittered letters spelled out names. One said *Helen*. The other, "Billy?"

"My homecoming mum. He left for boot camp the following Monday."

Tears stung Genevieve's eyes. Poor Helen. Genevieve's heart broke at the thought of all her sister had gone through, and yet, even as she had the thought, unanswered questions loomed in her mind. Primarily, what had happened to the baby and why

Helen had never once, in all these years, shared this story with Genevieve.

That one was going to hurt. Badly. Genevieve had shared everything with her sister and thought the practice was mutual. Obviously, she'd been wrong about that. However, for now, she would tuck that pain away. This moment was Helen's.

Her sister set aside the mum. For a long moment, she sat still as a statue while staring down into the box. Genevieve sat at such an angle that she couldn't see the contents that had Helen transfixed. When tears suddenly and silently overflowed Helen's eyes and trailed down her cheeks, Genevieve could no longer hold her own tears back.

Helen cleared her throat and, without looking up, asked, "Zoey, do you by chance have an old photograph of your father on your phone? One taken when he was a teen or in his twenties?"

"Actually, I do." Zoey pulled her phone from her pocket and started scrolling. "I scanned a bunch of family photographs and made a video montage for him for Christmas a few years ago. It may take me a few minutes to find it."

"Thank you," Helen replied as she reached into the box and pulled out a stack of photographs.

Genevieve leaned toward her sister in order to get a better view. The color photos were small, square, and faded. The first was of a couple, Helen—a young teenager—and a young man. He was tall and slim with broad shoulders and muscular arms—a basketball player's build, Genevieve thought. His shoulder-length, sun-bleached hair was typical of guys in the seventies. She couldn't tell his eye color from the picture. He was shirtless, barefooted, and wearing swim trunks. Helen wore a coverup that Genevieve vaguely recognized. She thought she'd worn it as a hand-me-down. She also recognized the diving boards in the background. The picture had been taken at the neighborhood pool where Genevieve had all but lived each summer.

Her gaze returned to the guy with his arm around a beaming Helen. Had she ever met him? She didn't recall.

Helen flipped to a second photo. This one was of the guy—Billy—alone. He'd cut his hair here, and this one showed his eyes. They were a beautiful, brilliant blue.

But Zoey looked so much like Willow. Did Genevieve see any of Zoey in this boy? Maybe his height.

"Here it is," Zoey said. "This was a photo my grandfather took when they dropped Dad off at college his freshman year." She rolled to her feet, approached the sofa, and held out her phone toward Genevieve and Helen.

"Oh my," breathed Genevieve. Zoey's father was the spitting image of the man in the photo Helen held. No wonder her sister had fainted dead away.

She could no longer hold back the question that had been bubbling inside since Helen admitted to a teenage pregnancy. "Helen, what happened to your baby?"

The look Helen turned toward Genevieve was haunted. "He lied to me, Genevieve. Daddy lied."

1974

Helen had never been so hot. She'd never been so fat. She'd never been so miserable. When she complained, her doctor, Uncle Ray, simply smiled and said, "Welcome to the last month of pregnancy."

She wondered what he'd say if she told him that all of that paled in comparison to the anger she felt right now. He probably wouldn't say anything. Just smile that kindly smile of his. She loved her uncle. She truly did. He and Aunt Grace had been nothing but kind to her during these five months she'd been living with them.

But Uncle Ray wouldn't put himself in the middle of the argument she'd just had with her father. He had retreated to his office, which was a free-standing building next door to the house, and ceded the field to her dad. Aunt Grace wasn't even around to help since this morning was her Women's Club meeting.

Helen waddled her way around the block from her uncle's house, this being her third walk of the day in the neighborhood where she'd lived since January. When she moved to this small, West Texas town, her walking route took her through the entire neighborhood and through downtown—such as that was—and back.

Today, at just over three weeks from her due date, she barely made it around the block.

Seriously. She didn't feel well at all. She wouldn't have gone on this third walk of the day had she not desperately needed to get away from her dad.

He'd paid her a visit this morning in order to argue his case against the decision she'd made a few days ago, the biggest decision of her life.

She'd changed her mind about giving her precious child up for adoption. She was going to keep her baby. Her little boy. Her William. Will. Named after his father, who'd lost his life in the service of his country.

To say Edward Bennett wasn't pleased with her decision was an understatement of enormous magnitude. He was, in fact, furious. He'd arrived at his brother's house this morning loaded for bear.

Helen fired right back. After all, she was a mama bear protecting her cub.

She and her dad had a loud and long argument that ended when she fled the house in a temper and started this walk around the block. She'd left in the nick of time. She'd come close to crossing the line and saying things she shouldn't.

Helen recognized that her dad sincerely believed that giving her baby up for adoption was best both for Helen and her son. She had believed that, too, for most of her pregnancy.

But during these past few weeks, as little Will grew and kicked and hiccupped inside her, Helen had formed an attachment with the child that was fierce and ferocious. She'd fallen in love, and it was a mother's love. Was any force on earth stronger?

Helen knew it would be hard to be a single mother raising a child on her own. Dad had made it clear that he and Mom would not help her in any way. Once she had her baby, if she failed to place him for the adoption her father had arranged, she and Will would be on their own.

Okay, then. She'd deal. She'd figure it out somehow, some way.

This baby was her baby. Her responsibility. She loved him, just like she'd loved his father. "I will take care of him, Billy. I will take care of both of us."

She turned the corner, and her uncle's house was in sight. Dad was outside, pacing the front yard. Inwardly, Helen groaned. *I'm not ready for round two.*

She didn't feel good enough to battle him again right now. She was going to go inside and lie down for a bit. He could just cool his jets and wait on her.

Helen lifted her chin and approached the house. She really, truly didn't feel good. She was sick to her stomach, and her head felt light. *Weak. So weak.*

That's when she felt it, when she realized something was wrong. *Warm and sticky. Pain. Oh, God, the pain.* Helen looked down, and all she saw was red. "Daddy!"

She collapsed in the neighbor's front yard, and after that, things became a blur. Dad was there. Lifting her. Rushing forward. "Ray! Ray! I need help. We need help!"

Vaguely, she heard voices. Her uncle, her dad. Urgent. But she was fading...fading...fading.

Pain. Such pain like she'd never known before.

Was that a baby's cry?

Helen's world went black.

Awareness returned on a wisp of a cloud. Helen was floating... drifting. She wanted to open her eyes, but her lids were so heavy.

She heard sounds...voices...soft murmurings. "I'll be right back." Mom? Was that Mom? Helen wrenched her eyelids up. Bright light stabbed, and she quickly shut her eyes against it and drifted back to sleep.

When next she awoke, the light was dimmed. She sensed she was not alone. With effort, she turned her head. A shadowed figure sat beside her bed. Her father, with his head in his hands. Helen opened her mouth and forced a word past dry lips. "Water."

Edward Bennett's head jerked up. His eyes met Helen's. *He's old. He's gotten old.*

"Hey, kiddo. It's great to see those pretty green eyes." Rising, he reached for a plastic mug on the bedside table and adjusted the straw. "I'm going to lift your head just a bit so you can more easily drink."

He pushed a button, and her upper body rose. He held the

mug before her and the straw to her lips. Helen sipped. Cool, sweet, wonderful water.

"There you go," her father said. "Now, that's probably enough for now. Want to make sure it sits all right on your stomach."

My stomach. What was it about her stomach? She tried to move, and pain sliced through her. "What...?"

"Careful now. Let me call the nurse to let them know you're awake."

Helen's mind was cold molasses. She ached everywhere. Why did she...oh! She moved her hand toward her belly. Agony washed through her. "The baby! Daddy?"

Edward took her hand, licked his lips, and then explained. "You hemorrhaged, sweetheart. Uncle Ray performed an emergency C-section. You developed an infection, and it went septic. An air ambulance brought you here to Fort Worth. You've been here for eight days now." His voice broke as he added, "We almost lost you."

"My baby! Daddy, where's my baby? I need my baby boy!"

Edward Bennett sucked in a deep breath, then exhaled in a rush. "I'm sorry, sweetheart. The baby didn't make it."

As Helen told her story, she had set aside her shoebox and rose to stand before the patio door, where she stared not toward the hummingbirds visiting her feeders but into the past.

Zoey held her hand over her mouth as she listened. Helen's voice remained relatively flat, and silent tears rolled down her face.

As an emergency room physician, Zoey had witnessed her fair share of heartbreak. And yet, this story touched her in a way that no other had.

This one was personal.

When Helen announced that the baby hadn't made it, a stricken Genevieve rushed toward her sister and wrapped her in a hug. Both women were crying.

Zoey wanted to join the embrace, but now wasn't the time.

After a moment, Helen stepped out of Genevieve's arms and once again gazed outside. She did maintain a hold on her sister's hand as she continued her story. "I wanted to see him, my little Will, but Dad told me they'd already buried him. He promised to take me to see the grave once I got out of the hospital."

With tears in her voice, Genevieve said, "Oh, Helen."

"At that point, I broke. I went a little crazy. They sedated me, and the next few days were... difficult. I ended up spending the rest of the summer at a psychiatric hospital. I didn't visit Will's grave until the anniversary of his death."

When it appeared that Helen had finished her story, Genevieve gave her sister's hand a squeeze. "That's the summer they sent me away to camp at the last minute." Abruptly, she added, "I need some water. Do you want some water?"

"No, thanks."

Genevieve walked into the kitchen, filled a glass with water from the tap, and tossed it back like whiskey. "I have so many questions. Helen, this is why you never came back home to live?"

"I couldn't. I was so depressed and angry, primarily at Dad. Intellectually, I knew the argument hadn't caused me to hemorrhage. Emotionally, I couldn't get past it. Uncle Ray and Aunt Grace were fine with me continuing to stay with them. Once I started school there, I liked it. So, I stayed until I graduated."

"I missed you."

"I know. I missed you, too. But it was weird between Dad and me after that. We were never comfortable around one another again. Until the day he died, a part of me blamed him for losing Will." Bitterness dripped from her tongue as she added, "For good reason."

Genevieve braced her hands on the counter, frowning. "So, what happened?"

"It's obvious, isn't it?" Helen whirled around to face her sister, her eyes flashing with fury. "He took advantage of the opportunity and followed through with the adoption. Our father stole my baby."

Now it was Genevieve's turn to have the color leach from her face. "No. He wouldn't. I can't believe that."

"It's the only explanation. It fits. Oh, I guess there is still a slight possibility that John or Paul fathered Zoey's dad. I don't believe it, though. The man looks just like my Billy. Plus, I just *know* it. I know it in my bones."

"I don't see how—"

"Think about it, Genevieve. That day, I went from Uncle Ray's office to the local, small-town hospital where Uncle Ray was a god. Then, once things went south, I arrived at the Fort Worth hospital sans baby. Staff at the local hospital probably saw Dad leave with the baby and never thought another word about it. Staff in Fort Worth saw me come in alone, and he would have told them the baby died."

Zoey couldn't restrain her question any longer. "Were you given a death certificate?"

"I was not. I never thought to ask for one. I was sixteen. Though, knowing Dad, he probably had one forged and waiting if I'd ever inquired about it."

"This is unbelievable," Genevieve said.

"Maybe that's not how it worked, but it doesn't really matter, does it? Bottom line. I've spent the past fifty years believing my son died."

"Oh my God." Genevieve covered her mouth with her hands and repeated, "Oh my God."

Helen focused on Zoey. "Tell me again what you know about your father's adoption?"

Now Zoey was teary-eyed, too. "I don't know that much. We could call him and ask."

At that, the Bennett sisters both froze. Genevieve repeated for a third time, "Oh my God."

Her gaze flew to Helen's. "You have a son. Helen, you have a son!"

Helen froze, her mouth agape. When she started to wobble, she reached for a nearby chair for support. "Oh my. I've been so caught up in the past that it hadn't hit me. I have a son. Oh, Genevieve. I have a son! Will is alive!"

The joy that burst upon Helen's face like a sunrise had Zoey shifting Cookie out of her lap so she could climb to her feet. She was crying now, too. Taking a step toward Helen, she said, "You have a granddaughter, too."

Helen audibly gasped before she covered her mouth with her hands.

Grinning, Zoey added, "What would you like me to call you? Grandmother? Gammie?"

"Nana!" Helen tore her gaze away from Zoey and looked at her sister. "Genevieve, I get to be a nana!"

Then she flew across the room toward Zoey, and grandmother and granddaughter embraced.

Chapter Eleven

WHILE ZOEY MADE A quick trip to the visitor's apartment to release Freeway from his crate, Genevieve and Helen broke out a bottle of champagne. They also called Willow and invited her to join them. Helen told her to hurry because they had a fabulous surprise. Helen had a few bottles of nonalcoholic bubbly that she'd stocked when her nieces began announcing pregnancies, so she chilled one of those while waiting for Willow to arrive.

At Helen's direction, Zoey put Freeway and Cookie out into the condo's small fenced-in yard to play. While they waited for Willow's arrival, Helen peppered Zoey with questions about Adam. "So, he celebrates his birthday on June eighth, and he's Adam Hillcrest. Does he have a middle name?"

"He does. Adam was my paternal grandfather's name. His middle name is his maternal grandfather's name." Zoey's eyes gleamed at Helen over the top of her champagne glass as she added, "It's William."

"No!" Helen and Genevieve spoke simultaneously.

"Yep."

"Wow," Genevieve breathed. "Just, wow."

"If I'm not careful, I'm going to start crying all over again. I don't want to do that. I want to take a little bit of time and enjoy the joy before I let loose the other emotions I have churning inside of me. So, tell me anything and everything else you can about him. When Willow arrives, we will read her in and then formulate a plan on how best to share this news with Adam."

Zoey considered Helen's request for a moment, then decided to jump in. "He is whip-smart and intense about his work. He can be forgetful when he gets lost in research. He has a sweet tooth. He's a real candy hound, the sweeter, the better. Not much of a drinker, although he does enjoy a good scotch upon occasion."

"What's his favorite food?" Helen asked. "Other than candy, I mean."

"Growing up in Florida, he learned to love fresh fish. Since he's moved to Texas, he's added steak and barbecue to his favorite list." She paused a moment, then added, "He despises broccoli."

Helen clapped her hand against her chest. "Billy didn't like broccoli, either!"

They heard a quick rap on the door, and Willow walked inside. Her gaze went first to Zoey, and she smiled. "Our bride! I'm so happy to see you again, Zoey. I'm sorry your trip was stressful. I hope you're feeling better after your nap?"

"Thank you. Yes, I'm feeling so much better." She glanced toward the two older women for a cue to how to proceed.

Helen took charge, handing Willow a flute and saying, "It's only apple juice, don't fret. You need something with which to toast."

"What are we toasting?" Willow responded, her eyes sparkling with happiness. "What's the big news? Tell me!"

Helen linked arms with Zoey and said, "Willow, love. Today, I have experienced a miracle. What was lost is now found. And I have you to thank for it."

Lifting her glass in salute, Helen said, "To Willow!"

Genevieve and Zoey raised their flutes and repeated, "To Willow!"

"Me? What did I do?" She clinked glasses with the others, then brought hers to her mouth for a sip.

Helen picked that moment to say, "You gave me a granddaughter."

Willow spit out her juice. "What?"

Helen laughed, and over the next ten to fifteen minutes, the story tumbled out. When it was finished, Willow gazed around the room in wonder and delight. "You know what this means? We're having another family wedding at the lake."

Just like that, Zoey's high evaporated. The wedding was a subject she wanted to avoid—just like she'd avoided the two phone calls she'd received from Cooper this afternoon. To divert attention from the subject, she focused on her father. "Well, first, we need to figure out how we're going to break this news to Dad."

Her diversion worked. The other women lost all interest in the subject of her wedding. Helen said, "Well, I guess I need to make a trip to Texas."

"You're not going alone," Genevieve declared. "I'm coming with you."

"Can I come, too?" Willow asked. "I want to come. I don't need to be there when you first meet him, but I'd like to be there for support."

"That would be nice." Helen glanced at Zoey. "Would that be okay, do you think?"

Zoey nodded. Willow beamed and clapped her hands together.

"Excellent. So, are you thinking road trip or will we fly? We might have trouble getting seats out of Durango this time of year. It's high tourist season." Glancing at her mother, she added, "I'll bet Gage would let us use his plane."

Genevieve frowned. "No, he is a generous man, but that is too big of an ask."

"Not for you," Willow fired back.

Helen nodded in agreement. "I think Gage Throckmorton would do just about anything for you."

Genevieve shook her head and folded her arms. "Nevertheless, I'm not asking. Period."

Helen shot Willow a meaningful look. "Now is not the time, but let's make a note to explore this topic at a later date."

The dogs scratched at the door, and Willow slipped off her seat on a bar stool and opened the patio door. As Freeway padded over to Zoey, Helen asked, "How do you think we should handle this, Zoey? Do we give him a warning ahead of time? A few days—if I can wait that long? A couple of hours? Or do I meet him first and then ease into the story? What is going to be best? And where? Just as long as it happens fast. I'm not getting any younger here."

Zoey rubbed Freeway behind the ears and considered the questions. Suddenly, she was feeling a bit overwhelmed. This was happening so fast.

She blew out a breath. "Well, I don't know. I need to think about it."

Surprising Dad wasn't the answer. Neither was telling him over the phone. Probably the thing to do would be for Zoey to tell her father the news in person first, then they could all meet somewhere. It would need to be private. Not Dad's place. He'd feel like he needed to play host. *Not my place, either.*

Since Cooper wasn't around for this momentous occasion in

Zoey's life, she didn't want to be smelling his aftershave during the big event.

Then, she had an idea. "My Dad has a beach house in Galveston that I use more often than he does. It's about an hour's drive from the hospital. But there's room for all of us. I think it would be a nice place for Dad to meet y'all."

"That sounds perfect," Helen said. "The next question is when do we leave? I know you just arrived today, Zoey, and the thought of climbing back into the car to make the return trip is exhausting but—"

"Whoa, there, Helen." Genevieve had been watching Zoey closely. "I know you're anxious, but Zoey just arrived today. You cannot ask her to get back in the car to make that grueling trip without at least one night's sleep. Besides, Ms. Mayor, you have to open the Christmas festival tonight at five."

"Oh no. The festival." Helen slapped her forehead. "I completely forgot."

Her brow furrowed as she thought the matter through. "I have something festival-related scheduled every day through the weekend. I guess I could ask Nicole to fill in for me." She looked at Genevieve. "Think we can find someone to run our booth for us?"

Genevieve shrugged. "If not, we hang a sign saying family emergency. It's a family-themed booth. It's appropriate."

"Oh no," Willow said, with a shake of her head. Disappointment wreathed her face. "I don't know what I was thinking of. I got ahead of myself. I can't go to Texas. I have three bridal appointments this week and an event on Saturday. I was going to help Noah in his dollhouse booth, but he could manage without me. I'll run your booth for you. We can close it down on Saturday if I can't find anyone else to cover during my event. Just promise to get your dad to Lake in the Clouds ASAP, Zoey. I hope before your wedding, although that'll be here sooner than we think."

"Thank you, Willow," Helen said fervently as Zoey's stomach sank.

The wedding again. Zoey took a long sip of her champagne.

"Why don't we see what sort of flight we can get out of Durango?" Genevieve suggested.

"I'll look for you," Willow said. She reached into her purse, pulled out her phone, and began searching a website. Genevieve and Helen discussed the logistics of driving while Zoey tried to ignore the fact that her phone had rung again.

She had a niggling fear that Cooper's father might have had a post-op issue, but surely he'd have texted that information like he had the other surgery-related details.

Guilt nudged her to finally check her phone. Three missed calls from Cooper. No voice mail. No texts. She typed out a message to him. Can't talk now. Update on Pat's status?

Almost immediately, three dots showed on her screen, and one word arrived. Fine.

Okay, then. Zoey tossed her phone back into her purse. She knew him. Dr. MacKenzie was pissed. Zoey continued, "I know you're anxious, but knowing my dad, he'll be more relaxed if we do this on the weekend."

"Looks like the earliest y'all could get a seat is on Friday evening," Willow said. "That puts you in Galveston at about the same time as it would take you to drive. Should I book them?"

Everyone looked at Zoey. "Make them refundable. I'll need to check with Dad and confirm he intends to be in town this weekend."

Helen said, "Use my credit card, please, Willow. The one in my desk drawer. You know where it is." To Genevieve, she added, "That will work out well. In the meantime, we can work the Christmas market. That'll give me something else to occupy my mind."

"It's a plan, then." Genevieve rose and picked up her bag. "Speaking of the festival, I have a few things to do before five o'clock tonight. I need to run by the bank and get money for our cash box and pick up our new brochures advertising the inn at the print shop, so I'm going to head out. Shall we plan to meet back at the courthouse booth at a quarter to five?" Following Helen's nod of agreement, she passed around hugs, hesitating a moment before taking her sister into her arms. "I'm so happy for you."

Genevieve's tone was genuine, but only Zoey was positioned in such a way that she could see Genevieve's expression as she embraced Helen. For just a moment, an odd expression flashed across her face. *Huh. Wonder what that's about?*

Willow departed shortly after her mother, leaving Zoey and Helen alone for the first time since the big revelation. Zoey gave Helen an awkward smile. "I think I'll go back to the apartment and catch up on a couple of phone calls and my e-mail if that's all right with you?"

"Of course. I'm sure you can use a little downtime to process everything. Honestly, I do, too." She approached Zoey and took her hands in hers. "I hope we haven't OD'd you on family. If you want me to back off, just say the word. I'm not promising I'll actually do it, mind you, but I will try to be more sensitive."

Zoey laughed softly. "No. No. I love it. It's what I've always dreamed about."

"Me, too. Oh, honey. Me, too!" Helen wrapped her in a quick, hard hug. Stepping back, she asked, "Before you go, will you say it? I haven't heard you say it."

At first, Zoey thought she was asking to hear the l-word. *Love* was a word Zoey didn't throw around indiscriminately.

She really liked Helen, but this was still a little too fast for her. Then, even as she hesitated, Zoey realized that Helen meant something else. Her heart did a little happy dance as she leaned over and kissed her grandmother's cheek.

"Nana. I'm so glad you're my nana. I'm so glad to be part of your family."

Zoey remained in the guest apartment only long enough to change clothes and don her running shoes. A section of Helen's condo community snaked alongside a bubbling creek, and Zoey headed for the meandering trail running beside it, indicated on a facility map she'd found in the apartment's kitchen. The myriad of emotions rolling through her would overcome her if she let them, so while she ran, she tried to clear her mind instead of dwelling on the events of the day.

She ran for almost an hour to the music of a burbling mountain stream and the perfume of Douglas fir and pine. At what point during her run she made the decision about her next move, she couldn't say. She didn't consciously work the problem. She simply went with her gut.

When she returned to the apartment, Zoey picked up her phone and sent a bat signal text to her dad.

"My family is going to be the death of me," Genevieve declared without so much as a hello when Gage opened the door of the Triple T Ranch house. His lips twisted in wry amusement as he stepped aside while Genevieve barreled her way into the house. "You won't believe what—"

She stopped abruptly upon realizing that Gage was not alone. His daughter Lindsay stood in the family room with her arms crossed and a smile on her face that didn't reach her eyes. "Oh. I'm interrupting. I'm sorry."

"You're not interrupting," Gage said. "This is my day for unexpected visitors. Lindsay dropped by to bring me a book by a new author that she thought I'd like. A juicy murder mystery."

"Oh? I'm always on the lookout for new authors. What's the title?"

Now, a gleam of emotion—was it malice?—lit the young woman's eyes. "It's called *The Black Widow's Demise.*"

Yes, definitely malice.

"It's a cozy mystery. I'm trying to book the author for a signing."

"I'll watch for it," Genevieve said, forcing a smile. She really wasn't in the mood to deal with Lindsay Higgins today. Meeting Gage's gaze, she said, "I'm going to run. I just wanted to stop by and remind you that the Christmas market opens tonight."

"No. You're not running anywhere. You are obviously upset about something, and Lindsay was actually about to leave. Weren't you, honey?"

She hesitated, but Genevieve could see the truth of Gage's claim in Lindsay's expression. She pursed her lips mulishly and nodded. "Yes, I was on my way out."

Gage walked over to her and smoothly ushered her toward the kitchen, saying, "I'll walk you to your car. Be right back, Genevieve."

Genevieve concluded that Lindsay had parked beside the kitchen door. That was why she hadn't seen the vehicle upon her arrival. Genevieve knew what kind of car Lindsay drove. Had she noticed it when she'd driven up to the ranch house, she'd have kept driving.

Spotting a pitcher of ice water sitting on Gage's bar, Genevieve crossed the room and filled a glass. Maybe something cold would help her cool down.

Now that Genevieve was away from Helen and Zoey, she could release her inner ire. She was not a happy camper. She was furious with her father and her mother. And had her brothers known about Helen's pregnancy? Had any of them known what her father had done with the baby?

Last, but definitely not least, Genevieve wasn't exactly happy with Helen.

Genevieve polished off her ice water and then set down her glass with a bang. Entering the room from the kitchen, Gage noted her movement and reacted by arching his brows. "All right, sweetheart. What have your children done now?"

"Believe it or not, my children aren't the troublemakers this time around. It's my sister."

Gage's eyes widened with surprise. "Well, this is different."

"You won't believe. I have a story to tell you, Gage, but I need to move while I'm doing it. Want to go for a walk with me?"

"Sure thing. Want your boots?"

Genevieve glanced down at her feet, noting the sandals. "Yes, I definitely need my boots."

Gage had given her a pair of hiking boots to leave at his house following the third time their plans changed because Genevieve was wearing inappropriate footwear. She might be living in Colorado now, but she'd yet to leave her Texas sandals-and–flip-flop lifestyle behind.

She didn't speak again until they were out of the house and headed for the trail that wound up the mountain behind Gage's house. It was an easy hike that required just enough exertion to help with stress relief without being so strenuous that Genevieve couldn't talk while she hiked. And talk, she did.

She relayed the story in a clear, concise manner. During

the telling, Gage whistled a time or two, but he didn't interrupt. Only when she concluded and fell silent, searching for the words to express the emotions churning inside her, did he begin to ask questions. "So, why are you upset with Helen?"

"Why am I upset?" Genevieve whirled on Gage. "Because we don't keep secrets. I tell her *everything*. I thought she did the same."

Gage tilted his cowboy hat back on his head, then folded his arms. "So, your feelings are hurt. You're upset because you think she didn't trust you enough to share it."

"She lied to me!" Genevieve bent and scooped up a handful of rocks. She sailed one into the forest as she added, "She lied to me about the biggest, most important, most devastating event of her life. She lied for fifty years!"

Gage opened his mouth to speak, but smartly reconsidered when Genevieve shot him a warning look.

"Listen, I understand why she didn't tell me when it happened," she said, throwing another stone. "I was too young to understand. But I grew up. We got to be best friends. Or, so I thought. *She. Never. Told. Me.* She never told me when I held her hand through her miscarriages. She never told me when our parents died. She never told me when my husband died, and I thought no adult around me could possibly understand the depth of my grief. And all of that time, she had lost a baby! A full-term child. I know it's not exactly the same thing as grief for a spouse, but it has to be pretty damned close. She understood, but I didn't *know* she understood! I didn't have all the facts!"

Genevieve threw the rest of her rocks one after the other before resuming her march uphill. Gage followed, offering silent support. She liked that about him. He understood her. Right now, she needed to vent, not answer questions or listen to his thoughts or observations.

Upon reaching the top of the hill, she wrapped her arms around herself and sighed. "It stinks, Gage. I had all those feeling simmering inside me, but I had to swallow my words. This was a wonderful moment for Helen, and I wasn't about to try to make it about me. Today wasn't about me. I couldn't throw a wet blanket on her joy."

His expression turned tender. "So you came to me."

"Yes, I came to you, Gage."

He reached out, cupped her chin, stared deeply into her eyes, and smiled. "You came to family. Your family."

"Oh, Gage," she said with a sigh. "That's not a subject for today either. My entire worldview has tilted on its axis."

Now he pulled her into his arms. She resisted for only an instant before melting against him. "I understand, sweetheart. You and Helen have a history that is unique and gives you a bond unlike any other. The relationship you have with your sister is the longest-lasting one of your life, and it will be until one of you passes. Helen *did* hurt your feelings."

She struggled just a tiny bit. He held her a little tighter. "That makes me sound like I'm six. Yes, she hurt my feelings, but it's bigger than that. I feel betrayed. *By my sister!* At the same time, I understand her position. She has a right to privacy."

"From everyone except you."

"Exactly. I knew you'd understand, Gage."

"You poor baby," he teased. He tucked her head against his shoulder.

"I feel like a baby. Helen and I will need to talk this through once the excitement dies down. I need to let it go. Why am I wasting even a moment of thought on this when we've had a miracle today? A real honest-to-goodness miracle. Helen has a son. His name is Adam. I can't wait to meet him."

"When is that going to happen?"

"Hopefully, this Sunday. Helen, Zoey, and I have seats on a Saturday night flight. I think Helen would have gone tonight if she could have gotten onto a plane."

"Y'all are welcome to use my plane."

Warmth bubbled up inside of Genevieve. Willow had been right. But then again, so had she. "You are the most generous man, Gage Throckmorton. Thank you, but no. What I need from you is this. You holding me. Listening to me. Letting me vent."

"You're leaving something out."

"Oh yeah? What's that?"

The gleam in his eyes telegraphed his intentions, so Genevieve wasn't surprised when his mouth captured hers.

This, she thought, as warmth seeped languidly through her body, was coming home.

Maybe Gage is right. Maybe he's already my family.

Had the time come for her resistance to end?

Zoey lay in bed that night and couldn't fall asleep. Never mind that she was as weary as she'd ever been, all those never-ending hospital shifts through her residency notwithstanding. But emotion was caffeine in her blood that kept her heart racing and her mind spinning.

She'd worked the Christmas market booth with Genevieve and Helen. Helen had introduced her as her granddaughter, telling those who had questioned this new addition to the family that the story was a long one, but the bottom line was that the expansion of Helen's family was a joyful thing.

And it had been a night of joy, with a little after-dark crisp in the air, the drifting fragrance of mulling spices and roasting nuts, and the sound of carols floating on the gentle breeze. A bit weird for July, but fun nonetheless. They'd sold an impressive amount of inventory for what Helen assured her would be the slowest night of the festival. Zoey herself had purchased a ridiculous number of family-themed tree ornaments, her excuse being a whole bunch of new cousins with whom she might wish to exchange gifts come December.

Light from a three-quarter moon beamed through the bedroom window and illuminated the handmade glass ornament that Helen had presented to her. Zoey had hung it from a suction cup hook. It was a gold angel holding a pink heart. The ribbon on the bottom read, "World's Best Granddaughter." Zoey focused on the ornament, and her heart did a little *thud-a-thump*.

She'd found family. A grandmother. Helen wouldn't replace Mimi, whom Zoey mourned deeply to this day, but a girl had room in her life for two grandmothers, especially when Nana brought an aunt and lots of cousins along with her.

She'd been looking forward to growing her family when she became a MacKenzie. Yet she sensed that forming a family with in-laws took time. While she adored Pat and Sherry MacKenzie, they were Cooper's family. Given time, she expected she and his parents would develop a family bond.

Given time.

Zoey's gaze drifted to the bedside table where her phone lay connected to a charging cord. She wanted to tell Cooper about today. He'd called her three times today, and she'd let it go to voice mail each time. He hadn't left messages.

He hadn't contacted her at all since their brief text exchange. Had he given up on her? If Zoey were being honest with herself, she couldn't really blame him.

She sat up, scooched back against the headboard, and reached for her phone. Her pulse speeding up, she scrolled to their latest communication. It was two hours later in Michigan, so it was after midnight on the East Coast. He wouldn't be awake.

Hesitating only a moment and not truly expecting an answer, she typed out You awake?

His response came almost at once. Yes. Let's talk.

She was still debating her response when the phone rang—a video call. Okay, video was not what she'd been expecting. Well, she'd started this. She couldn't ignore this call. She switched on the lamp, then connected. Cooper's image filled her screen.

He looked worried. She said, "Hi."

"Hello. I was getting worried. Where are you?"

"Colorado. Lake in the Clouds."

"Already? We're still a month away from the wedding."

"It's a long story. First, though, how is your dad?"

Cooper spent a few minutes telling her about his father's injury and prognosis. When he finished the update, Zoey responded, "I'm so glad. I'm sure he and your mom were relieved to have you there."

"They were."

After that, an awkward silence fell between them, and Zoey quickly surmised that he intended to wait her out. Okay, then. She'd wanted to tell him, hadn't she?

"Remember those DNA kits you left with me when my mother was dying?"

"You told me you didn't sample her."

"I didn't. I sent off a sample of my own DNA, and not long after you left our place, I received notification of a match. Except, the family I found is on my father's side."

Always a quick thinker, Cooper said, "Willow the wedding planner."

"Yes." Zoey gave him a rundown of the events of the past three days. While she talked, the frown he'd greeted her with transformed into a genuine smile. When she finished speaking, he said, "I'm both surprised and unsurprised. The resemblance between you and Willow was uncanny, but I've been focused on your mother. I don't know why I never considered that the link could be through your dad. Stupid of me."

"It's because we always thought of his parents as his parents and never really concentrated on his being adopted."

"But, man, a stolen child. How horrible for your grandmother. How did your dad take the news?"

Zoey exhaled a heavy breath. "I haven't told him yet. It's not the sort of thing I think I should do over the phone. Helen wants to meet him, of course. We were planning a quick trip to Texas, but I canceled the reservations because I managed to convince Dad to come to Lake in the Clouds. He'll be here Friday."

"That's good." Cooper raked his fingers through his hair. "How long do you plan to remain in Colorado?"

She shrugged. "I'm in no rush to return to Houston. I want to get to know my new family better."

"Speaking of family..." Cooper glanced away for a moment and appeared to brace himself. "Zoey, I think we need to talk about us."

From out of the blue, tears stung her eyes. "Now? It's late, Cooper."

"It is. You wouldn't take my calls earlier today. Or yesterday."

"It's been an eventful few days, and I'm exhausted. Please, can this wait until I've had a decent night's sleep?"

His brow creased with a frown. "If I agree, will you promise to quit dodging my calls?"

Zoey opened her mouth to deny the charge, but she couldn't do so in good faith. "I promise."

"Okay, then. We'll talk tomorrow. I need to be at the hospital early so I can catch Dad's doctor during his rounds. How about we schedule a time to talk? Say, after about ten?"

You're pushing, Cooper. "I'm not sure what Helen has planned for the day tomorrow. Why don't I text you when I have a better idea about what's on my agenda?"

"All right." Cooper exhaled heavily, then said, "I gotta hit the sack. I'm glad we talked, Zoey. Good night."

"Me, too. Good night."

It wasn't until she'd returned her phone to the nightstand that she realized they'd ended their call without the customary "I love you."

Zoey sank back into bed and pulled the covers over her head. How could this day have been both so extraordinarily wonderful and so extremely sad? How had she and Cooper gotten to the place where they didn't say "I love you" to each other less than a month ahead of their wedding?

She was too tired to try to figure it out.

Searching for a distraction from her thoughts, she grabbed her phone, pulled up the audiobook app, and swiped to a classic romance novel she listened to so often that she almost knew it by heart. Her last conscious thought before drifting off to sleep was that it had been nice to hear Cooper's voice.

She missed him.

Chapter Twelve

HELEN WOKE UP WITH a hangover. She'd stayed up late drinking on her own—and it hadn't been celebratory drinking. After the Christmas market, when Helen was home alone and reflecting on the events of the day, the glow of joy had begun to fade. Anger took its place.

Lots of anger. At her parents and aunt and uncle, definitely. But also, Helen was angry at herself. Why hadn't she asked more questions about what had happened? What hadn't she asked for a death certificate? In hindsight, she could see the holes in the story that she'd been fed, but yet, in all these years, she hadn't questioned it.

Guilt ghosted through her. Had she pushed harder she might have found out about Adam herself and done so a lot sooner than fifty years after the fact.

With all those monsters roaming through her head, she'd ended up drinking way more vodka than she should have done. Now, after downing half an ocean full of water, she had to admit that the booze hadn't done any good.

She remained as ticked off as she'd been last night when she'd started drinking.

Coffee. She needed a cup of good, strong coffee. Emphasis on the *good.* Also, she needed someone to whom she could vent. Because if she didn't get this poison out of her system, she just might blow. Picking up her phone, she made a call to the one person in the world who could possibly understand. "Genevieve? I'm a mess. Can I come over? Will you put the coffee on?"

"Of course."

"Thank you. I'll be there in fifteen."

Driving with a lead foot this morning, Helen arrived at her sister's in less than ten minutes. She entered through the kitchen door and sailed straight for the coffeepot, then with a steaming mug in hand, went in search of her sister. She found Genevieve outside on the patio, wearing gardening gloves and holding a trowel. Her sister glanced up in surprise. "Wow, that was fast."

Helen opened her mouth, and the words poured out like vomit. "I am so *angry,* Genevieve. It's a good thing Dad is already dead; otherwise, I'd find a weapon and do the deed myself. Do you know how badly I wanted children? Four miscarriages and a baby who died at birth. Do you know how deeply I mourned?"

She whirled around and, spying Genevieve's weed bucket, picked it up and carried it over to the rose bed. She went down on her knees and started yanking errant grasses and dandelions growing among the mulch. A moment later, Genevieve tossed a pair of gloves to the ground beside her. "Watch what you're doing there. That variety of rose has spectacular thorns."

"Perfect. Totally appropriate. I'm feeling pretty thorny myself." Helen tore a dandelion from the dirt. "Not having children of my own was my deepest sorrow and regret. The desire for children led me to marry men I never should have married. It's why I kept remarrying, you know. I was hoping to find what I'd lost. Lost, hah! What was stolen from me. He stole fifty years from me. He stole my family from me. He stole my child from me! And this was someone I loved. Why? Why did he do that, Genevieve? He was my father. He was supposed to love me!"

Helen rolled back on her butt and wrapped her arms around her legs. "Do you know how hard it has been all these years? Do you know how envious I've been of you? Every time you announced a pregnancy and then a successful birth, I was pea green with envy. It was so difficult to hide."

Genevieve opened her mouth, then abruptly shut it.

"I didn't hide it, did I?"

"Not very well, no. But you'd had all the miscarriages, so I understood. Of course, I didn't know that...well...that it was... bigger."

Bigger. Guess that's one way to put it. Helen closed her eyes and rubbed her temples. "I'm a mess today, Genevieve."

"That's understandable."

Helen glanced up and gave her sister a sharp look. There'd been a note in her voice. Just a hint of sharpness. Genevieve was stewing and trying not to show it.

Helen could guess what had her riled. "You're pissed at me, aren't you?"

Genevieve sighed. "Helen, you've supported me through a million crises over the years. Let me support you for a change. Today is about you and your feelings, not mine."

Helen almost let it go. However, she was spoiling for a fight and Genevieve was handy. "Okay, then. I'm *feeling* like I want to talk about this now. Let's just lay it out there and deal with it. That way it'll be behind us."

"Oh, Helen."

Helen picked up one of the gardening gloves and slapped it against her thigh as she plowed ahead. "You probably understand why I didn't tell you back when all this happened. You were young, and you wouldn't have understood. But today you're wondering why I didn't tell you later on. After you grew up and the two of us became close."

The light in Genevieve's eyes signaled *Bingo.* "I thought we were close," she said quietly, folding her arms. "I thought we shared everything."

"And now you find out I kept the biggest secret of all to myself, and it pisses you off."

Genevieve looked away, her gaze focusing on the pot of red geraniums decorating her front stoop. "Maybe you didn't want to upset my relationship with Mom and Dad, especially Dad. I can see how that might have been the case."

"Never mind that he's been dead a long time," Helen snapped and slung the glove away like a Frisbee.

Genevieve obviously didn't care for her tone. She shifted her gaze from the spot on the lawn where the glove had landed and glared down at her sister. "All right, then. If you're intent upon doing this, let's do it. Why *didn't* you tell me after Dad died?"

"Because I couldn't. I tried, but I couldn't." With that, Helen's anger drained away. After all, she wasn't angry at Genevieve. The emotion rolling through her stomach was guilt. "I started to tell you many times, but I never could get the words out. The pain was so deep and sharp. It was in the marrow of my bones, and I did everything I could to seal it off, so I wasn't forced to feel it." Tears misted Helen's eyes as she added, "Feeling it sucks. Yesterday, as wonderful as this news is, oh, Genevieve, it hurts. It's all brand new again. It hurts."

Helen broke then and tears spilled down her cheeks. She buried her head against her knees. "I'm sorry. I should have told you. I'm sorry."

"Oh, honey, it's okay. No, no, no. Don't cry like that." Helen felt her sister's hand on her shoulder. "Get up, Helen. You need a hug. I need to hug you. However, I'm afraid if we both get down on the ground, with our old and creaky knees, we might be stuck there. Get up and let's go sit on the garden glider. We'll talk this through."

Helen nodded and allowed her sister to help her up. Genevieve had a point about the knee thing.

Genevieve had a lovely white wicker set of furniture with deep cushions covered in a navy and pink floral pattern. She led Helen to the sofa, sat her down, and took a seat beside her. "First, I accept your apology, so that's behind us. Let's concentrate on your feelings. I think you need to open a vein and bleed. I'm here to make sure you don't bleed out and to wipe up the mess. Okay?"

"Okay."

"So, where do you want to start?"

"I don't know where to start."

"The beginning is always good."

"It's fifty years ago, Genevieve. In all honesty, I don't remember a lot of it. I just remember that I fell in love over the summer and he went away in the fall and my life fell apart in the winter. Mom and Dad and Uncle Ray and Aunt Grace convinced me that it was the best thing for me and for the baby that I put him up for adoption. So, that's what I agreed to do. But those last weeks, the last month, I knew I couldn't do it. I told them I wouldn't do it. That's when the shit hit the fan. Do you think he planned to steal my baby all along, Genevieve? Did I love someone that evil?"

Genevieve sucked in a long breath. "Okay, I really really, really hate to do this, but you asked. The act of taking your child and telling you the baby died was evil, yes. But I doubt he planned it. I imagine he saw an opportunity and took it. And this is the part that is going to get me into trouble. I think he probably acted out of love for you and maybe even the baby. Zoey has said the family who raised your son loved him dearly and were lovely people who gave him a wonderful childhood."

"He had no right," Helen snapped.

"He absolutely had no right. His actions were wrong. But, understandable. Times were different fifty years ago. It was still the beginning of the sexual revolution. Having children out of wedlock was frowned upon, especially in Wichita Falls, Texas. Listen, I am not defending what he did. I'm just trying to understand it. I think Mom and Dad knew how difficult your life would be as a single mother. By encouraging you to choose adoption, they were trying to save you from that struggle."

"Do you think she knew what he did?"

"Mom?" Genevieve considered a moment, then shook her head. "I sincerely doubt it. She was not a good secret keeper, and besides, the guilt would have eaten her alive. I could see Uncle Ray being in on it, but not Aunt Grace. Especially since you lived with them. The females of our family might have supported putting the baby up for adoption, but taking your child and telling you he died? No. That's something else entirely."

"I think you're probably right. Aunt Grace tried so hard to take care of me. I was such a mess."

"But you came out of it." Genevieve smiled encouragingly. "You survived and rose from the ashes and succeeded. Look at all you have achieved in your life."

"What have I achieved?" Helen asked with disdain. "I've had three failed marriages. So what if I've had a successful career? Big whoop. What did I do that matters? Law school taught me to think critically and look through every lens and at every angle. But I never looked back at my own tragedy and saw the holes."

Her tears flowed anew. "I wasn't there to raise my son. I never kissed his booboos or read him a bedtime story. I never held his hand on the first day of school or lectured him about getting home by curfew. I didn't caution him against drinking and driving or having unprotected sex! I wasn't there when he went off to college or got married or when his precious little girl was born. I missed so much, Genevieve, and I'm so angry!"

"I know you are. You have every right to be angry. I'm angry for you. But you can't say that your life hasn't mattered. It has mattered very much. You've mattered to me." Genevieve took hold of her sister's hands and squeezed them. "How many times did you catch me when I fell? Too many to count. I don't know how I would have survived without you. You've been the best sister and aunt to my children. And yes, your career mattered. You did a lot of good in your work, and your work provided you the means and opportunity to do a lot of good in your community. Feel sorry for yourself about missing half a century with your son, but you don't get to deny or belittle the difference you made to the people who were in your orbit. You're doing it still! Look at all the good you've done for Lake in the Clouds!"

Helen heard her sister's words. She took them into her heart and held them close.

Genevieve drew Helen into her arms and held her, her head pillowed against her little sister's bosom as Helen allowed herself to weep. She cried for what she had lost until her tears and much of her anger was spent, comforted by the arms of the person on this earth who knew her best and loved her most. Eventually, she said, "I don't know if I can ever forgive him."

"I know. You probably need to try, though."

"You're probably right."

"I usually am."

"I love you, Genevieve. I'm sorry I never told you."

"I love you, too, Helen. I forgive you for not telling me."

"Thank you. It's a powerful thing, forgiveness. Maybe someday I'll be able to find a little in my heart."

"Maybe someday," Genevieve repeated. "So, do you want a Bloody Mary?"

Helen chided her sister with a look and asked for two Tylenol instead.

Freeway gave a warning bark just before the doorbell sounded. Zoey set down the novel she'd been reading and hurried to answer the door. "Batman! Thank you for coming."

Then she threw herself into her father's arms.

"A promise is a promise," Adam Hillcrest said against her ear. He hugged her for a long minute, then stepped away and gave her a quick but thorough study. "What's the emergency, baby girl?"

"It's a really long story, Dad."

Adam bent over and gave Freeway a good scratch. Rising, he reached into his pocket and pulled out her engagement ring. "Does it have something to do with this? When I went by your condo to pick up the items you'd requested, I couldn't help but notice it."

Zoey's mouth twisted in a rueful grimace. "I left in a fit of temper."

She accepted the ring from her dad and held it in the palm of her hand. The apartment had a small safe like the ones found in hotel rooms. She could store it there. Instead, without giving it too much thought, she slipped the engagement ring onto her finger.

Where it belonged. Yes, it felt like it belonged. Zoey was instantly comforted by that fact.

She showed her father to the apartment's second bedroom and bath, then went to the kitchen to pour him a glass of iced tea while he stowed his stuff. When he rejoined her, he sipped his drink and studied her expectantly over the top of his glass.

Okay, show time. "I can't sit still and do this, Dad. Are you up for a little exercise following your long trip?"

"I'll do whatever you'd like."

"Let's play a little basketball. There's a court not far from here, and I saw a ball in one of the closets."

Adam smiled faintly. Many a time over the years, father and daughter had discussed the important news of the day during a game of "horse" beneath the basketball goal in their driveway.

"Sounds good."

"Give me five minutes to change and convince Freeway he needs a little crate time."

Zoey had checked out a handful of places they could use for this discussion, but she pinned her hopes on her first choice being free. Luck proved to be with her. Less than an hour after her dad had knocked on her apartment door, they took their places on the outdoor basketball court at Reflections Inn at Mirror Lake.

After a short warm-up, Adam held the ball and asked, "Standard rules?"

"Yes."

Their "standard" rules for the game were personal and unique, having developed as a way for father and daughter to learn about each other's day without it being an interrogation. In the Hillcrest version, the first player took his shot from the shooting spot of his choice. If player one made the shot, player two attempted the same shot. A miss by player two meant two earned a letter in the word-of-the-game, and player one got to ask a question. The word-of-the-game was invariably a medical term. The first person who spelled the WOG was deemed the loser.

Adam tossed the ball to Zoey. "And our word?"

"I had considered using *stethoscope*."

He arched a brow and smirked. "Anticipate your story will take that long, hmm?"

"Not necessarily. You could be off your game, and I could win quickly. However, I've decided to go with *flower*."

Adam frowned as Zoey flipped the coin. Her father won and the game began. Adam chose his spot, an easy-to-make warm-up bucket. He arced the basketball toward the net, and it sailed through with a whoosh. Zoey made the follow-up shot. After two more relatively easy shots, Adam stepped up the difficulty level. His ball fell through the net. Zoey's rimmed out.

Adam said, "You have an *F*. My question is this. Have you brought me to Lake in the Clouds to show me the retail space you want to lease for your flower shop?"

Zoey had anticipated that her father would suspect that her issues with Cooper were behind the summons to Colorado using their personal "I need help" signal. So she'd expected him to ask about Cooper first. Her choice of *flower* assured it.

She thought it best to get that subject out of the way.

She responded to the question with a shake of her head. "No, Dad. You can rest easy because I'm not ready to pull the trigger on a flower shop. Not that I've abandoned the idea entirely, but I have decided to place a moratorium on big career decisions until I get my personal life figured out."

"Well, that's a relief."

Having answered his question, she took position and sank her shot.

They traded three more shots before he stepped up the difficulty level and missed. Zoey made her attempt. "There's your *F*, Dad."

"Okay. What's your question?"

Here goes. Zoey cleared her throat and said, "You always said that you weren't bothered by the fact that you didn't know anything about your birth family. I'm curious if that's the whole story. Didn't you ever want to know something about your roots, Dad?"

His blue eyes widened in surprise. "That question is out of left field."

"We're playing basketball, not baseball," she quipped.

"Hmm." He studied her for a long moment, then nodded. "Well, that is pretty much the whole story, yes. I had loving parents who gave me a great childhood. I grew up knowing who I was—Tom and Mary Hillcrest's son—so I never felt anything lacking."

He glanced away at that point and stared out toward the sapphire lake where sunlight glittered on the wind-choppy surface. He frowned. Thinking, Zoey surmised. She knew him well, so she was able to read in his expression the moment he put two-and-two together. "This is about your mother, not Cooper."

No one could deny that her dad was quick. Zoey probably could have chosen a short word for today's game.

She bounced the ball twice, lined up, took another shot, and made it. He repeated it. They worked through three more positions before she missed, gaining an *L*, and handing the question to him.

Adam had his powder ready. He'd not only put two-and-two together, but he was well into double digits. Bordering on triple. "Did you take a sample of your mother's DNA and use it to discover her identity?"

Zoey hid a smile. This was working just as she'd hoped. Her dad was the ultimate problem-solver. He much preferred working his own way to a conclusion than being told the answer. She didn't want the news about finding his birth mother to slap him across the face. Zoey wanted it to bloom like a flower in his brain. Hence, her choice of word-of-the-game. She answered, "No, I did not sample Mom's DNA. I considered it, but that was a step too far for me. She'd protected her privacy all of these years. I couldn't betray that."

"Okay. Good. I went down that road myself in the past and reached the same conclusion."

Zoey wasn't surprised by the revelation, but she didn't waste any time thinking about it. Instead, bracing herself, she lobbed her verbal grenade. "I did submit a DNA sample of my own to a selection of databases."

His eyes widened, and he gave her a searching look. After a long moment, he said, "I thought you had decided against making your genetic data public."

"Things changed. I changed my mind." Zoey tossed the ball to her father. "Your turn."

Adam bounced the ball three times and took his shot—the most difficult one yet. When Zoey invariably missed, he caught the rebound and held the ball. "That's an *O* for you. So, things changed. Your mother passed away, taking her secrets with her. That brought your lack of family top of mind. Also, earlier this year, you met a young woman to whom you bear a striking resemblance. Now, you summon me to Lake in the Clouds, where this young woman lives. Zoey, have you found a genetic relative?"

"I have. Your shot, Dad."

"It frustrates me that you're using our game to dribble out information."

"Dribble. Good one, Dad. I have my reasons. Your shot again."

He missed it.

"That's an *L* for you," she announced. "Here's my question. You do know that you've been the perfect father for me and that this yearning I've had to know something about my family roots has nothing to do with you, right?"

He sighed. "Thank you for that."

Zoey deliberately missed her shot and retrieved the ball. "*W* for me." She tossed the basketball to her dad, saying, "Your question."

He caught it and began a slow, stationary dribble. "All this together leads me to believe that you are attempting to protect me, most likely from something your mother did while we were married. I think you've used this game in an attempt to turn a big bang into a pop."

She had never been very good at fooling her father.

"So, all that said, here's my question. Did you discover a long-lost half-sister?"

Bomb defused. "No. It's a logical conclusion, but no, Dad, I didn't find a sister. However, I was notified of a more distant genetic match. Not through Mom, though. Through you."

"Ah." He pivoted and executed a perfect jump shot. *Swish.*

Zoey rebounded and immediately shot a clunker. The rim clanged, and her father caught the ball and tucked it beneath his arm. "You found my birth parents?"

Game over. "I found your mother."

Adam stood as still as a statue for a long minute, absorbing the momentous news. Then, he nodded once. "Time out."

He took the ball down the court. For the next few minutes, he ran and shot and rebounded. Ran and shot and rebounded. Again and again and again.

Zoey stood by and silently watched, letting him work through his thoughts. It didn't take long.

"Head's up." He shot the ball toward her. "Two letters to go."

Zoey caught the basketball and immediately turned to shoot, her aim wild. Her dad caught the ball. "*E.*"

"She's related to this young woman you met and lives here in Lake in the Clouds?"

"Yes." She held out her hands for the ball. Adam threw it, and Zoey again took another poor shot.

The ball bounced off the board, and her dad caught it. "She wants to meet me?"

"Yes." She caught the pass and held it. *Game over.* "Her name is Helen. Helen McDaniel."

Adam tested the name on his lips. Then, as if the words were being pulled out of his mouth against his will, he asked, "Why didn't she raise me? Did she say? Let me guess, teen pregnancy."

Zoey hesitated. "I'll tell you the details she shared with me if you want, but honestly, I think it's her story to tell you, Dad. She doesn't know you are here. She's planning to travel to Texas on Saturday, but I thought doing it this way would be better."

He nodded. "Okay, then. Let's do it."

"Now? You're ready to meet her now?"

"Yeah. Unless..." He glanced down at his gym shorts and T-shirt, then sniffed his pits. "Should I shower and change first?"

"You didn't break a sweat. You're perfect. You're you. Well, you're you when you're not in a lab coat. There is a place here that I believe will make a perfect meeting spot. Let me make a call, and I'll see what sort of timeline we can put together."

Zoey walked over to the bench where she'd left the gear bag and dug around inside it for her phone. On the court, Adam resumed taking shots.

Scrolling through her contacts list, she hesitated and then made a game-day decision. The call connected after two rings.

"Hello, Zoey."

"Hi. Do you have a minute? I have some news to share."

"I have nothing to wear," Helen grumbled to Cookie as she rejected yet another dress.

Her gaze shifted from the opened suitcase on her bed to the pile of clothes lying beside it. She owned nothing appropriate for the biggest event in her life. She needed something new, something chic and stylish and slimming, but that wasn't happening out of her closet.

She'd have to run by Lake in the Clouds' only boutique later today. Maybe for once the fashion gods would smile upon her and she'd find the perfect thing.

Yeah, right. The lack of decent shopping was the biggest drawback she'd discovered since moving to Lake in the Clouds. Feeling a little desperate, she returned to her closet. Maybe she'd missed something spectacular hanging in the back.

She heard the ping of a text and checked her phone. Genevieve. Are you home?

Yes. Cleaning my closet.

Hah. Hah. Picking you up in five.

Where we going?

Meet me outside.

"Well." Helen looked at the dog. "I guess I'm going out."

She was outside visiting with the mail carrier when her sister pulled up. She climbed into the passenger seat and said, "What's up?"

"We need to run out to the lodge."

"Oh? Is there a problem?"

"No. No." Genevieve slowed to make a turn and flicked on her signal. "I had a call a few minutes ago. From Zoey."

"Oh?" Helen pinned her sister with a look and caught her breath. She knew Genevieve. Her sister looked oh-so-innocent. Something had happened. "What's wrong? What happened? Is everything okay?"

"Everything is great. It's wonderful. Honey..." Genevieve reached over and rested her hand on Helen's knee. "Adam is here."

Helen froze. "Adam? My Adam?"

"Yes. He's waiting to meet you at the Glass Chapel."

"But...but..." She glanced down at her jeans and Reflections Inn at Mirror Lake T-shirt. "We need to stop at Nina's Boutique first. I need an outfit."

"You're fine. You're perfectly dressed. Apparently, Adam and Zoey have been playing basketball at the lodge, and he's in gym shorts and a T."

"But I was going to wear the necklace Billy gave me for my birthday. I wanted to show it to him. Turn around, Genevieve. Let me get my necklace."

"You can show him the necklace later. He's waiting for you."

"He knows about me? That I'm his mother?"

"Yes. Knowing you both, Zoey decided that this was the best way to handle the introduction."

"Oh. Okay." Helen laced her fingers in her lap. "I'm not ready, Genevieve."

"You have about ten minutes to get that way. I suggest you get after it."

The rest of the drive to the inn passed in a blur of nervous anticipation. Helen rummaged around in her purse, looking for her hairbrush and hoping to find lipstick. Since moving to the mountains, she'd fallen in with local customs and only wore makeup on special occasions. "This is the most special occasion ever," she grumbled. "I should be wearing foundation."

"You're wearing a bra. That's the most important foundation, and it's one that way too many Lake in the Clouds women are choosing to forgo, in my opinion."

"It's mountain life. Can I borrow a lipstick?" Helen knew that Genevieve never left home without a selection of lipsticks. *You can take the girl out of Texas, but you can't take Texas out of the girl.*

"Sure. There's a dusty cinnamon gloss that will be perfect for you. It's just a touch of color."

"Should I put it on my cheeks? I feel like all the blood has drained from my head."

"Sure, put lipstick on your cheeks if you want to look like a clown when you meet your son."

Helen fell silent for another few minutes before saying, "I think I'm going to be sick. You'd better pull over, Genevieve."

Genevieve twisted her head sharply. "Seriously?"

"Yes."

"Oh, Helen. This is so not like you." Genevieve pulled off onto the road's shoulder and Helen immediately threw open the passenger door and hung her head outside of the car.

She didn't lose her breakfast. A few moments of fresh air settled both her stomach and her nerves. "Okay," she said, resuming her seat and shutting the door. "Let's do this thing."

Upon arriving at the inn property, Genevieve drove to the new parking lot beside the trailhead that led to the Glass Chapel. She parked, switched off the engine, then asked, "Want to do this alone or shall I go with you?"

"With me, please. I can't do this without you, Genevieve."

"Good. I really didn't want to miss this."

Before exiting the car, Helen opened her wallet and tugged the photograph of Billy that she'd taken to carrying from inside. She slipped the picture into her pocket, drew in a deep, bracing breath, then exited the car.

This distance from the parking lot to the chapel could be covered in an eight-minute casual walk. Helen and Genevieve made it in five. Approaching the front doors, Helen could make out two figures seated inside. She reached for Genevieve's hand and squeezed it tight.

She and her sister stepped into the chapel, and the figures rose from their seats. They turned. Zoey and... "Oh, Billy."

She had only seconds to see him clearly before tears flooded Helen's eyes. He was tall with sandy blond hair and his father's summer blue eyes. He smiled awkwardly as she approached. For a long moment, they stood staring at one another. Helen's heart pounded. Her mouth was dry as dust—probably because all the moisture in her body was leaking out her eyes.

Finally, Zoey took control of the moment by saying, "Nana, this is my father, Dr. Adam Hillcrest. Daddy, this is my nana, Helen McDaniel."

Helen couldn't have spoken had her life depended on it.

He smiled his father's bashful grin and opened his arms. "Would a hug be appropriate?"

Helen flew into his embrace. A dozen different emotions buffeted her as she held her only child for the first time. Joy, regret, euphoria, pain. Overriding all of it was love. Fierce, all-encompassing maternal love.

She could have remained in his arms forever, but eventually, his grip on her was released. He stepped backward and said, "Okay, I'm a little wobbly. Why don't we sit down before I tumble over?"

"Good idea," Helen said shakily.

It was only after he'd guided her to a seat that she remembered her sister. "Oh, Genevieve. Adam, this is my sister, my best friend. Your aunt Genevieve."

Smiling indulgently, Genevieve asked, "Do I get a hug, too?"

"Absolutely."

While her sister shared a hug with Helen's son—*my son!*—Helen feasted on the sight of the man and listened closely to his voice as he exchanged greetings with Genevieve. He had a deep, bass voice, but she didn't notice any accent.

Genevieve said, "I'm going to sit off to the side and let you and your mother get acquainted, but first, I want to tell you that our family just loves your Zoey."

Adam lit up with a smile. "Thank you. She's my heart."

That started Helen's waterworks again, and Genevieve retrieved a small packet of tissues from her purse. She handed it to Helen and then took a seat. Adam pulled a chair out of the row and angled it so that he and Helen could better see each other. Sitting down, he propped his elbows on his knees and clasped his hands. "Where do we begin?"

Helen had a ton of questions, and she was tempted to fire them off scattershot. However, her legal training's appreciation for organization kicked in. She said, "Tell me about your parents and your childhood. Zoey says it was a happy one?"

"It was. Mom and Dad had been trying to adopt for years."

Mom and Dad. Mom. Of course, he called the woman who'd

raised him *Mom.* They'd have to come up with a name for him to call her. "Mama," perhaps?

Don't get the cart before the horse, Helen.

"I grew up in Florida," Adam continued. "I played every youth sport imaginable. My dad liked to coach, so..."

He spoke for a full twenty minutes, prodded by questions, and finished with a summary of his current job. Helen still had a million questions, but when he asked her to tell him about herself, Helen realized she wanted him to know her, too.

She reached into her pocket and pulled out Billy's picture. "This is a photo of your father. Billy Poteet was the love of my life. What has Zoey shared about our story?"

He gave his daughter a quick glance. "Nothing. All I know is that a DNA database match led her to you."

Helen shared her story. His expression was easy for her to read—that similarity to his father, most likely—and his shock and the flash of anger he displayed on her behalf proved to be a soothing balm to her soul.

Adam said, "It might help you to know that I had a great life. I was happy and safe and given every opportunity. My parents were great people. I loved them deeply. I did wonder about my birth parents, but I never once felt unwanted or abandoned. In our house, giving a child up for adoption to an infertile couple was just about the greatest gift a mother can give. You were our hero, Helen."

In a shaky voice, she clarified, "You didn't resent me?"

"Absolutely not. I was grateful to you. We talked about it some as a family. We figured you were probably too young to raise a child."

"We were young. And Billy never got the chance to even know you were on the way. But I wanted you, Adam, and I was going to keep you and give you the best life I could manage.

Then my father betrayed me, and here we are." Bitterly, she added, "Fifty lost years."

"Well, we have now, and God willing, many more years ahead of us. That's good, isn't it?"

"Oh, it's very good."

Beyond the tale about his father, she didn't spend too much time on details about her life post-Billy. Frankly, there wasn't much to tell beyond a CV of her work history. At some point during the discussion, she heard Genevieve's phone ring. She stepped outside to answer the call and soon requested that Zoey join her.

That's when Helen decided to take advantage of her granddaughter's absence. "Would you tell me about Zoey's mother?"

Adam sat back in his chair and stretched out his legs. "That's a tough one. Has Zoey mentioned that she recently passed away?"

"She did." Helen summarized what the young woman had shared.

Adam absorbed the information, considered a few moments, then said, "Jennifer worked the early morning shift at a doughnut shop I frequented, and we got friendly. She had an air of sadness about her that I wanted to chase away. When I asked about her family, she said she had no one. She needed me, and well, I needed her, too. I fell for her hard. I believed then—I still believe—that she fell for me, too. So when she got pregnant, we got married, despite the fact that I was still in college. I was lucky in that my parents continued to pay for my education. Things were tight, but we were happy."

He paused for a moment, then added, "We were really happy."

Adam rose from his seat and walked toward the wall of windows. Facing the forest, he said, "I always knew she had secrets, but in the beginning, they didn't seem important. We were living in the now, looking toward the future. Things started to change after Zoey was born."

He fell quiet for a long moment. "Was it postpartum depression?" Helen asked. She had firsthand experience with that condition. For months after Adam's "death," she'd barely functioned.

"No. I don't think so. It was more paranoia than depression. She was scared of everything, and she wouldn't let me help her. It was always there, hovering in the background, but we managed. She had a bad spell when Zoey was three and didn't leave the house for a month."

"That must have been so hard."

"I was in medical school by then. I wanted to heal Jennifer. Lord knows, I tried. But she shut me out. She was hiding from something real or imagined—I never discovered which. It got a little better for a while, but then I came home from school one day and found a note that Zoey was at the neighbor's house. Jennifer had taken off. She stayed gone a few months, then showed back up with little explanation." He turned around and faced Helen. Lines of strain etched into his brow, and his voice sounded tired as he added, "That was the first of a series of disappearances. By the time Zoey was in third grade, I could see how destructive these jaunts of Jennifer's were. They tore Zoey up. Jennifer had no explanation or defense. Well, I'd had enough. I told her if she ever left again, I would divorce her. She did, and I did."

A faraway look came into his face. He added, "I wish I could have healed her—for Zoey, for myself. Whatever she was running from or hiding from, real or imagined, took over her world. It was more important to her than we were."

The need to comfort welled inside Helen. She rose and walked over to her son. "You did what was best for your daughter."

"Was it? I don't know. In hindsight, I think I might have

royally screwed up. The problems she's having with Cooper are connected to her mother."

Helen frowned and glanced toward the door through which Genevieve and Zoey had disappeared. "You don't think it's normal cold feet?"

"Is that what you think it is?" he asked, hope ringing in his tone.

"Honestly, I don't know. We're just hearing and seeing one side of the story, and I'm sure there's lots she hasn't shared. That said, I don't think giving her a big, thick pair of wool socks would hurt anything."

Adam smiled his father's crooked grin. Both he and Helen turned toward the sound of the door opening. Genevieve walked in, all smiles. Zoey appeared a little shell-shocked. Helen asked, "What's up?"

"Willow called," Genevieve said. "She's over at the inn getting ready for tomorrow's wedding, and she got a call from someone looking for a room this weekend."

Helen could read her sister like a book. Glancing at Adam, she said, "We might not need those wool socks after all."

Zoey looked at them and confirmed Helen's suspicions. "Cooper is on his way."

Chapter Thirteen

COOPER HAD TOLD WILLOW he wanted to surprise Zoey with the visit. However, since he was getting in very late and didn't want to disturb her until the following morning, he'd asked if he could get a room in the lodge near hers.

Of course, Cooper hadn't known that Zoey wasn't staying at Reflections Inn or that available rooms in Lake in the Clouds were next to impossible to find at the height of the summer season. Willow had no intention of ruining the surprise, however, so she had told Cooper she'd get back to him once she had his reservation handled. Then she called her mother for advice.

The first thing Genevieve did was spoil the surprise. To her mind, Zoey was over her limit for surprises that month. They all agreed that Zoey and Cooper needed privacy once he arrived. With no room in the inn, they debated different scenarios until Willow called back with a serendipitous solution. "Our weekend guests at the Hideaway canceled. Zoey and Cooper can stay there."

The Hideaway was the house where Noah had lived prior to the construction of the new home he shared with Willow and her children. The land upon which the Hideaway sat had been in his family for generations, so rather than sell it after moving into a larger place, they operated it as a vacation rental. Located a short distance outside of town, the Hideaway sat on a beautiful and isolated piece of property, the perfect place for... what? A breakup? A kiss-and-make-up?

Zoey honestly didn't know which. A trip like this wasn't like Cooper at all.

She had difficulty concentrating during the next few hours when, at Genevieve's suggestion, Zoey and her dad joined the Bennett sisters at Genevieve's house to review family photo albums. Her inattention accelerated after Cooper called Willow back with the news that he'd caught an earlier flight and anticipated an early evening check-in. Finally exasperated at Zoey's inattention, her father had told her to leave. "Go spruce yourself up for your man," he suggested.

Zoey bristled. "Please, Dad. This is a surprise visit. He gets me as I am."

"Of course he does, dear," Helen said, patting her arm. "Nevertheless, the better you look, the better you'll feel. It's just a fact of life."

She'd had a point. Zoey glanced at her dad. "Walk me to the car?"

"Of course."

Outside, she smiled up at him with a question in her eyes. "Are we okay, Dad? Did I make a mistake when—"

"No," he interrupted. "No mistake. We are good. I'm good." His expression held a hint of bemusement as he added, "I like her, Zoey. Today has been nice. I'm glad you made this meeting happen this way."

"Good. I'm so relieved. I've been worried about it ever since I got the e-mail about the match."

"No worries. No worries at all." Adam kissed Zoey on her forehead. "It's all good. I'm happy with this new development in my life. So you quit fretting about me and concentrate on yourself and Cooper. Just give me a call or send me a text tomorrow and let me know how you're doing. Okay?"

"I will. Thanks, Dad."

She returned to the guest apartment, showered, and "spruced herself up." After exchanging a series of e-mails with Willow about the status of supplies at the Hideaway, she stopped at the grocery store and loaded up with items that should meet her needs whichever way Cooper's wind blew. Steaks, potatoes, salad fixings for two, along with a couple of bottles of Cooper's favorite cabernet, and cookies-and-cream ice cream and brownies if she was eating for one.

She spent a bit checking airline schedules and attempting to deduce when he might arrive. The task was complicated by the fact that he could have flown into a handful of different airports. Eventually, she accepted the futility of the effort and decided to go on out to the Hideaway. She could just as easily twiddle her thumbs there as she did here. Cooper would arrive when he arrived.

She plugged the address into her phone and headed out. As she turned off onto the private road leading up to the house, she was glad she'd come. It was a beautiful spot with rockers on a wraparound porch and a breathtaking view of snow-capped mountains. She brought in her suitcase and unpacked her groceries. Then she took Freeway on an exploratory journey that proved to be half hike, half walk. Upon returning to the house, Zoey decided to open a bottle of wine and sit and sip and rock on the porch for a while.

Her phone rang. Cooper. She filled her lungs with air and then blew out a heavy breath. "Hello?"

"Hi, Zoey. How are you?"

"Um... I'm okay."

"Look, I called your dad to talk to him about something and, well, he doesn't lie worth a damn. You know I'm on my way to Lake in the Clouds."

Her mouth went dry, and her heartbeat pounded. "Yes."

"Well, I've had the travel day from hell. I had hoped to arrive in time for us to talk, but I'll be honest, I'm toast. I still have a four-hour drive ahead of me, longer if I stop for dinner. Could I make a breakfast date with you?"

"I'd love that." She checked her watch. He wouldn't arrive until close to nine. "I don't know if Dad told you anything about the accommodations Willow arranged, but it's a beautiful house out away from town. It has a great kitchen, and I was planning on cooking tonight. If I promise not to talk, do you want to have dinner with me? Unwind a bit before you crash?"

"That sounds great, Zoey. More than great. Thank you."

"You're welcome. Drive carefully, Cooper."

"I will. See you in a few hours."

Zoey stared at her phone for a long minute after they hung up. Four hours. She needed something to keep herself occupied, or she'd go crazy. She could track down Dad and Helen and let them occupy her time. No, that didn't feel right.

Cooper said he was having a horrible travel day. Did she really believe that he was making this trip to break up with her in person?

No. No, she didn't. She believed that he was being the grown-up in the room. They were a month out from their wedding day, and they desperately needed to have a heart-to-heart conversation. Circumstances had conspired against them in recent weeks. Cooper was making a gesture. Maybe she should make one in return.

An idea occurred to her. She checked the kitchen cabinets for cookware and bakeware and grinned. "Perfect." Grabbing her keys, she put Freeway into his crate and then headed back to town and the grocery store. The errand took her forty-five minutes. If she worked quickly, her timing should be just about right.

She hadn't made homemade lasagna for Cooper in over a year. Bad on her. It was his favorite comfort food.

Zoey had the lasagna keeping warm in the oven, the salad made, and the table set when she took a glass of wine out to the porch to watch the sunset. It was full-on dark when she spied the headlights headed her way.

For a reason she couldn't define, Zoey's eyes filled with tears. "Dang it," she muttered, rising to hurry inside in search of a tissue. The last thing she wanted were mascara tracks running down her cheeks when he arrived.

By the time she blotted away the mess, her tears had dried, and Cooper had pulled the car to a stop in the circular drive next to hers. Zoey wiped her suddenly sweaty palms on her jeans and stepped out onto the porch to meet Cooper.

The interior lights illuminated his face as he opened the driver's side door of his rental. He looked exhausted, and Zoey immediately felt her concern grow. Could it be that this trip was not about the two of them after all? Was he bringing bad news about his father?

He exited the car and pulled an overnighter from the backseat as she descended the porch steps. They met halfway between the car and the house. Following a moment of hesitation on both sides, they exchanged a quick kiss. "Hi," Zoey said.

"Hey." Zoey could sense the tension inside him as he gazed up at the house, where a warm, welcoming light glowed in the windows. "This looks nice. Is it just the two of us?"

"Yes. This is where Noah lived before he and Willow married. They use it as a vacation rental and had a last-minute cancellation."

"Nice to have a family connection, I guess?" he observed as they started up the steps. "I only met them once before and thought they were nice people, but what do you think of your newfound family? It's a lot for you, but a good thing, I hope?"

"Yes, I think so. They are very nice people. However, the whole thing sort of blows my mind, to be honest."

She led him inside. He took two steps in, then abruptly stopped. "What do I smell? Zoey, is that my mother's lasagna?"

The hope on his face made her smile. "It is."

He dropped his bag, pulled her against him, and repeated his kiss, this time with enthusiasm. When he released her, Zoey took her first calm breath in what felt like weeks. Maybe months. "Everything is ready. Are you starved, or would you like to have a glass of wine first?"

"Dinner, please. I haven't eaten since breakfast, and that was at the hospital with Dad this morning."

"How is Pat doing?"

"Ornery as hell. He's doing fine. We busted him out right after breakfast, and he's settled in at home. He refused to go to a rehab hospital, so I hired a private physical therapist for him. She paid her first visit this afternoon. I talked to my mother on the drive over here, and she said he did great. I'm a little worried about her, though. She's exhausted."

"I'm sure she is." Zoey made a mental note to send some food to the Hillcrest home.

Cooper rubbed the back of his neck and said, "All in all, things are going well."

"That's great news. I'm so glad."

"Me, too." His gaze trailed toward the kitchen and the oven, his hunger apparent.

Zoey chuckled and pointed down the hallway. "The powder room is that way if you want to wash up. I'll get supper on the table."

"Great. Thanks."

When he returned a few minutes later, Zoey nodded toward the open bottle of wine. "I started without you. The glasses are in the cabinet beside the fridge."

While he poured wine for himself, she dished up the lasagna and set plates on the table. Moments later, he took his first bite, closed his eyes, and groaned. "Oh, Zoey. This is the best thing I've ever tasted. Don't tell my mom, but this is even better than hers."

"That's just because you're hungry. I followed her recipe to the letter."

"Well, it's true." He shrugged and took another bite.

Zoey had to admit that the lasagna was pretty darned good. She asked him more about how his mother was doing in the wake of his father's fall and the repercussions from it. He gave her a summary of his actions since leaving their Houston condo to catch a flight to Michigan.

They both made a point to stay away from personal topics. When she broke out the brownies, he gave a halfhearted protest—right before he polished off three of them.

Finally, he pushed away from the table. "I'm done. That was delicious, Zoey. This was really nice of you to do."

"I was happy to do it." She hesitated a moment and said, "I'm glad you're here."

"Me, too."

Despite their seemingly easy conversation, the evening had

an awkwardness to it. They never were like this before. Was this chasm permanent? she wondered. Was it all too much?

Family drama. Career drama. Wedding stress. It's no wonder they were a little crazy. But this was the guy she wanted to spend her life with. She hoped he still felt the same way. That was the bottom line, wasn't it?

He helped her clean up after dinner. Once that was done, they topped off their glasses and went out to the porch. It was dark and chilly and moonless, but the sky was full of stars. Just as they took a seat next to each other in a double rocker, his phone rang. Cooper groaned. "That's Mom. I'd better take it."

"Of course."

He didn't return for almost ten minutes. He looked even more tired than he had before supper. Zoey dreaded asking, "What's happened?"

"Stubborn man won't take his pain meds. I think I made a mistake about setting up private rehab. My mom is going to have her hands full." He paused before saying expressively, "What a day. What a week!"

"Go to bed, Cooper. You're exhausted."

"Yeah. Food gave me a second wind, but I think the carbs are hitting me now. I'm dead on my feet." He raked his fingers through his hair, then met her gaze. "Where do I sleep?"

"The master is downstairs."

"Where are you sleeping?"

"Where should I sleep?"

"With me," he said without hesitation.

Again, relief rolled through her. "Go to sleep, Cooper. I'll be in after a bit."

She sat on the porch and watched the moon rise, enjoying the peace of the night and that in her heart. She didn't yet know why he'd made the trip to Colorado, but she knew enough. A little before ten, she crawled into bed beside a sound-asleep Cooper. Naked.

She awoke to a hazy dawn and his finger painting circles on her stomach. They made slow, sweet, healing love and held each other afterward. Cooper lay on his back with her tucked against him. He twirled a lock of her hair around his finger and said, "I intended to ask you to come with me to Boston."

"Why didn't you?"

"When I was invited to apply to be part of the project, I didn't say anything because you were caught up with your mother, and I honestly didn't expect I'd be selected. By the time it became a sure thing, well, life was tense. It got weird. No matter what I said, it wasn't the right thing. I kept upsetting you, so I thought I'd better just keep my mouth shut. You were going through a lot. You were prickly, and I was walking on eggshells around the house. I didn't know the prescription, Zoey, and I hated that. I decided that having some space before the wedding might be a good thing, so I thought I'd make it easy on you and not ask you."

"Well, that was stupid." *He's such a man.*

"Yes, I figured that out pretty quick when our argument went sideways. But then Dad fell, and we didn't have the chance to talk before I had to leave. You dodged my phone calls, and, well... this whole flower shop thing has me off-kilter. Will you tell me about that?"

Suddenly feeling naked, Zoey sat up. Her suitcase lay open on the cedar chest at the foot of the bed, and she reached for her sleepshirt and pulled it on. Cooper sat up and rested his back against the padded headboard, watching her, the bright white sheet pooled in his lap. He looked tanned and tousled and a little bit worried.

Zoey sat at the end of the bed, finger-combed her hair, and

searched for the right words. "I thought it was burnout at first and that I'd get over it. I thought it was my mother dying and finally finishing my education and being resistant to change. Honestly, now, I don't think that's it. Something has changed, Cooper. *I've* changed. I don't want to work in the ER anymore. Saving babies is supposed to balance the ones that we lose, but it doesn't. We're losing too many. For stupid reasons. And since I can't stop it, I don't want to watch it happen. Maybe that makes me selfish, but there's too much grief. I don't know if selling flowers is the answer, but I'm not strong enough to handle the ER anymore."

He held her gaze for a long moment, then nodded. "It's your call. I will support whatever decision you make. Truly, I will. However, I do have a few thoughts on the subject. May I share them?"

Zoey nodded, and Cooper held out his hand toward her. When she took it, he pulled her in against him. "I hear what you are saying. I've always had so much respect for you and for the work you do. It's something I knew I never could handle. So if you're done with it, like I said, that's your call. I just have to say that in the past eight years, I've heard you talk a lot about diagnosing RSV and meningitis and leukemia. Until you brought it up last week, I never once heard you mention a desire to arrange flowers. Shoot, when I bring you roses, I'm usually the one who cuts the stems and arranges them in a vase."

"You're better than me at it."

"Were we discussing someone other than you, I'd say that proves my point. However, we both know that the only reason why I might be better than you at flower arranging is because you have not yet attempted to learn it. Once you do, you'll be great. Nevertheless, this makes me wonder if the decision to give up medicine and run a flower shop is a bit premature."

"I haven't decided that's what I want for sure," she mumbled.

He laced their fingers and lifted her knuckles to his mouth for a kiss. "Have you considered going into private practice?"

She gave a long sigh. "I have, but that feels like quitting."

He opened his mouth, thought better of it, and shut it again. Zoey couldn't help but laugh. "I know. I know. Flowers. I'm just a mess, Cooper. I don't know who I am."

She felt the sudden tension in him and turned her head to give him a questioning look. "What?"

"I need a shower. Let me get a shower, and then I'd like to go fishing. I flipped through the guest book that was sitting on the bar last night. They have gear for guests. We can catch some trout for breakfast and talk while we fish."

Cooper rolled from the bed and disappeared into the bathroom before Zoey quite knew what had happened. Talk while they fish? You don't talk while you fish if you expect to catch anything. And Cooper knew that!

Cooper had grown up fly-fishing, and he'd taught Zoey the basics of the sport when they first started dating. She loved the outdoors, and she'd enjoyed the hours they'd spent on various creeks and streams around the country on the long weekends and holidays they'd managed to steal during med school. By now, she knew her way around a tackle box. If he planned to talk while he was rocking his waders, their chances of having fresh rainbow trout for breakfast hovered between slim and none.

She'd bring the bagels with her.

Zoey decided she wanted a shower, too, but she wasn't about to join Cooper, so she grabbed a change of clothes from her suitcase and went upstairs to use one of the bathrooms there. She didn't rush, choosing to shampoo and blow-dry her hair. When she returned downstairs twenty minutes later, Cooper was nowhere in sight, but a steaming travel-sized tumbler filled with coffee waited for her on the bar along with a note that read. "I'm outside in the barn."

He smiled sheepishly when she joined him. "Sorry, I ran out on you there."

"It's getting to be a habit of yours."

"My bad." He handed her a fishing pole. "I wanted to ask about your dad, and I felt weird doing it bare-assed naked."

Zoey wasn't certain she bought that, but she felt better after having taken a shower. The coffee was excellent, and the morning was spectacular. Dew sparkled on the petals of wildflowers blooming in colorful swaths in the meadow behind the house. Zoey drew in a breath of mountain-scented air and drank in the beauty of the vista before her. Peace washed through her like a song. Fortified, she asked, "What do you want to know about Dad?"

Cooper pulled on his own backpack over a fishing vest he must have found with the gear. On his head, he wore his own floppy fishing hat that he never traveled without. "You introduced him to Helen yesterday. How did that go?"

"Good. Better than I had hoped, honestly."

He handed her a copy of a small, hand-drawn map before he bent and picked up a tackle box. "I'm glad for you both. Tell me about it as we walk."

As they followed a well-traveled footpath across the meadow toward forest-covered hills, Zoey summarized yesterday's events. She told him about playing basketball with her dad as she stopped to pick a purple wildflower. While describing Helen's expression at her first glimpse of her son, Zoey lifted her gaze to watch what she thought might be a hawk sail across the sky.

"That's a special moment you'll remember the rest of your life," Cooper observed.

"It was." Zoey knew then that she'd remember this moment, too. She was suddenly fiercely glad to be here in Colorado with Cooper.

When they entered the forest, and the sound of rushing water grew louder, he asked a more probing question about recent events. "So, how does it feel to have all this new family, Zoey? A little strange?"

"Yes." Zoey pulled the fishing pole she carried lower and closer to her body after it clipped the branch of a pine tree. "Definitely good. Definitely strange."

"Do you feel a connection to them? A bond?"

"I sense something. Not a bond. More, the possibility of a bond."

Cooper held back a bough of a tree that blocked the path, allowing Zoey to pass. "Like I mentioned yesterday, I really liked them when we met them in January." He paused, then added, "We're going to need a name for this new family of yours. The women I met all have different last names. Do you know what Helen and Genevieve's maiden name was?"

Zoey nodded. "Bennett. Helen mentioned it while going over the photos with Dad."

"How about we call them that? The Bennett family as opposed to the Hillcrests?"

"Works for me," Zoey responded, then offered him a smile when he reached out a hand to steady her after she twisted an ankle on a rock.

"How many Bennetts are there, do you know?"

Okay, whatever he is working up the nerve to say has something to do with my family. This beating around the bush was so unlike Cooper.

And wasn't it weird to think that her family consisted of more than her dad?

"No, I don't know," she responded. "Quite a few, I believe."

"The more the merrier, I guess. It does make me wonder about something. While no one will replace your grandmother—and I'm talking about the woman who raised your dad—I'm wondering if having this family full of Bennetts might help to soothe that ache inside of you that missing your mother has created. What do you think?"

Impatience finally sparked inside her. "I don't know, Cooper. It's too soon for me to know that. Besides, it's not accurate to say I'm missing my mother. She's been gone since I was a girl."

"Nevertheless, her illness and death triggered a need to know inside you. That's why you did the ancestry test."

"What? Have you earned a psychiatry specialty when I wasn't looking? Cooper, what is this all about? What are we doing?"

"Getting ready to catch breakfast, I hope," he replied in a blatant effort to change the subject. "I hear the creek. We must be getting close. When was the last time we went fishing, honey? Not since you moved to Houston for your fellowship."

Zoey was happy to change the subject because talking about her mother left her feeling…achy. "No, we went fishing for red snapper on that colleague of Dad's boat the summer before last."

"True, but saltwater fishing in the gulf and hooking a trout in the mountains are two different experiences." He shot her a grin over his shoulder and teased, "I'm glad you decided to run away to Colorado rather than Port Aransas."

Technically, she had not run away. She'd run to her newly discovered family. However, with the sound of gurgling water in the near distance and the memories of those days of escape during medical school hovering in her mind, she didn't call him on it. Living in California, most of their peers had headed for the beaches on days off. She and Cooper almost always chose the mountains.

She'd fallen in love with him in the mountains. That's one of the reasons why she'd wanted to marry him in the mountains.

They arrived at the creek, and Zoey knew they'd located the correct spot when she spied the wooden bench placed near the bank along a stretch of the creek marked on the Hideaway's fishing map. "This is nice."

"Yeah, it is." Cooper propped his pole up against the bench, set down the tackle box, and then slipped out of his backpack. "The guestbook said there's a storage shed somewhere close that has waders in addition to more supplies. Want to see if you can find it while I tie the flies on our lines?"

"Sure."

Zoey discovered the shed a little farther down the path and up the hill. She found wading boots in Cooper's size, then hesitated over searching for a pair of her own. That bench had sure looked inviting. The morning was pure bliss. Maybe she'd sit and observe today rather than participate.

She carried the waders back to Cooper and shared her plan. "Whatever trips your trigger," he said with a shrug.

A few minutes later, Zoey sat with her legs outstretched on the bench, sipping her coffee and absorbing the scene. Towering fir trees surrounded them and cast dappled shadows upon the surface of the crystalline creek. The fragrance of evergreens and earth combined with a floral hint of summer wildflowers to perfume the crisp mountain air. Where water crashed and frothed against rocks in the stream, mist rose in the air. Sunlight reflected off the mist in a rainbow of color. *It's paradise,* Zoey thought as her gaze strayed toward Cooper.

Dressed in waders, a fishing vest, and a hat, he took to the stream like a boss.

He was beautiful, his movements a symphony of precision and grace as he wielded the supple fly rod with confidence. The flick of his wrist sent the tiny fly on the end of the translucent line sailing. It drifted down like a feather to land softly on the water.

He caught two fish within the first five minutes, one brown trout and a rainbow. "There's breakfast," she called.

Looking up from the stringer, he shot her a grin, and her heart went *pit-a-pat.*

After securing the stringer in the water, Cooper rinsed his hands and shook them dry. He climbed out of the water and walked over to where Zoey sat on the bench. "Care if I sit down?"

She swung her feet to the ground and gestured for him to sit. "Be my guest."

"I have a confession to make."

Oh. Don't say you cheated. Please, don't be a cheater. It was one thing she'd never worried about with Cooper. Had she been wrong?

"I stuck my nose in your family business."

Okay. Whew. Wait, what? "What did you do?"

"I tried to take care of you. After your mother came to Houston, you were a mess, Zoey. For good reason. I wanted to help."

"I repeat. What did you do?"

He exhaled a heavy breath. "Okay. Well, do you remember asking me to deal with all the estate sale matters?"

"Yes."

"I did that. I asked both the estate sale company and the attorney we hired to go through everything with a fine-tooth comb for clues about Jennifer's true identity."

"I remember." Zoey went still. "You said they didn't find anything."

"They didn't. They didn't find any clues about her past. So..." Cooper propped his elbows on his knees, clasped his hands, and leaned forward. He didn't look at Zoey as he said, "That's when I decided to hire an investigator. He went into her apartment before we had it cleaned to put on the market. He lifted her fingerprints from her apartment, and he got a hit."

Zoey covered her mouth with her hands, but she didn't so much as squeak. Her heart was pounding like a piston.

Cooper continued. "It's taken some time to compile a report, but I have it. If you want the information, it's yours. Maybe you don't need to know now that you have the Bennetts in your life. If you want me to deep-six it, it's gone. If you want me to put it on ice until you're ready to learn it, we can do that, too. If you want to read the report right now, well, it's in my backpack. The ball is in your court, honey."

Zoey sat for a long minute, her mind spinning like a twister. Finally, she asked, "You're sure the fingerprints were hers?"

"We're sure."

"Was she horrible?"

Cooper sat up straight, turned his head, and met her gaze. "No. She wasn't horrible at all. Her story was a sad one. Really sad. Some might call her a hero, in fact. Her sister, in particular."

"There really was a Becca?"

"There *is* a Becca."

Laughter that held an edge of hysteria bubbled up inside of Zoey. "A grandmother and an aunt? In the same week?"

"I know. Threw me for a loop, I'm telling you."

Zoey's gaze shifted to his backpack. "So, you've read the report."

"I have. More than once. It's thorough. Forty pages. I can give you the bullet points if you'd like, but knowing you, I figured you'd want to read it yourself. You'll want to absorb it all."

"That's why you came to Lake in the Clouds? To give me this report?"

"That's part of the reason. I was hoping to get laid, too."

"You took care of business first."

"I'm no fool." He risked a grin and added, "Maybe I am a fool. Jury is still out at the moment."

All her life. All her life, she'd wanted family. She'd wanted to know her mother. "Does Dad know?"

"No. This information is for you. What you do with it is up to you."

Cooper had found her mother for her. Zoey blinked back sudden tears and exhaled a heavy sigh. "Well, okay, then. Go catch some more fish, Dr. Mac. Reading makes me hungry."

Chapter Fourteen

GENEVIEVE'S IMAGINATION WAS CAUGHT. Trapped. Snagged like a fishhook in a tree. She could see the home that Gage had just described.

They stood atop a hill above an alpine valley on a section of the Triple T Ranch that was a good distance from the ranch house. Currently, this parcel of land was inaccessible by road. But building a road was no step for a stepper, as the saying goes. Not when the stepper was a rancher who owned half of Colorado.

Okay, that was an exaggeration, but the man owned a lot of property.

And he was thinking about building a new house.

For her.

"You are relentless, Gage Throckmorton," Genevieve told him. She could see the house he described in the spot he'd indicated. She'd change the roofline, she thought. And she wasn't sure about the logs. She'd come to appreciate modern architecture in recent years. But Gage was definitely a log house kind of guy.

Well, maybe it was time for a change.

For both of them.

That's what he was proposing, after all. Well, not that he'd proposed yet. A hunter from way back, he was still laying his traps.

"Relentless has served me well throughout my life." He turned to look at her, his light blue eyes keen. "You like the idea, don't you?"

"I do." In truth, Genevieve loved the idea. No matter the decorative changes he made at his house, it was still another woman's home. Genevieve would never feel truly comfortable there. If, that is, she allowed his relentlessness to win.

Gage wore a satisfied smile as he shoved his hands in his pockets and rolled back on his heels. "I got the idea from Noah, you know. The best thing I ever did was to hire your son-in-law as my mini-me."

Genevieve laughed. "You do know how much he hates it when you call him that."

"Of course. That's why I do it. Anyway, it never would have occurred to me to build a new home for a new start if he and Willow hadn't decided to build a new place despite having a perfectly good one in the Hideaway. I saw firsthand how excited they were while planning the place. Then when we helped them move in after their wedding when they were beginning their new life together as a family, well, it made an impression. The Hideaway was Noah's house. The new place is theirs."

Genevieve nodded. "I'll admit I thought they were crazy when they decided to build. But the Hideaway is a great vacation property, and they're doing well with the rental business." She gave the rancher a sidelong look. "So, if you build a new home, what will you do with the one you're in now? Tell me you're not going to turn the Triple T into a dude ranch."

He snorted a laugh and casually draped an arm around Genevieve's shoulders. She leaned into him as he replied, "Not hardly. I'll keep it as a true headquarters for all my enterprises. We will do a little remodeling. Noah will be able to expand his office. My ranch foreman can move his office into the main house and give his assistants more room in the outbuilding."

"I'm surprised. I thought you might offer it to Lindsay and Frank. Isn't she looking for a place in town?"

"She is, but how can I offer her the house and not Zach or his brother? If you do for one, you have to do for them all. Emily hammered that lesson into my head from the day our number two was born. I have enough trouble with my kids as it is." He gave a rueful smile, then added, "I've had my lawyers divvy up my estate as even-Steven as possible. I'm not messing with that now by giving one of them the ranch house."

"Thoughtful and fair estate planning is one of the best gifts you can give your children," Genevieve said. "My family still has PTSD from my former father-in-law's attempt to control his family from the grave."

"Yeah, I have no interest in that. So, Genevieve, what do you think?"

"It's a beautiful spot for a home."

"Want to meet me for lunch to look at house plans?"

"You're pushing, Gage."

"I know. I'm pretty good at it, don't you think?"

"This is a masterful effort, I'll give you that."

He took both of her hands in his and stared down at her. "I'm giving you the time you asked for, but I'll remind you that we're not getting any younger."

"I know." Genevieve went up on her tiptoes and kissed his cheek. "This is a wonderful idea, Gage. I think you've stumbled on a way to remove a roadblock I didn't realize existed. That said, I'll remind you that I'm still shaky from the bomb that went off in my family in the past couple of days. We have a month until Zoey's wedding. What if I ask for these next four weeks, and we revisit this idea after that?"

Always one to negotiate, Gage studied her with a narrow-eyed gaze. "What if I give you these next four weeks, but in the meantime—just for fun—we start looking at house plans?"

"Just for fun? No commitments?"

"No commitments."

"All right, then," Genevieve said, her heart taking flight. "You do know that HGTV is my favorite television network. I have some definite ideas. If you think you're going to get your way on everything, you've got another think coming."

He tipped his hat. "I look forward to the battle, ma'am."

"Now, you'd better take me back to my car. I have to be at our Christmas market booth when it opens at ten, and I need to be ready. We're expecting a big crowd today."

"Do you need an extra pair of hands? My afternoon is fairly free."

"Thank you, but we're good. We've actually figured out that with this size booth, we only have room for one of us there at a time. Otherwise, customers don't have room to shop. One person can handle transactions quickly enough because technology makes checking a customer out easy. So, I'm taking the first shift and Helen the second. This evening, Nicole is going to cover for us so we can all get together for a family dinner. Noah is cooking steaks. Would you like to join us?"

"At a family dinner?" His eyes gleamed. "Damn right I would."

Half an hour later, Genevieve parked in the lot reserved for market vendors three blocks off the square. She climbed out of her car in the parking lot, grabbed her purse and the tote bag containing their cash box and the tablet they used to process credit cards, and headed for the square. "Oh, what a beautiful morning," she sang as she smiled up at the sun. Today was shaping up to be an extra special day.

A house. He wanted to build her a house.

She would have skipped all the way to the Bennett sisters' booth if she weren't worried that her knees might give out if she tried.

Their predictions of a brisk business held true. Genevieve barely had time to put her purse away before making the first sale of the day. The first hour was constant, the second busy. Only in the third hour was she able to slow down and visit with her customers.

She was glad of that when Zach Throckmorton and his nephew, nicknamed Scamp, stepped into the booth to browse. "Hello, you two. I'm happy to see you. Are you enjoying your visit to our Christmas in July market?"

The boy nodded. "It's great. We came for the food and to buy presents for my family because giving surprise presents is a lot of fun. Have you tried the fried rattlesnake, Mrs. Prentice?"

"I have not."

"It's really good. You should get some. And slather it with the venom sauce. It's spi-i-i-cy."

"Well, I do like spicy food, but I draw the line when it comes to eating reptiles."

"How come?"

"They give me the creeps."

"Huh," the boy said, obviously thinking about it. "Just snakes or all reptiles? Do you not eat alligators, either? There's another booth selling fried alligator. I haven't tried it yet, but Uncle Zach said I can have some if I'm still hungry after we shop a bit."

"I am anti-reptile all the way. Now, I have tried the fresh corn on the cob they sell at the alligator booth. It's delicious."

"Good to know," Zach said, a grin playing on his face.

He pointed toward a plaque hanging on a display. "Look at this, Scamp. I think we should get it for your dad, don't you? His birthday is coming up."

The plaque read: "Remember. What Dad really wants is a nap."

The boy laughed. "Perfect. That's totally my dad! Let's get it." His interest engaged, he soon picked out a paperweight for his grandfather and a sign for his aunt's bookstore. Reading the sign, Zach frowned. "I dunno, Scamp. This might not be Aunt Lindsay's type of thing."

The sign read: "You can pick your nose, but you can't pick your family!"

Scamp protested. "It's perfect for her. Every time I see her, she tells me not to pick my nose."

"Maybe you ought to stop picking your nose," Zach pointed out.

Scamp waved away the suggestion. "I do it just to bug her. It's our thing, Uncle Zach."

"Okay, then. Wrap it up, please, Genevieve."

"Now we gotta get something for you, too, Uncle Zach. I still have money left over from what Dad gave me, don't I?"

"Well, that depends. What's our total so far, Genevieve?"

She told him, and Zach winced. "You have three dollars left in your gift budget, big guy."

When the boy's face fell, Genevieve jumped in to save the day. "We have the perfect thing, and it's part of our buy-two-get-one-free special." She handed him a photo frame tree ornament that read, "World's Craziest Uncle."

Scamp's eyes went wide, and he lit up like a string of Christmas lights. "It *is* perfect. I know just the picture to put in it, too. So this ornament is free?" When Genevieve nodded, he said, "Awesome! I'll take it."

He met his uncle's gaze. "I'll put the picture in and then give it to you. That'll be the surprise. Okay?"

"Works for me."

The boy cupped his hands around his mouth and whispered loudly. "In the picture, he's got his fingers in his ears, and he's sticking out his tongue."

Genevieve winked at him. "I love it."

She put the three different items in three different gift bags, accepted the cash the boy handed over, and gave him his change.

Traffic picked up again after the Throckmorton guys moved on, and Genevieve finally had a chance to restock her shelves about twenty minutes later. She had her back to the booth's entrance when a familiar voice scraped along her nerves. "Excuse me? Genevieve?"

Lindsay. Pasting a smile on her face, she turned around. "Yes. Hello, Lindsay. How are you?"

"Well, I'm a little upset. I've come to return this." She plopped the gift bag on an empty spot on a shelf.

"Um..."

"You sold something vulgar to a child. Totally inappropriate."

Vulgar? Because it refers to boogers without using the b-word? "I'm sorry, is that the gift Scamp bought for you?"

"Nicholas. His name is Nicholas."

"Yes. Okay. Nicholas."

"I know that all the profits from the Christmas market go to support our local women's shelter, so I'm not going to ask for a refund. I just think you need to understand that the Throckmorton family doesn't do crude."

Lindsay whirled around and marched away before Genevieve could even get out a "Bless your heart."

Genevieve had almost an hour before Helen showed up for her shift. She fumed. She brooded. She stewed.

She loaded for bear.

When Helen arrived happy and bubbling about the morning she'd spent showing Adam around town, Genevieve barely listened. "I have an errand I must do now. I'll see you tonight at dinner."

Then, carrying a tote bag filled with her purse, the plaque Scamp had bought for his aunt, and a little something she'd chosen to gift, she marched across the town square toward the bookstore.

She blew in like a Cat 5 hurricane. Standing at the cash wrap in the process of checking out a young mother buying books for her preschooler, Lindsay turned toward the door as the bell jangled. The smile on her face died in an instant. Genevieve ignored her, flipped the Open sign in the window to Closed, and then breezed through the store in search of other customers. She spied only one more, an older man she recognized as a neighbor of Helen's, and told him the store was closed for the next twenty minutes and to please return later.

Genevieve escorted him to the front of the store, where a red-faced Lindsay slipped a copy of *Chicka Chicka Boom Boom* into a bag. Lindsay thanked the customer and wished her a good day. Once the mother exited the store, Genevieve twisted the door's lock hard and turned around.

"How dare you!" Gage's daughter exclaimed.

"Oh, honey, you might as well save all that offense. I'm just getting started."

Lindsay was smart enough to keep the counter between them. Genevieve advanced toward her, set down her tote bag, and folded her arms. "I have been patient. I have been kind. But it appears that I'm going to have to talk to you like I do my own children. I have a few things to say, young lady, and you are going to listen to me. When I'm done talking, you can have your say. I'll stand here and take it. However, I get to go first."

"But—"

Genevieve cut her off with the index-finger-up, circle-in-the-air flourish that ended by pointing at Lindsay and snapping, "No. Hush."

"You can't tell me what to do!"

"Oh, but I can. You don't want to make me stop this car, Little Miss Sunshine."

"What? Stop the car? You're crazy!"

"I'm a mother of four, so I have lots of experience dealing with brats. Now, shut your mouth and listen. The sooner I have my say, the sooner I will leave this store."

Lindsay snapped her mouth shut, folded her arms, and lifted her chin pugnaciously.

Genevieve lobbed her first grenade. "I am not a threat to you. Period. Full stop. I am not after your father's money. I'm blessed to have plenty of my own. *If*—note the word there—*if* your father and I decide to marry, we will absolutely sign a prenup."

"Dad won't do that," Lindsay scoffed.

"Then we won't be getting married. I'm not going to marry him without one. My sister wouldn't allow it. She practiced as an attorney for thirty years, and the things she witnessed will curl your hair. Now, if neither your father nor I had any assets, that might be different. But it's not the case, and a prenup protects us both, so you can drag that particular bee out of your bonnet."

Lindsay's lips pursed like she'd sucked on a lemon.

"Next, I am not trying to take your mother's place in your father's life and heart. I would never do that. I'm a widow myself, and my David will always own a piece of my heart. But that's the thing about hearts. There's always room for more love."

Lindsay began, "You're not—"

"Still my turn," Genevieve interrupted. "Here's the thing, Lindsay. You don't have to like me. What you do have to do is respect your father and the choices he makes. If he chooses to marry me, then you have to figure out a way to make peace with it. Or, at the very least, figure out a way to hide the fact you're still feeling pissy about it. Because you will treat me with respect. I deserve that. Your father deserves it. And from everything Gage has told me about your mother, I suspect that she would expect it."

"You don't know anything about my relationship with my mother!" Lindsay snapped.

"No, I don't. Why don't you tell me?"

"She was there for me when I needed her. Always!" Tears suddenly flooded Lindsay's eyes and overflowed. "I could tell her anything. I told her everything. She listened to me and let me cry on her shoulder, and she always made things better. I could tell her things I couldn't tell Dad. She understood. If Mom were here today, she would understand what we are going through. I could tell her about it. How hard it is. How scared I am."

Scared about what? Genevieve's anger evaporated in an instant. Gentling her voice and her manner, she took a step forward. "What's happening, Lindsay?"

"We can't get pregnant," she said with a sob. "At first, I thought it was the stress from dealing with Mom, but finally we saw a fertility specialist. It hasn't worked."

Now in mother mode, Genevieve stepped around the counter and lifted her arms, offering a hug. After only a moment's hesitation, the young woman melted into her arms.

"We've tried three times. It's just crushing. Now we're stepping up to IVF, but... what if... I don't know if I can keep doing this."

"Oh, sweetheart. I'm so sorry. I know it must be so hard."

"I'm just a mess. The hormones!"

Genevieve clucked her tongue. "Yes, they're a killer."

"They make me want to kill someone."

"You poor thing."

"I just... I need my mom!"

"Oh, Lindsay, I know you do. At times like this, a woman needs her mother so badly. I'm so, so sorry that Emily isn't here to help you navigate these stormy waters. Sometimes, life just sucks."

"It does." Lindsay buried her head against Genevieve's shoulder and wept.

Genevieve held Gage's daughter, patted her back, and murmured soothingly. Eventually, Lindsay's tears eased, and Genevieve could feel her slowly stiffening. Genevieve released her and took a step back. She spied a tissue box on the counter, grabbed one, and handed it to the distraught young woman.

Then she retreated back around the counter. Calmly, she picked up her tote bag and decided to wait for Gage's daughter to break the silence. Eventually, Lindsay said, "I owe you an apology about this morning. I was totally out of line about Nicholas's gift. I talked to Dad this morning, and he told me he's thinking about building a new house, and it set me off. I was looking for a reason to go off on you, and I used the plaque as an excuse."

Genevieve debated how best to respond to that. If Lindsay had stopped after saying she was out of line, Genevieve would have replied with a gracious thank you. Bringing up the house shifted them back into uncomfortable territory.

She reached into the tote bag and pulled out the bag containing Scamp's gift. "I thought you should know why your nephew chose this particular gift for you. He—"

Lindsay interrupted. "I know. He teases me. It's actually a sweet gift. Please don't tell him I was witchy about it. Like I said, it was just an excuse."

The young woman closed her eyes, drew in a deep breath, then exhaled sharply. "I apologize for how I've acted toward you. You're right. My mother would not be happy with me. As much as I'd like to blame it all on hormones, the truth is I don't understand how Dad has been able to move on romantically so fast."

"Fair enough." Genevieve acknowledged the point with a nod. "After my husband died, it took me a long time to be ready to date again. However, in the grief counseling groups I attended, I saw firsthand how people grieve differently and on different schedules. It's natural that you and your dad and your brothers will be on different schedules." She hesitated a moment before asking, "Have you tried discussing your concerns with Gage, Lindsay?"

"Oh yes. He shuts me down. He won't listen to anything I have to say about..."

"Me?"

Lindsay winced. "He gives me that dark scowl of his and tells me to grow up. I had some legitimate worries." She glanced at Genevieve and added, "Like a prenup."

Genevieve nodded. "Perfectly fine question. He shouldn't shut you down. But men can be hardheaded."

"Tell me about it." Lindsay's expression turned glum.

"I will. Come to me with your questions, dear, and I'll listen and answer if I can. We will all be happier if we have openness and honesty between us. Lindsay, your father hasn't mentioned your fertility struggles to me. Does he know you're going through treatment?"

She shook her head. "No. He'd worry about me. He wants more grandchildren, and it's been a dream of mine to surprise him with baby news."

"In that case, I won't spoil the surprise. As I said, I'm here if you need a friendly ear or a shoulder to cry on. And if not me, have you considered counseling, Lindsay?"

A smile flickered on her lips. "Our fertility clinic recommended it. I've been waiting to get in to see someone who has been recommended to me by a friend. My first appointment is next week."

"That's good. Counseling has helped me tremendously at various times in my life." Her lips twisted in a smile as she added, "Now that the subject's come up, it occurs to me that a visit with my therapist wouldn't be a bad idea for me now. I don't know if you've heard, but a volcano exploded in my family this week."

Lindsay's brows arched. "No, I hadn't heard that." A gleam entered her eyes that suddenly reminded Genevieve of Gage. "Maybe you should check out our self-help section before you go."

"Nah, but I'll take a gander at your murder mystery section."

"Your volcano was that explosive?"

Genevieve's mouth twisted. "Well, the person I'd like to kill is already dead, so maybe what I need is something from the fantasy section."

Lindsay actually laughed. "Well, my fantasy section is extensive."

Genevieve decided that she'd made significant forward progress today. It was probably time for a strategic retreat. "I'll stop in again when I have some time to browse. Right now, I'd better get moving. I have a whole list of errands to run before a family event tonight."

She reached into her tote bag and withdrew the four-by-six-inch framed print she'd brought from the booth. "I'm glad we talked, Lindsay. I will keep you and Frank in my thoughts and prayers in the coming weeks. Now, I brought a little gift."

Genevieve handed the print to Lindsay with a smile. "I thought of you and Emily when I saw this."

Lindsay read it and said, "Oh, Genevieve. I'm going to start crying again."

"Happy tears, though, right? You'll feel it whenever you see the sign."

"I will. Thank you so much. I'm glad we talked, too."

Genevieve flipped the Closed sign back to Open, unlocked the door, and turned to wave as she left.

Lindsay had placed her gift in a position of honor on a shelf behind the sales counter.

The sign read: "A mom's hug lasts long after she lets go."

Helen floated through her afternoon shift at the Christmas market on a cloud of happiness. She'd spent the morning with her son, and life simply couldn't be better. She was enjoying the Christmas market, too. Genevieve had been right. As much fun as the sisters had together during the planning, the actual operation of the vendor booth lacked something important. Space. They simply didn't have enough space once the shoppers arrived. Next year they'd need to get a bigger booth.

If I'm here next year.

A little wave of apprehension rolled over Helen at the thought. She was going to have to have a talk with Genevieve about the future, and she wasn't looking forward to it.

Well, she didn't have time to worry about it today. She was in charge of dinner for ten tonight. She was hosting her first family dinner where she had skin in the game—*ha ha!*—and she couldn't wait.

They'd decided to use the Hideaway since it had a fully equipped kitchen, dishes for everyone, and room for everyone to spread out. Helen's condo simply wouldn't do. It had been the perfect home for her when she moved to Lake in the Clouds. Two bedrooms and little upkeep. She'd been alone.

She wasn't alone anymore. She'd need to get a bigger place. Wherever she ended up.

After stopping at the grocery store, she headed up to the Hideaway. Zoey and Cooper weren't there. They'd gone over to Reflections to take a look at the Glass Chapel and discuss their wedding with Willow once her afternoon event ended. Adam had some work to do on his computer this afternoon, so he was holed up in the guest apartment. Helen figured that folks would start showing up between five and six. She planned to serve dinner at seven.

Not a culinary queen like her sister, Helen chose to keep the menu simple. Steaks, salad, baked potatoes. Also, she planned to prepare a cheese board. Helen was a master at building a charcuterie board.

At the Hideaway, she released Freeway from his crate and let him outside to take care of business. He puppy-dog-eyed her into throwing a tennis ball for ten minutes or so, then they retired indoors, and Helen got to work. By the time she heard the first car arrive, she had everything ready. Adam sauntered in and, to her delight, greeted her with a casual kiss on the cheek. "Hi, Mum."

He'd decided to call her "Mum." He'd explained that the mother who raised him had a generous heart, and she would never begrudge his calling Helen "Mom," but Adam believed that two unique women deserved unique names. *Mum* was a perfect solution, to Helen's way of thinking. Her heart still skipped with joy each time she heard the word coming from Adam.

"Did you get the work done that needed doing?" she asked.

"I did. I had a bit of a breakthrough, in fact. That patio is an excellent place to think. Now I'm looking forward to having a relaxing evening."

At Helen's invitation, Adam chose a beer from the fridge and filled a small plate with cheese, meat, and olives. Following a brief debate, they decided to enjoy their snack on the porch and wait for the others to join them.

Zoey and Cooper were the first to arrive. Helen studied them closely as they approached. "They look happy."

"Yes," Adam agreed. "I'm glad to see it. I'll admit I was getting a little worried about them. Although..."

Helen looked at him sharply. "What?"

"Something's on her mind."

"Hmm." Helen invited Zoey and Cooper to grab a drink and a plate and join them. "I made a pitcher of vodka martinis if you'd like a cocktail. Glasses are chilling in the fridge."

Cooper said, "Helen, you are my hero."

The couple rejoined them a few minutes later. Cooper shifted a second pair of porch rockers closer to Adam and Helen so they could easily converse. Helen asked, "So, what did you think of the Glass Chapel?"

"It's glorious," Zoey said. "Willow did an awesome job bringing her vision to life."

"Will you use it for your ceremony?"

Zoey and Cooper shared a look, then Cooper said, "No, I think we're going to stay with the rose-covered arbor."

"I've been dreaming about Dad walking me down the aisle toward it ever since Willow painted the picture for us in January."

Helen accepted the verdict with a nod. "I think you'll be happier with the lakeside ceremony at a summer wedding. The chapel will be wonderful for rainy days and winter, but nothing beats a summer ceremony beside Mirror Lake."

"I'm really excited about it," Zoey said. "I'm also glad that I waited until today to go out to Reflections with Cooper."

Adam said, "Your wedding day will be here before we know it. I'm glad to have the lay of the land myself. It'll be a big day for all of us."

"Have you thought about your dress, Nana?" Zoey asked.

Helen's eyes went wide, and she lifted a hand to cover her mouth. She'd be escorted down the aisle in a position of honor! It would be a first for her. This was a moment! "I haven't thought about it."

"Well, you'd better think about it," Cooper said with a laugh. "My mother has been shopping for months and months. Dad said she's ordered and returned a dozen different dresses."

"The bridesmaids are wearing dusty rose, and the men will be in gray suits. Cooper's mom is wearing navy. If you can find a dress you like that is navy, that would be great, but honestly, wear whatever makes you feel good. I'm not going to fret over color-coordinated photographs. What matters is the people who are in the pictures, not what they're wearing."

"Well, I guess a shopping excursion is now on my calendar. I'll get with Genevieve tonight and decide where we want to go."

Helen launched into a story about shopping with Genevieve for her mother-of-the-groom dress when her son Jake got married. All the while, Adam didn't take his gaze off his daughter. When Helen finally finished her tale, he sipped his beer, then asked, "You're chewing on something, little girl. What is it?"

Zoey and Cooper shared a telling look, then Zoey nodded. "This is why you're such a great researcher, Dad. You notice every little thing."

"No. Not always. But ever since I failed and forgot your school program, I try not to miss things with you. What do have to tell me, sweetheart?"

"I know who Mom really was. I know why she hid her identity."

Adam sucked in an audible breath. "Well, hell."

"Do you want me to share?" Zoey offered him an apologetic smile as she continued. "I know it's something you put behind you, but I never did. I'm sorry if it causes you pain. We considered keeping you out of the loop on this now, but that's a huge secret that I don't want standing between us."

"No, I don't want that, either, but I don't know..." He set down his drink and stood. "Give me a few minutes."

He walked off the porch, and when Freeway rose from his spot in the sunshine and followed him, Adam reached down and scratched his ruff. Helen suggested, "Maybe I should give y'all some privacy."

"No," Zoey said, her gaze on her father. Recognizing an easy mark, Freeway had gone for one of the tennis balls. "He won't mind you hearing the story."

"You think he'll want to know?"

"Oh yes," Zoey said. "I do. He just needs a little time to prepare."

Adam threw the tennis ball for the dog to retrieve ten times before he turned around and walked back toward the house, his manner resolute. Helen's breath caught. "He looks so much like his father."

Adam climbed the steps, smiled at Zoey, and said, "Let's hear it."

"Okay." She moved over to a glider and patted the seat beside her. "Come sit with me, Dad."

Once Adam was seated, she took his hand in hers. "Cooper hired an investigator who collected Jennifer's fingerprints from her apartment, and he traced her from those."

So, she was in a system somewhere, Helen realized.

"Her name was Anne-Marie Olsen. There's a warrant for her arrest in New York for the murder of a forty-five-year-old man named Misha Vasilyeva. He was her stepfather."

Adam closed his eyes. The veins in his arms bulged as he gripped Zoey's hand more tightly.

Zoey continued, "She had a mother and a younger sister."

"The Becca she told you about?"

"Yes, Rebecca Olsen. She was four years younger than Mom.

The investigator found her. She lives in Kentucky now, and she's married and has two children. She told the investigator what happened."

"The stepfather assaulted Jennifer," Adam said, his tone flat. "I always suspected that."

"Yes, he had. For years."

"Oh, that poor girl," Helen murmured.

"Becca said she'd had no idea until the night he came to Becca's room and attempted to rape her. Jennifer—Anne-Marie—stabbed the bastard with a kitchen knife. Repeatedly. Becca was twelve at the time."

Adam muttered an expletive. Helen closed her eyes and shook her head. She said, "I hope there's a special place in hell for men like that."

"Becca said the aftermath was a nightmare. Their mother acted like she didn't believe Anne-Marie, and then she blamed her and said she'd asked for it, that Anne-Marie was a 'husband-stealing slut.' She went into hysterics and said that Vasilyeva's family would kill them all. She gave Anne-Marie what cash she had in the house and told her to get out and never come back. Jennifer ran. She never came back."

"His family?" Helen asked. "Were they in the mafia or something?"

"Becca believes they were connected to that world, yes. She said they were scary men, and they did look for Anne-Marie. For years afterward. Her mother remarried someone else who was 'friends' with her late husband. He wasn't a pedophile, however."

Adam cleared his throat and asked, "Becca never heard anything from her sister?"

"One time. She received an envelope postmarked from New York City with a typewritten address. There was no note. Just a photograph inside. Becca kept it. Took a photo of the photo and gave it to the investigator."

Zoey looked at Cooper. He slipped his wallet from his pocket and removed a photograph, which he handed to Adam. "It's you. Your hospital picture." He glanced up at Zoey. "When did she send this?"

"Spring of 1999. I recognized the photo, but the year throws me off."

"I went to New York for an interview. I took you girls with me." Adam brushed his thumb over the photo. "She didn't want to go, but there was an event for spouses. Not long after that, she took off for the first time."

"Maybe they found her," Zoey said. "Do you think someone found her? Maybe that's why she ran?"

"I don't know." Adam's lips twisted in a wistful smile. "I guess we'll never know." He paused a moment before adding, "I wish she'd told me."

Helen said, "Well, it sounds like you know one thing for sure. She was protective of those she loved."

Adam lifted Zoey's hands to his lips and gave her knuckles a kiss. "That's nice to know. I'm glad to know this truth, honey. Thank you for your effort."

"It wasn't me. It was Cooper." She beamed love toward her fiancé and added, "He's protective of whom he loves, too."

Helen observed, "I guess it runs in the family."

They all shared a smile, and the sound of an approaching vehicle signaled the arrival of more of tonight's guests. Adam glanced around the small circle of people—his mother, his daughter, his soon-to-be son-in-law. "Before I go get another beer and snacks, is there any other big family secret y'all have to reveal to me? If there is, I think I'll switch to martinis."

"No more secrets I know about," Zoey said. "How about you, Nana?"

Helen sipped her martini, and her eyes glittered with amusement. "Oh, I might have a secret or two tucked away, but nothing so exciting as secret babies or newly discovered aunts. Speaking of your aunt Becca, Zoey, shall we invite her to the wedding? You'll want to give her plenty of time to find a dress."

Chapter Fifteen

THE NEXT MONTH PASSED in a flurry of activity. Zoey and Cooper decided that the most efficient way to meet all the new family members was to invite them to the wedding. That grew the numbers and sent their wedding planner scrambling to find rooms for everyone. While the summer season was winding down in the middle of August, Lake in the Clouds was enjoying a strong tourist season.

Genevieve was excited that all four of her children planned to attend their cousin's wedding. The decision had been made to ditch the once-removed thing. Zoey's mother's sister and her family planned to attend. Becca was the mother of three children, so Zoey's family had grown significantly.

After spending a week with Cooper in Boston as he began his research project, Zoey flew to Houston, where she met Helen. They made the short trip down to Galveston, where Helen looked at beach houses in the neighborhood where Adam owned a home.

Zoey had warned her grandmother that if she decided to buy a place near Houston, she needed to prepare for Adam's tendency to get lost in his research and forget things like dinner dates. Helen returned from the trip with the interesting tidbit that Zoey was exploring professional options that would take her out of the hospital emergency room with Cooper's full support.

"She's giving up the flower shop idea?" Genevieve asked her sister when they met for lunch following Helen's return from Texas.

"Yes." Helen passed Genevieve a tablet containing photos she'd taken on her trip. "That was never a serious desire. It was a depository for all her unhappiness. I believe she's coming to the conclusion that she'll be happier joining a pediatric practice and getting to work making babies with Cooper."

"You'll be a great-grandmother!" Genevieve crowed, scrolling to the photo app.

"I am a great grandmother. Just ask Zoey."

The sisters were distracted from their catching-up when Lindsay Higgins walked into Cloudwiches. "Uh-oh," Helen murmured in warning. "Trouble incoming."

Genevieve straightened and braced herself. Then, spying Lindsay, she relaxed. Helen had been away during this month's book club meeting. Genevieve had not yet had the opportunity to share the latest. Lindsay approached their table wearing a scowl that was at odds with the twinkle in her eyes. "Well, Genevieve, I hope you're happy." She pointed to her eyes and added, "These bags are all your fault."

Genevieve chortled gleefully, which obviously shocked her sister. Speaking to Gage's daughter, she said, "I take it you started *Kill Me Once Again*?"

"Started and finished. At ten after three this morning."

"I warned you," Genevieve said with a laugh. She motioned

toward an empty chair at their table. "Would you like to join us?"

"No, thanks. I'm meeting Frank for lunch. I just wanted to stop by and thank you for the recommendation. I'm going to stock that novel in the store from now on." Then she turned an apologetic smile toward Helen. "Hi, Helen. Welcome home. We missed you at book club last week."

"Thank you. I'm glad to be back."

Lindsay spied her husband, waved, and excused herself. Helen arched a questioning brow toward Genevieve, who said, "She and I have had a breakthrough of sorts. It happened during the Christmas market, but with everything else that went down then, I never had the opportunity to share."

"Well, spill the tea now, sister."

"She and I had a heart-to-heart discussion. I can't say too much without betraying Lindsay's confidence. Suffice to say she's going through a very difficult time, and I am totally sympathetic to her troubles."

Helen gave Genevieve a long look. And because the sisters knew each other so well, Helen put two-and-two together. "Hormones? Does she have…oh. She and Frank have been married for some time. Fertility treatments? That can mess with a woman's emotions big time."

Genevieve made a zipping motion over her lips, then reached for the menu, saying, "Dessert. I think I'm going to order dessert today. Want to split a piece of chocolate cake?"

Helen nodded her acceptance of the subject change but refused dessert. "I can't eat chocolate cake. I've got to get my zipper zipped on Saturday. Speaking of Saturday, has Willow figured out where to put all the extra flowers?"

Grinning, Genevieve nodded and signaled to the waiter.

After ordering her cake—with two extra forks because she, too, knew her sister—she addressed the question. It turned out that Zoey's aunt Becca and her husband made their living as floral wholesalers, and they wanted to provide flowers—a whole lot of flowers—in memory of Zoey's mother. "Yes. She's filling the patio with flowers to frame Zoey when she comes out to take Adam's arm to descend the steps."

"That's perfect." Helen clapped her hands together. "It's a metaphor."

This was an idea Genevieve couldn't follow. "How so?"

"It'll be her flower shop. She's leaving the unhappiness behind and marching up the aisle toward her future."

Genevieve rolled her eyes. "Or else it'll be one more beautiful spot to take photographs."

It proved to be exactly that. On Saturday, a radiant Zoey stood at the top of the steps on her father's arm, surrounded by pale pink and white roses. Standing in the front row, Helen reached into the row behind her and grabbed hold of Genevieve's hand. "Oh, Sissy."

It was an old nickname for Genevieve, one she hadn't used in decades. Hearing it brought a lump to Genevieve's throat.

"I can't believe this is happening," Helen murmured. "Can you believe this? My family!"

"I know."

The ceremony went off without a hitch beneath a flower-covered arbor right at sunset, as beautiful a sunset as they'd seen all summer. Afterward, at Helen's request, Genevieve stayed near her sister as they were introduced to dozens of people, mostly from Texas, but also a fair number of family and friends of the groom there from Michigan. Genevieve found Cooper's parents to be delightful. She was so glad for Cooper and his entire family that his father had healed to the extent that he could make the trip.

As the cocktail hour drew to a close, Genevieve found her way to the table reserved for her immediate family. That was when she realized that for this family wedding, for the first time ever, her sister wouldn't be sharing Genevieve's. Helen had her own family table. Genevieve clapped her hand against her heart. "Wow. This is bittersweet."

"What's bittersweet?" asked her son Jake as he came up behind her and slipped his arm around her waist.

Genevieve smiled up at her eldest. "Helen won't be sitting at our table tonight."

"Well, now. I hadn't thought of that." His gaze settled on Helen, who stood with Adam, talking to some guests whom Genevieve didn't know. "How cool is that? We're a two-table family now. And that's before all our babies are born. I have to tell you that the Texas contingent of the family is thrilled to have Zoey, Cooper, and Adam in the neighborhood. And I've never seen Auntie so happy."

"I second that notion," Genevieve's son Lucas agreed as he joined the conversation. "She's shining brighter than a spotlight."

Genevieve's youngest child, her daughter Brooke, said, "Zoey reminds me of Auntie. She's sharp as a tack."

"I still can't get over how much she looks like Willow," Lucas observed. Then, sensing his sister's approach, he added, "Of course, Zoey's a lot prettier than Willow."

"You're a jerk, bro," Willow said, unfazed by the teasing. "So, how do you all think everything's going?"

"Perfect," Genevieve said with confidence. "It's the prettiest wedding we've done, for sure."

Willow nodded. "I think so, too. The food is delicious. They are getting ready to serve it now."

"Good, because I'm starving." Lucas chose a seat and sat down.

Willow looked at her mother. "Where are our dates? I get twenty minutes to sit down and enjoy the meal with our family."

"Well, cocktail hour got a little boring for Drew and Emma," Genevieve replied. "Gage proposed a rock-skipping contest on the lake before dinner. They tapped Noah to be the referee. I'll go tell them it's time to eat."

"Thanks, Mom." Willow noticed Cooper's mother waving to her, so she hurried off to help.

Genevieve made her way to the lake, where she rounded up her peeps and herded them back to the dinner tables. As usual, during a Prentice family meal, the conversation was chaotic and fun. It didn't escape Genevieve's notice that Gage fit right in. In fact, her children all acted like he belonged there.

He does belong here, whispered her heart. Genevieve didn't hear the usual arguments rising up against the idea.

The evening progressed with the traditional speeches, toasts, and dances. Helen and Genevieve held hands as they watched Adam and Zoey waltz to Stevie Wonder's "Isn't She Lovely." Helen said, "My heart is so full right now."

"I know, hon. He's such a handsome man, your Adam. It's a shame he's never remarried."

"I know. I've been thinking about that. Maybe we should put finding Adam a bride on our project list."

Genevieve laughed, not certain if her sister was being serious or not. She was saved from responding when the father-daughter dance ended, and applause erupted. The bride and her father walked over to stand beside Helen and Genevieve while

Cooper danced with his mother. Genevieve took the opportunity to give Zoey a hug. "That was a beautiful moment. It was our family's lucky day when Celeste Blessing recommended our lodge for your wedding venue."

"I couldn't agree more," Zoey replied. "I like to think we'd have found each other eventually, but this made it happen faster."

"Yes. Time is too precious to waste."

The mother-son dance ended, and while the crowd applauded, Adam winked at Zoey, and she joined Cooper on the dance floor and motioned for the DJ to hand over the microphone. She said, "Cooper and I want to again thank you all for joining us on this special night. Right now, we'd like to do something a little different. Most of you who have joined us tonight know about the miracle our family experienced this summer. For those of you who don't know, the CliffsNotes version is that my father found his birth mother, and it's been a joyous event in our family. To mark the occasion, Cooper and I want to have a second mother-son dance at our wedding. Dad?"

Adam smiled tenderly at Helen and held out a hand to her. "Mum?"

"Oh," Genevieve said, the moment bringing shivers to her skin. Then, when the first bars of Simon & Garfunkel's "Bridge Over Troubled Water" sounded—Helen's favorite song in the world—Genevieve steepled her hands over her mouth and repeated, "Oh. Oh, Helen."

Tears poured down her cheeks as she watched her sister have what had to be one of the top moments of her life.

In the middle of the song, she felt a hand on the small of her back. She glanced away from the dance floor long enough to smile up at Gage. "Did you know about this?"

"Nope. She sure looks happy, though, doesn't she?"

"I'm surprised her feet aren't a foot above the dance floor. What a beautiful moment for Helen."

When the song ended, mother and son embraced each other, and then the bride and groom. Glancing around, Genevieve saw that hers weren't the only cheeks sporting tear tracks.

The DJ kicked off the dance party with an upbeat tune as Adam escorted Helen off the dance floor. Genevieve met her, and the sisters embraced. "Did you see that?" Helen asked. "Can you believe that?"

"It was wonderful."

"I'm never complaining about your going to see Simon and Garfunkel in concert without me ever again. This was a million times better than any concert."

"I totally agree!" Genevieve hugged her sister hard and added, "And, hey, no more complaints? Win-win for me."

At that point, Helen was swarmed with well-wishers, and Gage whisked Genevieve out onto the dance floor. For the next hour, she danced until her feet hurt. She was standing off to one side, sipping on a glass of water that Jake had brought her after they'd danced to a Frank Sinatra tune, watching Gage dance with six-year-old Emma. Once again, she found herself blinking back tears.

Gage Throckmorton was a wonderful man. He had a huge heart and a strong, constant, steadfast spirit. His word was gold.

His love was real.

Genevieve knew she could count on Gage Throckmorton. She could trust him.

His love was real.

He must have felt her gaze. At that moment, he looked up from her granddaughter's face and met her stare. With a twinkle in his eyes, he gave her a wink.

His love was real...and so was hers. Genevieve caught her breath and, for the first time, admitted to the emotion swelling in her heart. *Love. It's love.*

She'd fallen in love with Gage.

With the realization, inevitably, fear fluttered through her.

Been there, done this, it hadn't ended well.

Oh my. What was she going to do?

The dance ended, and Gage escorted a beaming Emma back to her mother and Noah, then returned to his date. As he arrived, the DJ cued up Frank Sinatra's "All My Tomorrows."

"Aah, he's playing our song," Gage said. "Dance with me?"

Genevieve's smile was just a little shaky as she beamed up at him and let him lead her onto the dance floor. His arm came around her, and he held her close. When he spoke against her ear, the deep timbre of his voice sent shivers running up her spine.

"Really nice wedding, Genevieve."

"I know. Willow did an awesome job."

"This is my third, you know."

"Third what?" Genevieve asked, despite knowing the answer.

"Prentice family wedding. Jake's, Willow's, and now Zoey's. They come along like clockwork, don't they?"

"Hmm," Genevieve responded. She closed her eyes and rested her head on his broad shoulder.

"Wonder who will be next?" He nuzzled her ear.

"Lucas brought a date," she suggested. The desire to tease him surprisingly overcame her fear of the subject under discussion.

He chuckled softly. "That woman is firmly in the friend zone."

Genevieve lifted her head and glanced up at him. "Seriously? How do you know?"

"She told me while you were dancing with Lucas."

Genevieve sighed. "That boy."

"Yeah, I've got a couple of those, too. We have to let them live their own lives, Genevieve. Just like we have to live ours. I'm putting a capital letter on that *L*, by the way."

A capital *L*. She returned her head to his shoulder and spoke softly, "I hear you, Gage."

He heard her, too. He pressed a kiss against her head and asked, "Do you? Do you really?"

She waited the entire length of a chorus to respond. While they danced, a million memories fluttered through her mind. Life. So many ups and downs. So many twists and turns. Her heart pounded as she lifted her head and gazed up into his intense stare. "I have to make a trip to Texas."

"Come again?"

"There's something I need to do before I can change my lowercase *l* to a capital. That said, I have two things I need to say to you."

Interest lit his eyes. "Let's hear 'em."

She stepped back out of his arms, took hold of his hand, and tugged him off the dance floor. She wanted privacy for this. "Come with me."

Being part-owner of Reflections Inn at Mirror Lake meant she knew all the nooks and crannies available even when the inn was bursting at its seams with guests. Of course, there were dozens of outdoor places she could take him, but she wanted to see his face, and moonlight wasn't enough.

A few minutes later, she pushed open a door to a small outbuilding. The lights automatically flickered on. "The laundry? You brought me to the laundry?"

"The fragrance of dryer lint and fabric softener do it for me. Besides, I've spent a good chunk of my life in laundry rooms.

It's real life, and that's a good reminder where you're concerned. Because you, Gage Throckmorton, are in many ways a fantasy."

His lips twitched. "I am, huh? Do you mean like Gandalf? Dumbledore? Bilbo Baggins?"

Genevieve giggled like a schoolgirl. "Feeling literary tonight, are you, cowboy? Alas, you're not right off the pages of books. I've said since the first day I saw you that you stepped right out of the television screen. You're *Yellowstone*'s John Dutton—without all the wickedness."

"Hey, I'm a little wicked. You just haven't seen that part of me yet because we're not sleeping together."

Coquettishly, Genevieve said, "I'll look forward to it."

He arched a brow and slid his arms around her waist. "What are telling me, Genevieve?"

She reached up and stroked her fingers through his thick, silver hair at his temples. "I'm telling you that I love you. It frightens me more than a little bit, but I've gone and done it. I've fallen in love with you."

"About damned time." He brought his mouth down to hers and kissed her like a man who'd won a hard-fought victory. It was sweet. It was steamy. It was perfect. When he ended the kiss and lifted his head, he asked, "So, are you gonna marry me?"

Genevieve tilted her head. "I'm going to assume that's a question and not a proposal. My answer to your question brings us to the second thing I need to say to you. I need to take that quick trip with my sister that I mentioned earlier, but when I get back, I'll be ready to be romanced."

"Romance, huh?"

"Yep. Just because it's our second time around doesn't mean we shouldn't have romance."

Gage nodded thoughtfully. "I can do romance."

"I'm counting on it."

Before Genevieve could say more, a booming sound distracted her. "The fireworks have begun. We'd better get back, or we might miss the send-off."

She turned and started for the laundry room door, but Gage snagged her hand and pulled her back into his arms. "Honey, you just told me you loved me. I've got your fireworks right here."

Gage's mouth captured Genevieve's once again.

Standing in front of one of the double sinks in Genevieve's en suite bathroom a little after midnight, Helen rubbed night cream onto her face. Her gaze met that of her sister's in the mirror. Genevieve was cleaning her face with a makeup remover wipe. "Look at my feet, would you, Genevieve? Are they touching the ground yet?"

Genevieve glanced down. "I dunno. I might see about six inches of distance between you and the tile."

"Hmm. I'm thinking it's more like a foot."

Tonight, having divvied up available beds like musical chairs for family, both new and old, the sisters were sharing a bathroom and Genevieve's king-sized bed, chatting about the wedding while they got ready to go to sleep. Helen noted the glow about her sister. Under other circumstances, she probably would have asked about it. Tonight, however, she was wrapped up in herself.

So she didn't ask. Instead, she crawled into bed and plumped up her feather pillows. Genevieve asked, "I usually sleep with the windows open in the summertime. That work for you?"

"Absolutely. I do the same thing. It reminds me of home. Only cooler and comfortable." Helen stretched to turn off the bedside light. "Good night, Genevieve."

"Good night." Genevieve switched off her light. "It was a good night, wasn't it?"

"The best."

Helen closed her eyes and began reliving snapshots of the evening. In her mind's eye, she pictured Zoey gazing up into Cooper's face as she repeated her wedding vows.

From out of the darkness, Genevieve said, "You've reminded me of home. I'll never forget those summer nights when we'd lie in bed sweating like dogs because the folks wouldn't turn on the air conditioner yet. We felt like having a party when May fifteenth rolled around, and they allowed the switch to be flipped."

Helen said, "I'm old enough to remember when they rolled back the start date from June first to the middle of May. I think the boys were threatening to fill up a plastic swimming pool with ice and put it in the living room."

"You know, Dad was a successful attorney," Genevieve pointed out. "He didn't have to be so tightfisted."

"Dad was a child of the Depression. It's how he rolled."

Genevieve allowed silence to settle for a minute before she began again. "Home was never the same after you left. A light went out of the house. Life went out of the house."

"It didn't have to be that way," Helen replied, a touch of bitterness in her tone.

"No, it didn't." Genevieve recalled the pall that had hung over the family home in the months and first few years after Helen had gone to live with their aunt and uncle. She'd missed her sister so much.

But life had gone on. She'd grown up. Fell in love. Got

married, had children, and was widowed. Raised her kids. Lived her life. And Helen's life had gone on. She'd aced college and law school and established an extremely successful legal career. There had been failed marriages and tragic miscarriages, but Helen claimed to have had a happy life.

And now, tonight...tonight, her life had been perfect.

Genevieve turned her head toward her sister and asked, "Do you think you can ever forgive him?"

"Dad?"

"Yes."

The silence dragged on so long that Genevieve began to think that Helen wouldn't respond. Finally, though, she let out a long sigh. "I don't want to forgive him. What he did was absolutely, positively horrible. And yet...oh, Genevieve. Look at how William's turned out. My Adam William."

"I know."

"It was a perfect night."

"It was that." Genevieve smiled into the darkness and said, "I told Gage that I love him."

"Well, it's about damned time. So, when's the wedding? Not too long, I hope. We're not getting any younger."

"He hasn't officially proposed. I told him tonight I have something I need to do first. I'm hoping you will go with me."

Helen sat up in bed and switched on the light. "Go with you where? I hope you're not going to say one last sisters' trip, because I'm making a rule right here and now. I don't care whether you are married and I'm living in Texas or not. We are still taking our sisters' trips together. That's nonnegotiable."

"You're moving to Texas? I knew you would."

"You did? You're not upset?"

Genevieve shrugged. "Well, I'm a little sad, but that's selfish of me, so I'm trying not to be upset."

"I'm only going for six months out of the year," Helen explained. "I'm going to resign from the mayor's office next month. Nicole is ready to step up and do the job until the next election. I bought a beach house."

"Really!" Genevieve gazed at her with delight. "In Galveston near Adam's?"

"Yes."

"That's great. You've always loved the beach. Maybe we can go on down, and you can show it to me after I complete my task."

"What task?" Helen demanded. "And again, where are we going?"

"Home." Genevieve's throat closed up with emotion. "I have to go home and visit David's grave. I have to get his blessing."

"Oh, Genevieve." Helen chided her with a look. "Of course you have David's blessing. He loved you. He would never have wanted you to be alone this long."

"Nevertheless, it's something I have to do. Will you go with me, please, Helen?"

"Of course I'll go." Helen patted her hand. "When are we leaving?"

"All my crowd will be gone by Tuesday. Adam and the newlyweds, too. Right?"

"Right."

"So, how about we leave Wednesday morning?"

"Works for me. I'll make arrangements at the office. Now, will you finally be quiet and let me get some sleep? I'm crashing." Helen switched off the light and rolled over, placing her back toward Genevieve.

With a smile on her face, Genevieve closed her eyes. Harkening back to a popular TV drama of the '70s and how she and her sister used to say good night when they shared a bedroom, she said, "Good night, John-Boy."

"Good night, Elizabeth."

Then Genevieve started to giggle. "Did you know there's a nightclub in Florida and a restaurant in Chicago named Good Night John Boy?"

Helen hit her with a pillow.

Chapter Sixteen

THE BENNETT SISTERS MADE the decision in Amarillo to take the route that offered more drive time on the interstate than on back roads. They put in a very long day behind the wheel and spent the night in a motel on the outskirts of their hometown of Wichita Falls. They awoke early the following morning, and as they ate yogurt and granola in the breakfast room, Genevieve eyed her sister over a steaming cup of coffee. "Shall we drive past the house?"

"It's been a long time," Helen replied. The last time she'd visited had been when they'd buried their mother eighteen years ago. "Why not?"

Thus began an extended trip down memory lane. They exited off the highway and drove past the church they had attended every Sunday and the restaurant across the street where, on extra special Sundays, they ate out.

After that, they drove through town and past the schools they'd attended. Then they made their way to the neighborhood where they'd grown up. The house looked good. The current owners had made improvements that both Genevieve and Helen liked. When they drove around to the neighborhood pool, Helen asked Genevieve to park, and they went inside. A teenage lifeguard met them at the front desk, and Helen explained they were former members looking around for nostalgia's sake. He allowed them in, and they walked out of the office and onto the property grounds.

It was a hot summer day, and the Olympic-sized pool was filled with swimmers, mostly under the age of twenty. Genevieve's gaze went immediately to the deep end, and she gasped. "They took down the high dive!"

Helen the attorney said, "Safety liability issues, I'm sure."

"That's so sad." Genevieve's gaze swept around. "Not much else has changed. They still have the baby pool. The teen hut sign is gone."

A bittersweet smile spread across Helen's face. "This is where I fell in love. That summer was a magical time for me."

"I can't believe I didn't notice what was happening with you."

"You were a child, Genevieve. You were too busy catching tadpoles in the flower beds and hunting lost change to buy a candy bar at the concession stand to pay attention to me."

"Remember that time I found the five-dollar bill?" Genevieve grinned at the memory. "That kept me in Paydays for a month."

Helen shook her head. "I don't recall that. I don't recall many details, to be honest. I think the subsequent developments overshadowed the summer." She sighed and added, "I was so young. Too young." Her gaze drifted toward the baby pool where a group of adults, mostly in their thirties, watched over toddlers and young children. "Way too young to be a mother."

Genevieve took hold of her sister's hand and gave it a comforting squeeze.

"Okay." Helen straightened and spoke with purpose. "How about a candy bar, for old time's sake? My treat."

"Heck yeah," Genevieve agreed.

"A Payday?"

Genevieve pursed her lips. "Nope. Think I have to go with a Big Hunk under the circumstances."

"Oh, those were awful. Do they even still make them?"

"I'll guess we will find out."

The candy bars remained in production, and the concession stand still stocked them. The sisters retreated to their car carrying candy bars and Cokes. They sat inside with the engine and air conditioner running while they enjoyed their snacks. When they were done, Genevieve asked, "Where to next?"

Helen filled her lungs with air, then exhaled in a rush. "We've come to Texas to visit a cemetery. Guess we could make it a two-fer."

"You want to visit Billy's grave?" Genevieve asked with sympathy in her voice.

"I think I do. I think I should." Helen waited until they'd exited the swimming pool's parking lot to add, "Let's put some flowers on Mom's grave while we're there."

Genevieve nodded. "You read my mind."

They drove to the cemetery and stopped at the flower shop at the entrance. Each woman bought two bouquets. Genevieve said, "I know where Mom is buried. Do we need to look up Billy's location?"

"I remember it," said Helen. The number was burned into her memory.

Genevieve drove to the section Helen indicated and parked the car. She asked, "Do you want me with you, or do you prefer to do this alone?"

"Come with." Helen led her sister toward the grave, marked only with a simple plaque that stated Billy's name and the dates of his birth and death. As a rule, Helen didn't "do" cemeteries.

She didn't need to visit a plot in the ground to remember those whom she had lost. In fact, this was the first time she'd visited Billy's grave since the day he was buried.

She'd only visited Will's grave once.

"I wonder if it's empty," she mused aloud.

Genevieve obviously knew exactly what she meant. "Probably so, unless Dad buried something that symbolized his integrity."

Helen snorted at that, then went silent as she spent some time reliving memories of that magical year when she'd been Billy Poteet's girl. When she was done, she dipped down and placed the flowers beneath his headstone. She kissed two fingers, then brushed them across his name. *Rest in peace, my love. You'd be very proud of our son.*

Rising, she smiled and turned to Genevieve. She had a lightness of heart she hadn't felt in years. "I'm done. Which way to Mom?"

"It's about a five-minute walk. You up for that, or should we drive?"

Helen glanced up at the afternoon sun. "It's August in Texas."

"We'll drive." A few minutes later, they approached their mother's resting place. Helen asked, "When you still lived in Texas, did you visit here very often?"

"I always tried to visit on their birthdays."

Their. It was a fact that Helen had been shying away from—her mother had been laid to rest next to their father.

Helen kept her gaze on her mother's marker as she said a brief, silent prayer while Genevieve placed one of the bouquets she held beneath Mom's headstone. Genevieve, it turned out, was a talker. She said, "You missed a heck of a wedding last week, Mom." Then she spent a good five minutes catching their mother up on family events.

Helen decided to roll with it, and she placed her own bouquet and chimed in a couple of times.

Finally, Genevieve was done, and she moved on to their dad's grave. She glanced at Helen, then frowned down at Edward Bennett's grave marker. "Okay, Dad. I don't see any sense in berating you over what you did to Helen. You've already had to stand in judgment before your Maker. But, dang it, you had a lot of nerve. It wasn't right."

Genevieve placed the second bouquet and then spoke to her sister. "I'm done here. You ready to head to New Braunfels?"

Helen read the marker. *Edward J. Bennett. Born January 23, 1918. Died July 19, 1989.*

She reached down and tugged a white rose from the ribbon-wrapped bouquet her sister had placed on their father's grave. Holding it by its stem, she twirled it in her fingers. Had she been Genevieve, she might have started talking and not finished before Halloween.

However, she was Helen Bennett McDaniel, innkeeper, attorney, and mother.

She laid the rose on her father's grave and said the only thing that mattered. "I forgive you."

New Braunfels, Texas

They made good time on the final leg of their journey. Arriving in the late afternoon, they checked into the vacation property overlooking the beautiful spring-fed Comal River that they had rented. Following the long day of travel with an emotional pit stop, Helen fixed a drink and took a seat on the deck to watch an unending stream of people floating the river in inner tubes—a popular activity for visitors from all over the state. Genevieve refreshed her makeup, then told her sister she'd be back in time for a late supper, and she departed.

Genevieve had wanted her sister to accompany her on this excursion to Texas, but she needed to do this last part alone. It took her twenty minutes to drive to a cemetery a bit outside of town along the Guadalupe River.

This time, Genevieve didn't take flowers with her. She took the quilt she'd brought from home, the same quilt she'd kept when she'd rid herself of most of her belongings before moving to Colorado. It was the same quilt she'd been bringing to the cemetery since her first visit following David's burial.

Today had already been an emotional day, and she teared up a little as she walked the familiar path. Upon reaching her husband's grave, she was surprised to see fresh flowers in the receptacle. But then she recalled that Lucas would have driven past here on his way home from Colorado. Her younger son visited his father's grave often, even after all these years. He'd told her once that walking beneath these towering oak and pecan trees where his dad had been laid to rest was better therapy than any visit to a shrink.

Genevieve spread out her quilt next to David's grave and sat down. "Hey, babe," she said softly. "It's been a while, I know. Let me tell you what's been happening since last I visited."

She started with the children, eldest to youngest, and gave an update on each of their lives. Then she shared the big bomb that had been Adam's existence and ended with Zoey's wedding.

At that point, she'd reached the part of her story that had brought her here today.

She wrapped her arms around her legs and began to speak. "Now I need to tell you about Gage. Oh, David. I've been such a fool. I knew I still had a heart. I loved the kids, loved my sister and mom. My brothers. But I believed I could never love another man as much as I loved you. I thought it couldn't happen. You'll recall—because I came and told you—that a few years after you died, for a few years, I tried. I dated some nice men, but I couldn't fall in love. And frankly, I was okay with that. I've lived a happy life. Not full, but happy enough. I've been content. That's more than a lot of people can say."

Genevieve absently picked at a loose thread on the quilt.

"All this time, David, I thought that part of me had died with you. Well, it turns out I was wrong. I just hadn't met the right man.

"You'd like Gage, David. He's a man's man, loving and protective. He's a widow, too. He understands grief, and he's taught me that the heart is big enough to hold two great loves. That's what I have now. Two great loves. One doesn't diminish the other. I have a great big heart that loves two phenomenal men."

She lay back on the quilt and pillowed her head in her hands with her elbows outstretched. She stared up at the summer blue sky where puffy white clouds shielded the worst of the hot August sun. "I'm going to marry him, David. I hope you're happy for me."

A single tear leaked from her eye and trailed slowly down her cheek. "I know you're happy for me."

And Genevieve did know that in her heart.

She spoke no more but lay there beside her David's grave as she had so many times before. Peace surrounded her, warm and comforting like a hug. Finally, her heart lightened, and she sat up and climbed to her feet. She picked up the quilt, gave it a snap, then folded it quickly and efficiently.

She pressed a kiss to her fingertips, then bent and touched her husband's name. "This is not good-bye. I'll never say good-bye. Until next time, rest easy, my love. We are doing well. I am doing well."

Genevieve turned and walked back to where she'd left her car, feeling a little like the Grinch at the end of the book—her heart had grown three sizes. So many emotions for it to hold—love, sadness, joy, excitement, regret, anticipation—and more for which she didn't have words.

Although, on second thought, couldn't they all be summed up in one word?

Life.

"That's pretty profound, Genevieve," she said to herself. "You'll have to share it with Helen."

And then, as if she'd conjured her up, Genevieve saw her sister leaning against the car, her arms folded, a pleasant smile on her face. "What are you doing here?"

"I Ubered over. I wanted to be here when you were done."

That's nice. It's so Helen. "You thought I'd be an emotional mess?"

"Nope. The river is rowdy with all the tubers. I wanted some peace and quiet, and I knew this stretch of the Guadalupe was lovely. I've got everything ready for us."

She pointed toward the riverbank, where a pair of lawn chairs, a cooler, and two yellow rubber tubes sat beneath the spreading branches of a huge pecan tree. Genevieve's chin gaped. "What crazy idea have you cooked up now, Helen?"

"Those are rocking chairs. See the pistons on the back legs? They're awesome. Come sit down, Genevieve. There's a bit of a breeze coming off the river. I brought alcohol."

"And the tubes? I'm not floating the river, Helen."

"No, that would be silly. We'd have to walk back to the car."

It was only when they approached the chairs and tubes that

Genevieve spied the ropes tied around the tubes. She shot her sister an incredulous look. Helen shrugged and said, "Have a seat, sis. I brought Bloody Marys."

Genevieve plopped herself down. She had to admit that her sister had chosen a great spot. Sunset was beginning to paint the sky in a palette of purples and pinks. Somewhere along the river, a bullfrog began to croak. In the trees, cicadas buzzed.

Helen handed her a red Solo cup filled with their favorite adult beverage. Genevieve gave the celery stick a stir and tasted it. "Yum. That is delicious. Thank you, Helen."

"You are welcome, dear."

They sat side by side in their rocking lawn chairs, sipping their drinks and gazing out across the river at the sunset. They didn't speak for the longest time until finally Helen asked, "Did you find what you came for?"

Genevieve gave a satisfied smile. "I did."

"Good."

They rocked for a few more minutes. Genevieve said, "Thanks for coming with me."

"Of course. Turned out to be a trip I needed, too. I'm glad we made the stop in Wichita Falls."

"I am, too. You seem... at peace."

Helen nodded. "I am. I've been filled to the brim with happiness these past weeks, but underneath it all simmered a rage. I think I've come to terms with it. The past, with all of its regrets, is in my rearview mirror. I'm driving toward the light, baby."

"Wait a minute. That sounds a little too spiritual. We are sitting in a graveyard, remember."

"We are. And I'll admit to some symbolism there. Allow me to point out that our backs are facing the graves, and we're looking toward..."

"Sunset."

"Speak for yourself, Ms. Maudlin. I'm looking toward the future."

"Hey, all I'm saying is that in this particular setting, moving toward the light makes me think of endings, and right now, you and I are all about new beginnings."

Helen smiled at that. "You have a point. Definitely new beginnings and second chances. I have a second bite at the Mom apple, and you have a second bite at being a wife."

Genevieve snorted. "What are we, a couple of horses?"

"Apparently, one of us is the grammar police."

"You're misusing the word *grammar.* It's not—"

"Genevieve!"

She laughed, threw her arm around her sister's shoulder, and gave her a hug. "I love you, Helen."

"I love you, too, Genevieve."

"I'm going to miss you when you're in Texas."

"No, you won't. You won't have time. You'll be busy having all of that newlywed sex."

Genevieve stirred her drink. "Yeah, you're probably right."

Helen elbowed her in the ribs. "Witch."

They sat in silence as the colors in the sky turned brilliant. As often happened at the end of the day, the wind stilled, and the August evening grew stifling. Genevieve eyed the tubes. "It's awfully hot."

"You ready to take a dip?"

"Did you bring swimsuits?" When Helen simply looked at her and rolled her eyes, Genevieve said, "I'm not skinny-dipping, and neither are you. Nobody needs to see that."

"There's nobody here."

Genevieve jerked her thumb over her shoulder. "I believe in the afterlife."

"Oh, for heaven's sake." Helen flipped open the cooler and removed the libation-filled thermos. She topped off their Solo cups, rose, and said, "Live a little."

Live, with a capital L. Genevieve's teeth nibbled at her lower lip. "I haven't skinny-dipped since I was seventeen."

"See? There you go. Second chances, baby!" Helen set down her cup and reached for the hem of her shirt.

"Can't we wait until it's a little bit darker?" Genevieve asked as her sister's top came off.

Helen was wearing a sports bra. Genevieve had to admit that was more swimsuit than what many women floating the river past their vacation rental had been wearing. Helen reached into her tote bag and pulled out a pair of towels. She tossed one to her sister. "The tubes will hide everything important."

Helen slid out of her shorts and stacked them on top of her shirt. She picked up the tube and hooked it and her towel over her left shoulder. With her right hand, she grabbed her Bloody Mary and then started down the riverbank, saying, "See this cottonwood? We're going to tie our ropes around it so we don't drift away."

Genevieve turned and cast a wary gaze around the cemetery. "They close the cemetery at dark. There's bound to be a security check."

"Would you stop it? If worse comes to worst, we can call Lucas. He'll bail us out."

"That's all I need," Genevieve grumbled.

The inner tube splashed. Helen climbed aboard. Genevieve was relieved to see that her sister had kept her bra and panties on.

"Come on in, dear. The water is so perfect."

"Live, with a capital *L*," Genevieve murmured. Laughing, she stripped down to her underwear and gathered her supplies. Then, just like she'd been doing all of her life, Genevieve followed her sister.

This time, she followed her into trouble.

If only Genevieve had left the thermos up the riverbank with their clothes, they wouldn't have had that third drink. If they hadn't had that third drink, they wouldn't have started playing "Remember When" and telling stories mostly about their brothers, which set them off into giggling fits. Had they not been making so much noise, the security guard wouldn't have guided his spotlight in their direction.

They received tickets for public intoxication and trespassing. To Genevieve's relief, the law enforcement officer had declined to write them up for public indecency. They'd had trouble getting an Uber to come to the cemetery at night, so the kind officer had driven them back to their rental and even arranged to have their car driven home.

Genevieve wasn't certain, but she thought she might have heard him ask Helen for her phone number.

The following morning during breakfast, Genevieve and Helen both declared they'd slept like the dead. This morning's giggles had nothing to do with vodka and everything to do with the shared joys of sisterhood.

That and thankfulness that they hadn't drowned or spent the night in jail.

Genevieve drained her second cup of coffee and was glad to note that the final little twinges of her hangover had disappeared. Helen leaned against the kitchen counter with her phone in her hands. Her thumbs moved across the screen as she sent a text. A wave of affection washed through Genevieve. She'd meant it last night when she'd said she would miss Helen.

She was inordinately glad that she intended to keep her condo and split her time between Texas and Colorado.

Then she recalled Helen's comment about the newlywed sex, and she wanted to giggle again. Instead, she asked brightly, "Is there anything you want to do in town before we head down to the coast? I'm looking forward to seeing your new place."

"Hmm?" Helen glanced up from her phone. "What did you say?"

Genevieve repeated the question. Her sister glanced at her watch and said, "No, I think I'll be cool with hitting the road. I need to finish gathering my stuff. Want to shoot for leaving in about ten?"

"Works for me. I just have to finish packing."

"Be sure to put your blood pressure meds in your purse and not in your suitcase."

That's weird. "Why? Am I going to need extra today?"

Helen snickered. "Well, it *is* my turn to drive."

Genevieve shrugged and retreated to her room to finish packing. When she loaded up her toiletries in the bathroom, she eyed the bottle of pills and shrugged again. She tossed the bottle in her purse and murmured, "That's what little sisters do."

Ten minutes later, she wheeled her overnight bag out the front door, punched the lock on her key fob, and opened the rear hatch. She'd just stored the suitcase in the back of the SUV when two things caught her attention. Helen was peeking through the front curtains.

And the roar of a motorcycle had died right behind her.

Genevieve whirled around. At the foot of the driveway, a man swung his leg off the saddle of a Harley and turned to face her. Even before he lifted both hands to remove his helmet, Genevieve had recognized the stance. The man.

She gaped at Gage Throckmorton.

He sauntered toward her, a half-smile on his face, a determined glint in his blue eyes. "Hello, Genevieve."

"What are you doing here? How did you get here?"

"Now, honey." He hooked a thumb over his shoulder. "That should be obvious."

Her gaze shifted from him to the bike, and back to him again. "Okay, the how, yes. The what, no."

And yet, even as she said it, she knew. A smile flirted on her lips.

Gage took her hand. "I'm here because I'm in love with you and you're in love with me and we've been waiting long enough, don't you think?"

She nodded.

"Good. Now, I'm going to give this a shot. If I can't get up, I'm counting on you to help." He took hold of her left hand with his and reached into his pocket, saying, "I'm counting on you, Genevieve."

Then Gage went down on one knee and held up a sparkling diamond ring. "Genevieve Prentice, will you do me the immense honor of becoming my wife?"

"Yes. I will. Oh yes, Gage. I will."

"Thank God." He slid the breathtaking square-cut diamond onto her ring finger. With only the hint of a creaking knee, he rose back to his feet and pulled her into his arms for a kiss.

Behind the buzzing in her head, Genevieve could hear Helen clapping and cheering.

Finally, he ended the kiss, lifted his head, and smiled down into her eyes. "So, you're through making me wait?"

"I am."

"Great. Let's go get married." He captured her hand and pulled her toward the motorcycle. "I thought we'd elope."

"Elope?" Genevieve planted her feet like a stubborn mule and repeated, "Elope!"

"Yes, elope. We're not getting any younger, Genevieve. I'm not wasting another day. Or night."

"But...but...but...wait. I can't elope. What about the kids? The kids should be there."

Behind her, Helen called out. "No, Genevieve. It's just weird to have your own kids at your wedding. It's backward."

"No, it's not." She lifted a panicked gaze to Gage. "I thought... well...I figured we'd get married at the Glass Chapel in the winter. It'll be so beautiful in the snow."

"Sounds great. We can renew our vows at the Glass Chapel this winter. But we're getting married today. I don't want to sleep without you for another night."

"We're engaged! We don't have to wait!"

He chastised her with a narrow-eyed stare.

"But, Gage, we can't just ride off into the sunset on a motorcycle and elope. We don't have a license. I don't have a helmet! I'm wearing shorts!"

"Now, sweetheart." He tenderly stroked a thumb across her cheek. "First, it's only nine in the morning. Not near sunset. I have everything taken care of. I have a license and leathers and a helmet for you to wear."

"Leathers! It's August, and we're in Texas! It's going to be a hundred and five degrees today!"

"Not where we're going, it's not. It's only a short ride to the plane."

The plane. Genevieve's new engagement ring sparkled in the morning sunshine. *Elope.* Her heart hammering, her mouth as dry as New Braunfels in August, Genevieve cast an imploring look behind her and met Helen's gaze. "Don't look at me," her sister said. "I'm going to the beach. Actually, I have a hot date with a cop, so you're not invited, Genevieve."

Genevieve's mouth dropped open. "He *did* ask you out!"

Helen shrugged a shoulder. "What can I say? He liked my underwear."

Happiness pooled inside her and bubbled like champagne. And yet... she was such a mother. "The kids will kill me. Kill us."

"They might," Gage agreed.

"Oh, wait. We can't. I promised Lindsay we'd do a prenup."

"She told me," Gage said. "I had my guy talk to your gal. Paperwork is all ready for you to sign. Right Helen?"

"That's right. You have an excellent attorney, Genevieve."

"Think she can help smooth things over with our kids?"

"Genevieve," Gage said. "Listen. We love our kids to the moon and back. My three, your four. They are our hearts. Since the day they were born, we've done our level best to give them a good life. We've done that. Actually, we've done a damned fine job of that. But they are all adults. They have to live their lives. We get to live ours."

Tears stung Genevieve's eyes. He was right. Not just "get" to, but "need" to. As much as they loved their children, they needed to let them go. Only then could they, themselves, fly.

Genevieve ripped away from Gage's grip and ran back toward her sister. Hugging Helen hard, she said, "I love you. I'm going to do this. I will see you soon. We'll still take sisters' trips together."

"Damned right we will. I told Gage that before I gave him this address."

"Thank you, Helen. You have always been there for me. Every single time, all of our lives. I love you more than words can say."

"I know, baby sister. Right back at you. Now, go marry your hot cowboy so I can get to know my hot cop."

Genevieve turned around and hurried back toward Gage. Holding his hand, she took three steps toward the Harley, then abruptly stopped. "I don't…it's been years. I'm not sure I can do this!"

"Get married?"

"Ride a motorcycle."

Gage imitated an exaggerated Texan drawl. "Don't worry, sweetheart. You've got this. You'll remember. Marriage… motorcycles…it's like riding a bike. Or a horse. It'll come back to you."

"Promise?"

"Oh, baby. I promise." Gage extended his arm to her. "Come, Genevieve. Come take a ride with me."

Acknowledgments

The time I've spent in Lake in the Clouds has been a bittersweet joy for me. I've written many books over the course of my career, but none have been so personal. As I sit down to compose the acknowledgments for *Second Chance Season*, I want to say a special thank-you to those people who are at the heart of every story I tell.

First, to my readers. Your support and enthusiasm for my work mean the world to me. I cannot express how much joy you have brought to my world through your letters, e-mails, social media messages, and visits to my table at book events. Over time, some of you have become dear friends. A special shout-out to our Emily March Book Club Facebook group members for your friendship and support, and a big hug to Kelly Green for going above and beyond so often. You are a blessing! Thank you for your generous friendship and the offer of prayers whenever they're needed. Our book club has become a bit of a sisterhood, I think.

Speaking of sisters...Mary Lou. How lucky I am to have you in my life. You are wise and wonderful and always, *always*, there for me. I love you. Thank you for everything. I can't wait to share this next stage of life with you and our girls and our grands. Nana play days rule!

Speaking of nanas...I also have to thank my children—Steven, John, and Caitlin—for giving me my beloved littles and for providing fodder for Lake in the Clouds and all my work over the past thirty years. There are bits of each of you in every one of my books. Sorry. (Not sorry.) The old saw that says write what you know is legit. In order to write authentically about family, love, and laughter, I needed to live it. I did so in spades with you three. We've shared enough heartache to bring emotional depth to my tales, and it's true that sometimes raising you all made me consider switching genres and gleefully write murder, but I have never doubted that we'd always find our way as a family to that all-important happy ending. I love you dearly.

Speaking of dear loves, I think the most appropriate way to say it is to repeat the dedication I wrote for my very first book, *The Texan's Bride*, which was published in 1993: "For Steve. Thanks for the time, the understanding, and the support. You've shown me what a true Texan hero is all about."

Some things never change. Drink your water. Wear your sunscreen. Leave Mom alone when she's on deadline. I wrote many heroes over the years—they all begin and end with you.

Finally, I'd be remiss if I didn't thank my publishing team at Forever, especially my fabulous editor, Junessa Viloria. Junessa, I've so enjoyed working with you! From Eternity Springs to Lake in the Clouds, I've always known that my book babies were in good hands with you. Thank you for making us shine.

Reading Group Guide

Questions for Discussion

1. In *Second Chance Season*, we learn about Helen's relationship with her parents and her father's decision to give Helen's baby away for adoption. How do you think this situation should have been handled differently?
2. Zoey chooses to stay by her mother's deathbed even though her mother abandoned her repeatedly throughout her life and refused to provide the family identity that Zoey so badly craved. Do you agree that a person should always stand by and forgive their family members regardless of how much pain they have caused? Why or why not?
3. How do you think Helen's life would be different if she had raised her son from birth? Do you think she would have ended up in Lake in the Clouds and have become mayor?
4. In the beginning of the book, Zoey and Cooper are a picture-perfect betrothed couple but then begin to struggle as Zoey feels buried under the stress of working in an ER, caring for her dying mother, and the emotional turmoil she feels. How do you think Zoey and Cooper could have better managed the hardships they faced, without shutting each other out and nearly destroying their relationship?
5. Gage's daughter, Lindsay, dislikes her father's relationship with Genevieve. During the Christmas market, we learn

that Lindsay and her husband are struggling with infertility. Lindsay and Genevieve are able to bond and share a maternal moment. Have you ever experienced a parental-type relationship with anyone other than your parents?

6. Zoey uses a DNA test kit to find clues about her mother's family. What are your thoughts on finding long-lost relatives through DNA?
7. Forgiveness is a theme throughout this novel—Helen forgives her father, Zoey forgives her mother, Zoey and Cooper forgive each other, and so on. What are some other themes that you noticed?
8. Genevieve and Helen share a number of special traditions. What traditions do you have with your family and friends?
9. Which character's storyline can you relate with the most? Why?
10. Helen and Genevieve celebrate their mother by swapping some of her classic sayings, such as "This too shall pass" and "Don't take any wooden nickels." Does your family have any mantras or sayings that have become staples in your life?

About the Author

Emily March is the *New York Times, Publishers Weekly,* and *USA Today* bestselling author of more than forty novels, including the critically acclaimed Eternity Springs series. *Publishers Weekly* calls March a "master of delightful banter," and her heartwarming, emotionally charged stories have been named to Best of the Year lists by *Publishers Weekly, Library Journal,* and Romance Writers of America.

A graduate of Texas A&M University, Emily is an avid fan of Aggie sports, and her recipe for jalapeño relish has made her a tailgating legend.

You can learn more at:
EmilyMarch.com
X @EmilyMarchBooks
Facebook.com/EmilyMarchBooks
Instagram @EmilyMarchBooks
Pinterest.com/EmilyMarch

YOUR
BOOK
CLUB
RESOURCE

VISIT
GCPClubCar.com

to sign up for the **GCP Club Car** newsletter, featuring exclusive promotions, info on other **Club Car** titles, and more.